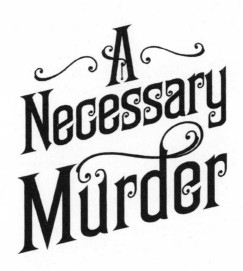

A Necessary Murder

A Heloise Chancey Mystery

M. J. TJIA

Legend Press Ltd, 107-111 Fleet Street, London, EC4A 2AB
info@legend-paperbooks.co.uk | www.legendpress.co.uk

Contents © M. J. Tjia 2018
The right of the above author to be identified as the author of this work has
been asserted in accordance with the Copyright, Designs and Patents Act
1988. British Library Cataloguing in Publication Data available.

Print ISBN 978-1-78-719879-1
Ebook ISBN 978-1-78-719878-4
Set in Times. Printing managed by Jellyfish Solutions Ltd
Cover design by Simon Levy | www.simonlevyassociates.co.uk

M.J. Tjia is a Brisbane-based writer. Her work has been longlisted for the Crime Writers Association (UK) Debut Dagger and the Margery Allingham Short Story Competition. She was awarded a Scarlet Stiletto Award (Australia) in the historical category. She is the author of *She Be Damned (2017),* the first novel in the Heloise Chancey Mystery series. *A Necessary Murder* is the second novel in the series.

Follow M. J. on Twitter
@mjtjia

For Dave,
You are gold to me

"With what wonderful wisdom has George Eliot told us that people are not any better because they have long eyelashes!"

Mary Elizabeth Braddon, *Aurora Floyd*

PROLOGUE

The heavy slop-pail bumps against Ruth's leg as she walks down the path to the privy.

She holds her breath, careful that its malodorous contents don't spill over the sides. She wishes the master would lay off the claret. The wire handle cuts into her fingers as she takes quick, short steps over the cobblestones and, keeping her nose averted from her burden, she fails to see the sparkle of dew on the heather florets that line the path, and the dawn rain that washes the dust from the wisteria leaves. A feathery, cool mist lights upon her upturned face, as she espies the brick outhouse at the bottom of the path.

She admires its sturdy lines just as she always does each morning when she empties the household's chamber pots. Much more handsome than the servants' privy, set a long way into the orchard, within a rickety, splintered structure. And most certainly fancier than anything Ruth's grandmother experienced when she served up at the Dodds' farm—leant up against a tree, was all, according to the old woman. Ruth shakes her head at the thought.

But, despite its promise of gentility, the household's privy retains the sour stench to be found around any outhouse. Its pong mingles with the sweetness of the honeysuckles creeping up its walls, and the flowers' rosy buds and thin, white tongues reach for her skirts as she brushes past to pull open the door.

There are two seats, one for the adults, and off to the left a smaller hole for the children of the house. Ruth sees that young Miss Margaret is on the smaller of the seats, and she apologises, starts to back out, but stops herself. The girl's small feet are bare, not in her silk slippers, and Ruth notices that her nightdress neatly covers her legs, and is not drawn up to her waist as would be expected. She pauses, confused, and steps closer, peering in the dimness.

There is a dark stain down the front of the Miss Margaret's linen nightdress.

Ruth feels bile rise to her throat, even as she reaches forward, and says, "Miss Margaret, have you had a nose-bleed?"

The girl falls to the side, jaw slack, her head at an awkward angle, exposing a raw, livid slice to her throat.

Ruth stumbles backwards into the fresh sunlight, the breath so heavily drawn from her body she thinks it will never enter again. She drops the pail, the master's shit seeping into the earth, trickling a path through the pebbles into the last of the marigolds.

Finally, after moments of what feels like a vacuum of riotous clarity—the stench of the outhouse, the shivering of the flowers, the horror to be found slumped on the privy—Ruth's breath returns, and she opens her mouth so that what trembles forth as a forced, harsh screech, transforms into a piercing clamour.

CHAPTER 1

I peer into the mirror and run my tongue along the ridge of my teeth until it catches on the tiny chip in my right canine tooth.

"Stop worriting at it, Heloise," says Amah, lifting my hair from the nape of my neck as she brushes. "You can't even see it."

"Yes, but I can still feel it." A reminder of that ghastly day. Each time my tongue catches on that chip, something slips in my stomach. I see the knife's blade, as mottled as an old shilling piece. I feel the sting to my lip, the strain upon my limbs.

"Well, Sir Thomas paid you handsomely for clearing up that mess, so go to a dentist, have it fixed."

I know she's not serious. She has that smirk on her face, knows I won't have some hairy brute of a dentist gouge around in my mouth. I've seen the pictures. She wouldn't either, the old mosquito.

I bare my teeth again in the mirror. It's true what Amah says. I can't even see the chip. My teeth are bright and even. Maybe that Marie Duplessis was right—telling lies whitens the teeth. I smile, bunch my cheek so the dimple fades in and out.

"Stop admiring yourself." Amah parts my hair down the middle, taking the left side of my hair to roll back from my face. Her hands are cold—have always been cold. I remember those winter evenings in Liverpool when I was small, when she'd pull my bloomers up for bed, how I used to hop away from her chilly fingers. "Who do you have coming tonight?" she asks.

"Well, Hatterleigh, of course, and Cunningham."

"Naturally." She twists the roll tight at the back of my head, and forces it into place with a hairpin. I'm sure my scalp curls away under the force of that hairpin, like potato skin under a peeler. "Who else will there be? Agneau hasn't prepared all that food for only three people."

"Well, the Pidgeons." I smile, as I dust pearl powder across my forehead. Sir Henry and his daughter.

Amah's brow lifts. "I do not like them."

"What are you talking about?" I think of dear Isobel Pidgeon. Of her sweet-serious countenance, of her pretty, flaxen hair. And her father, with his long face and kind eyes. "They're two of the nicest people I know." Of this I am certain. How many other respectable ladies would sit quietly in my house, conversing civilly with the notorious *paon de nuit*, Heloise Chancey? Of course, it's because Isobel has travelled to many other countries with her father, seen things that even I've not experienced. She's seen men, naked, except for long, long sheaths covering their cocks, and she's nibbled on fried spiders, as big as my palm. But still, in London, she could certainly choose to act differently towards me if so inclined.

Amah simply nods, with that irritating look on her face, as if she thinks she's the bloody moon goddess, Chang'e. "Who else will be here?"

"Maurice Cosgrove." Hatterleigh's friend from his time at Oxford. I feel warmth in my face. I lean forward so that Amah tuts, and pour myself a glass of sherry. Sweeping aside the curtain of hair that still hangs across the right side of my face, I take a sip. Then another. "And some of his cronies. His admirers really."

Amah coils the remaining hair back. "Ah. So tonight it is a meeting of your friends who think they've mastered the world."

I frown. "They've explored some of the world, yes."

"Explored. I can think of other words."

"Well, do so elsewhere, please. I rather like these people."

Amah breathes out through her nose, a sniff of derision. "At least they're a bit better than those pretty poets you have around—with all their languishing and posing." She scrapes more hairpins into my scalp, securing the second roll.

"How on earth would you know?"

Her mouth twists to the side again. "Sometimes I watch through the peacock tail, when I have nothing better to do. Although the stench of their cologne reaches all the way to my room."

I have another sip of sherry, and watch as a dappled blush rises to my chest. It resembles the first moments a tincture of carmine bleeds into a bowl of water, clouding it crimson. The blush is from the wine. It often happens with those first few sips. But I know it'll fade within minutes—definitely within half an hour—which is why I often have at least one drink in my boudoir before my guests arrive. Amah has told me that the same happened to her grandfather when he drank too much rice wine. My great-grandfather. I pick up the locket that was once his, that has found its way to me after all these years. It's now attached to the pearl choker I wear most days.

"He used to wear it on a gold chain," says Amah, nodding towards the gold dragon on the underside of the jade. "My mother had earrings made from the same gold."

"Where are they?" I tilt my head with the question but Amah tugs it back into line. She loops my remaining hair into a chignon at the nape of my neck.

"Lost them." Her mouth is set firm. I don't ask her to tell me more. I know she's lost a lot. More than she will ever admit.

She helps me clasp the choker around my neck as I gaze in the mirror. I don't like how Amah has done my hair tonight. It makes my face look wide.

"What's wrong?" Amah stands behind me, arms crossed.

I tease at the hair flattened to the top of my head, try to encourage a little more height. "Nothing."

"It's the same as that picture you showed me in the magazine," she insists. Of course she's right. She's done a superb job as usual. But I don't like it.

I angle my face from side to side. Maybe if I accentuate my eyes a little more. Or rub more rouge into my cheekbones.

Amah rolls her eyes, takes hold of my head to pull pins out. "I'll start again."

I duck away, laugh. "Don't be silly. Pass me that bunch of cherries I bought the other day. Or the pheasant feathers I wore to the play on Saturday night. It just needs a little decoration."

Amah's face softens. "Good idea. Your guests will be here before long anyway."

I watch her as she rummages through the trinkets, hair pieces and pomades on my dressing table. Her hands are tiny. Her fingers are thinner than mine, taper at the tips. I must have gotten my long fingers from my father.

I take another sip of sherry. Poor Amah. How bored she must be. What does she do with her time when I'm entertaining? I feel an urge to take her downstairs with me, to have her sit on the sofa with my friends. Surely they will find her stories enthralling? And how wonderful it would be to share her. But my thoughts snag. She's not simply an oddity at the fair, nor an exotic artefact from the East. And I think of how stiff my guests might be, of their shocked whispers as they climb into their carriages, how insufferably polite the Pidgeons would be to her. It can never be. And Amah would never agree anyway. Like most people in London, my guests do not realise she is more to me than a mere lady's maid. They don't realise I carry Amah's blood. How could they? I take great pains to hide it.

Amah's hand brushes some pins aside, and she picks up the newspaper. "Ghastly Murder at Stoke Newington," she reads. She mumbles over a few sentences and then reads aloud again. "The house was locked and secured as usual by the housekeeper, but found opened upon the morning. A way was evidently taken through the drawing room…"

"Appalling, isn't it? Their little girl was found in the privy. Murdered."

"Sir Thomas isn't involved, surely?" Amah's voice is sharp. "He doesn't want you to stick your nose in?"

"No." I dab some colour onto my lips. "Not at all."

Amah reads from the paper again, and nods. "Ah. Well, that is good. They will use real detectives this time."

I catch her eye in the mirror. It's just like the old wasp. Right when I start to feel a little sorry for her, she stings me in the neck.

CHAPTER 2

What Amah Li Leen really feels like eating is a steamed dumpling—the dewy dough between her fingers, the crunch of chives between her teeth.

She can hear people arriving, two floors down, shedding their coats and talking brightly with Heloise as she ushers them into the drawing room. Amah knows the side tables are laden with cheeses, pastries and sweetmeats because she'd assisted Heloise's chef, Agneau, with preparing the menu. She helped herself to three olives and an Indian pie, but what she really craves is one of Miriam's dumplings.

She glances out her window. Heavy clouds have replaced the sun, and the red bricks of the building across the way have taken on a muddy cast. Really, though, it isn't too late to make her way to Limehouse. Taff will be too busy to take her in the carriage, but she'll find a cab if need be.

Amah's rooms are on the third floor of the terraced house and used to be the nursery suite. The damask wallpaper's faded to the colour of courgette flesh, but she still feels remnants of its velvety texture when she runs her fingers over its surface. A picture border of shrubs and fruit trees, rabbits and leaping deer, circles the room, waist high. According to the nicks scraped into the door jamb, the previous tenants' son, Tom, was over seventy inches when he escaped the schoolroom, while Eliza was almost as tall as Amah herself. But poor Will stopped short at thirty-four inches. Amah always feels a splinter of sadness when that low notch in the timber catches her eye.

She riffles through her trinket tray for the pearl earrings Heloise had given her as a birthday present. As she settles her velveteen bonnet snug onto her head, the lace netting ready to pull down over her face, she pauses for a moment, staring at her reflection. Eyes the shape of almonds and the colour of cacao beans stare back at her. Her hair is mostly black—apart from the threads that are as fine and silvery as the silk of a spider's web. Heloise has threatened to wash the white strands away with a dark dye, but Amah steadfastly refuses. She isn't sure why. Maybe as a snub to the vanities that rule Heloise's life. Or maybe it's just a feeble bid to stay true to herself. But which self? The fierce, grief-stricken girl forced out of Makassar, or the young woman, as determined and clever as a weaverbird, who had made her own way to these cold shores of England? Looking at herself now, in her white blouse with the high collar and full pagoda sleeves, Amah wonders where that young woman has gone.

Sweeping her silk gloves to the side of the oak dressing table, she pulls its middle miniature drawers out from their casings. Easing her fingertips around the edges of the cavity, she slides out the whole frame, revealing a secret drawer. She pokes amongst the silk purses filled with beads and coins until she pulls forth one pendant earring—a golden orb, with a figure of a dragon entwined around its circumference, tiny feet splayed, tail teetering from the earring's base. It's the one thing she has left of her mother's. It nestles in the palm of her hand, its smooth surface surprisingly warm, and there's a tightness in her chest.

Amah's mother always wore these earrings, even when Amah's stepfather gave her the large diamonds, as square and cloudy as shattered window glass. She'd worn those diamond earrings for one day and night, before slipping the golden dragons into her earlobes again. When Amah was young, really young, she'd lie tucked in her mother's arm, so that she could smell the sour-sweetness of the sweat caught between her mother's hairline and throat. She'd suck her thumb, gently patting at the dragon earring with her fingertip so that it swung to and fro against her mother's neck. At that time, they shared a room out the back of her grandfather's house, a room her mother had painted bright red—lacquer red, the colour of joss sticks and Chinese altars. She'd even glossed the timber flooring. A sumptuous, warm room it was, with a large, hard mattress strewn with silk clothing and jars of her mother's unguents.

Amah looks up for a moment, at her cheerfully faded room, and wonders if she should also have her walls painted red. Her lip curls into a grim smile. How Heloise would rant at her if she did. Heloise likes her rooms to be reminiscent of the stylised Orient favoured by her more artistic, wealthy friends—of peacock feathers, silk turbans and cold porcelain. She has limited humour for pork dumplings and timber that holds the scent of sandalwood.

Amah stares down at the earring again, until her eyesight blurs—at the dragon as thin as a serpent, at the gold that's deeper in colour than any to be found in London. She can't help but wonder about its twin.

A shout of laughter from the drawing room breaks into her reverie. What use is it to wonder about the past? She puts the earring back amongst her hidden treasures and replaces all the drawers. Taking up her gloves and reticule, she treads down the servants' stairs at the back of the house in order to avoid her daughter's visitors.

Once out on the street she pulls the black netting over her face so people won't stare at her brown skin, or worse. Rounding the corner, a little further on from Heloise's house, she passes a young couple. As they stroll along, they gaze into each other's faces with an openness, a tenderness, born of intimacy and care. Amah once knew that look, but never beyond a room lightened by a lamp, or sometimes the dawn's unwelcome light. The memory makes her both happy and sad.

Across the road, a man, lean and of medium height, pauses at the corner, turning sharply to glance into the apothecary's window. His black hat, peculiar in shape—wide-brimmed, but curled up at the sides—is pulled low over his brow, but there's something familiar about the slope of his shoulders, the curve of his back.

"Pardon me," says a voice, as she bundles into someone walking in the opposite direction. The rough texture of his wool coat rubs against her ear, just as her eye catches the blue and green tartan tie at his neck.

Amah takes a sharp breath as she pulls away, and her fingers curl around an iron fence paling. That voice, it's still as deep as a bronze gong. And that scent that rises from his body, the sweet pungency of *nilam* oil. She stares into his face, at the pores on his cheeks that resemble the oily skin of an orange.

McBride.

He takes a step back, bows, lifts his top hat from his head. "Please forgive me. I was searching my way and didn't see you in my path."

He doesn't recognise her. Of course he wouldn't. She's so much older now, and the veil covers her face, thank heavens.

"That is no problem, sir," she murmurs, as she veers around him to move on down the street. Her legs tremble and the skin on her neck feels clammy.

She glances back once she reaches the main thoroughfare. He's staring up at Heloise's house. Pushing the gate open, he strides up her front steps.

Seeing that horrible, orange man takes Amah back.

She presses her eyes shut in the back of the hansom cab. Ignoring the sound of carriage wheels crunching across gravel, and the call of a costermonger by the side of the road, she thinks of Makassar. The pallid men who rode through town towards the port, and the Arabs and Chinese men who hawked silks, birdcages and bamboo chopsticks. She recalls the smoky fragrance of teak and cloves, and the sweetness of rambutan, how sometimes ants hid in its spiky skin, and bit into her tongue as she slurped on the fruit's flesh.

But London's wretched cold seeps back into her mind. Months and months go by and it feels like her bones cannot thaw. Her right hand is puckered with arthritis, and her skin is papery. Not like that last night she spent in Makassar, when her skin was plump and had the lustre of an olive.

She still had droplets of Tiri's blood on her arms when her mother's youngest brother, Chee, fetched her. The blood had dried into her skin, staining it. She wanted the spots to stay there forever, a memory of revenge, a mark of her anger, etched into her like the tattoos the dark sailors had scored into their flesh.

With the servant's help, Chee made Amah pack a few pieces of clothing. He said he had to take her far away, before the governor found out what she'd done and hanged her from the persimmon tree by the marketplace. She took no notice of what the silly servant packed, but she made sure her mother's bangles and earrings were tied into a piece of silk. Chee hurried her along, so all she had time to grab from her mother's dressing table was her comb, made of carved sandalwood. Even now, if Amah closes her eyes and breathes in, she can smell its spiced fragrance. But the comb is gone. Lost on that first voyage to this chill land.

It was almost dawn by the time they left Tiri's house. The light of the moon glimmered across the slate sky, lighting the clouds. Uncle Chee held her tightly by the wrist as they scampered towards the waterfront, her bare feet wobbling across the rocks in the road. Finally, they arrived at the *Dukano*, a dark mass that rose out of the sea, blocking Amah's view of the sky.

"Come," he said, ushering her forward on the gangway. "You will be a maid for my master's wife, Mrs Preston."

A white woman's maid? Never. She did not know this Mrs Preston. She barely knew her Uncle Chee. He had only been in port for a matter of days to take care of her mother's things. "But…"

Again, Uncle Chee gripped Amah's wrist. "Li Leen, you come with me, or you stay behind. It is this or death."

CHAPTER 3

I place the bunch of Michaelmas daisies my friend Charles Cunningham has given me in the porcelain vase on the window ledge. They're a simple flower—really, lilies or roses would have been better—but I do love their warm lilac hue. As I plump them in the vase, I catch sight of Amah walking along the footpath in front of our house. She's covered head to foot in dark colours—there's only a peep of her white linen blouse at the neckline of her overcoat—but I know it's her from that tight, determined gait of hers. Where the hell is she off to?

I pick up my champagne glass again, and survey the guests gathered in my drawing room. The fashion is, of course, to entertain pretty poets and elegant men of words—I do myself, at times—but I prefer the company of these men of science, and their more intrepid compatriots who discover and conquer new worlds. I love the earnestness with which they bow their heads towards each other, discuss whatever new theorem they have formulated or reptile they have discovered. They have colour in their cheeks, their arms are sturdy and, sometimes, they carry the scent of faraway— bergamot, clove tobacco, aged leather.

Tonight there are seven men and two women in my drawing room. Sir Henry Pidgeon—who doesn't look like a bird at all, more like a spaniel with drooping cheeks and sad, sagging eyes—stands under my portrait above the fireplace with young Charles Cunningham.

I come up to them, sipping champagne. My third glass; I

mustn't drink so fast. I pretend to frown at Charles. "You are blocking all the warmth, gentlemen."

"Pidgeon here was just telling me of his time in the Orient, Heloise," says Charles, not budging from his position in front of the fireplace. In fact, to speak to me, he faces his broad back to the fire even more squarely. "I'm to go to Hong Kong soon with my uncle. I'm starting out as his clerk, but he says that's how I will learn most quickly."

I can see he is about to embark on an eager litany of his father's past adventures in the East, which usually I would enjoy hearing of, but I don't want to concentrate, or nod at the right moments in his monologue. It almost feels like the bubbles of the champagne have risen to the top of my skull, floating, bursting with sweet little pops. So I pat him on the forearm and leave him with Pidgeon.

Maurice Cosgrove—explorer, some-time professor in medicine at King's College—holds court at the card table in the corner of the room. Although middle-aged now, he's as trim and handsome as ever he was; more so perhaps. His skin is still tanned from his time in India, and there's always something appealing about a man who has a fan of laugh lines at the corner of his eyes and the pepper of silver at his temple. Mostly, I like the stories of his scars: the nick above his left brow from when he clipped his head falling from a steamboat on the Ganges; the welts across his wrist from a stinging sea-monster; the red line on his palm that's repeated on the back of his hand, from where a Chinese pirate ran his sword straight through his hand. I take a cigarette from the lacquer box on the table, and Cosgrove lights it for me. He smiles at me with that lazy smile of his and turns back to the others.

Three budding scientists are seated around him. I know Milly Simpson; she nurses at a dispensary in Bloomsbury, but really she wants to be a doctor. When I first met her I thought she was Cosgrove's lover, but I don't think she is, somehow. I think he admires her tenacity, enjoys her devotion to him and her work. The other two youngsters I've never met before.

Cosgrove jabs his finger on the table, explains something to the chubby young man to his right. The third one ignores the conversation. He's as tall and well-built as Cosgrove himself, and his eyes are trained on me, over the top of Milly's head. He licks his fat, lower lip as he stares, as if I'm a platter of glossy steamed lobster. I want to stick out my tongue and pretend to heave, but I smile instead. I don't know who he is yet. He might be important. Rich.

I try to slide onto the sofa next to Isobel, Pidgeon's daughter, but the space is too small for my wide skirts and she laughs as she shifts over to make room for me. We're quite similar, really. Her father has dragged her around the world and society for so many years, she is at home in any situation.

"Who is that oily creature?" she whispers to me, lifting her fan. Her eyes dart to the card table and back.

"I don't know," I say, blowing my cigarette smoke away from her. "But he's a toady-looking thing, isn't he?"

I look across at Hatterleigh, who is on the opposite sofa, talking with Hunt. There's a pleasant hum in my ear from the champagne.

My butler, Bundle, ushers a tall man into the room. I've never seen him before. His hair has that gingery colour of a red fox fur, and his skin is ruddy, bodes of time spent in foreign climes. He strides straight over to Pidgeon, takes his hand, shakes it vigorously. There's surprise in Pidgeon's face, and he smiles, grips the handshake with his other hand—but is there something else? A slight shadow across his cheeks, a furrow between his brows?

"Heloise, listen to this," says Hatterleigh. "Hunt was just telling us of a dinosaur feather that's been unearthed. A *feather*. From some beast that is a cross between a bird and a dinosaur. I don't believe it can be true."

Bundle pours more champagne into my glass, so fresh its bubbles tickle my nose as I lift the glass to my mouth. This will be my fourth glass.

Through the hum in my ears, I can hear Hunt talking about his next dig in somewhere called Bernissart, but I've lost the thread of the conversation. As he speaks, the gold tip of his front, right tooth glints in the candlelight and I watch as his grey whiskers lift and separate, like the legs of a prone hairy caterpillar. I wonder what it must be like to kiss him, but only for a moment. He's a bit old, even for me. I glance across the room, catch Cosgrove's eye. He cocks an eyebrow, smiles. I smile back, only briefly though, return my attention to Hatterleigh and Hunt. I take two more sips of my champagne, and am surprised I'm at the bottom of my glass already.

Four men follow Bundle into the room, chums of Cunningham's, one of whom I've met before, but the others are new to me. I spy the bottle of champagne on the piano. I'll pour myself a glass on my way to greeting the newcomers. Pushing myself up from the sofa, I squeeze past Isobel's knees. Lovely Isobel. Her hair is so pretty, so golden. I've always wanted hair like that. I thread my way between the sofa and the low table. I'm in that nice, floaty stage, when the wine has relaxed my shoulders, mellowed my thoughts.

Isobel's father, Pidgeon, is across the room from us, still by the door, talking with his gingery friend, and as I reach for the bottle I hear his voice rise in surprise. I can't quite hear what's been said though, because the chatter in the drawing room has reached a low roar. The gingery fellow looks over towards me, and there's something in his face—is it recognition, or perhaps realisation? He turns and shakes Pidgeon's hand vigorously, rushes from the room, bowling Bundle to the side so that his tray of canapes almost slides to the floor.

Cosgrove takes the bottle from my hand. "What very strange behaviour," he murmurs, topping up my glass. His fingers brush mine as he hands my glass back.

There's something about Cosgrove, something unsettling. Whenever I'm near him I have to remind myself to be still, slow things down. I will my face to be as tranquil as that of the carved Javanese mask on the wall, while my heart judders, my breath shortens, like the time I tried belladonna drops in my eyes. I probably would avoid inviting him if I could, but he's one of this set. It'd be odd if he wasn't included. I glance over at Hatterleigh. He's laughing at something Hunt has said.

Pidgeon makes his way to the others and collapses onto the settee that is adjacent to the sofa, gestures for Isobel to join him. He takes her hand and says something in a low voice, and she gasps.

I look up at Cosgrove, pull a face. "I wonder what that's about?"

"It seems Pidgeon's Scottish friend left him with some unhappy tidings."

"Oh, yes, I've been reading about that in the papers," Hatterleigh says to Pidgeon, his voice booming above the others. He twists around, gestures to me. "Heloise and I were just discussing it earlier today."

I brush past Cosgrove, note the scent of his cologne— cedar bark, and something that reminds me of the woodlands near Paris—and lean on the back of the sofa, place my hand on Hatterleigh's shoulder. Cosgrove stands a little behind me. "What were we discussing?"

Pidgeon frowns, shakes his head. "I won't burden you with it."

"But you must," says Hatterleigh. "Didn't I tell you she's been working for that charlatan—Avery? He runs some sort of detective agency, apparently. He has my Heloise stick her nose in here and there." He looks up at me. There's pride in his eyes, but, deeper, I can see concern. "She was in quite a bit of a mess the last time he had her look into something."

Suddenly, it feels like there's a slippery eel in my guts. I think of that time in Waterloo again as my tongue finds the chip in my tooth. The gleaming, blonde curls. The chill morgue. The blood. My grip on my glass is tight as I take a long sip of champagne.

Isobel, too, urges her father to tell me about what's happened. As I make my way to a seat opposite him, he glances around the room. Cunningham and his coterie have joined the three young ones at the card table. They've set up a game of loo and are busily betting and drinking great gulps of my burgundy.

"What were you discussing?" I ask again.

"Yes, tell us of what you are talking," says Hunt. His voice has that querulous note found in those who are hard of hearing. "And speak up."

"It's Lovejoy." Pidgeon digs a finger in under his tie, loosens it. "His little girl—what's her name again, Isobel?"

"Meggie," she says. A tear hovers on her lower eyelid, looks like a bead of hot wax ready to streak its way down the side of a candle. "Margaret."

Pidgeon nods, sadly, swallows hard. "She's been murdered."

My eyes find Hatterleigh's. "Not the murder we've been reading about in *The Times?*" The child found in the outhouse. Throat cut.

"Yes, it would seem so."

Margaret Lovejoy, then. Only three years old.

"Not Bob Lovejoy?" Hunt looks aghast.

Pidgeon's face is ashen as he nods again. "I'm afraid so. That was McBride just then. He tracked me here to tell me of it."

"Don't tell me that was McBride!" says Hunt. "He did not greet me. Very strange. Travelled with him years ago."

We're silent for a few moments, listen to playing cards whisk across the felt surface of the card table, to Cunningham exhorting Milly to play fair.

"Cosgrove, you were in Sarawak with him, too, weren't you?" says Hunt. "That's right. Young cub, you were, arrived in town just after all the trouble. Helped patch poor Wilkins up, from memory."

"Where? What trouble?" Hatterleigh asks.

Hunt frowns. A cloud of film, as murky as a fish scale,

partially covers his left iris, from too much time in the sun. "Sarawak. Must be over twenty-five years ago now."

"You weren't there during that riot, were you?" Hatterleigh looks from Hunt to Pidgeon. "I remember my father reading about it in *The Times*." His face is even ruddier than usual. He looks more like a farmer than ever. Hatterleigh is utterly fascinated with the expeditions and adventures of these older men, but not enough to stir himself further than his own library or his club. Which suits me. What would I do if he were to wander off for some godforsaken place every few months like Cunningham does?

"Yes, that's when we were there. Blasted Chinamen, tried to force us out," says Hunt.

He's cross, but it's Pidgeon's hand I notice, how it trembles slightly against his knee.

"What is it, Papa?" asks Isobel.

Pidgeon's jowls sink low, giving him more than ever the appearance of a hound. "Remember there was that Chinese man outside our house a few days ago? I was sure he'd been trying to break in through the parlour window." Sir Henry squeezes Isobel's hand. "He moved off quickly when I called out to him, but not before I saw a damned dagger in his hand."

"You think he meant you harm?" I ask.

Pidgeon opens his mouth to say something, closes it again.

"Papa thinks the man is threatening us in some way, that it wasn't just a simple burglary," explains Isobel. Her eyes widen as she looks at me, like she thinks he's being a little silly.

Hunt snorts. "Pidgeon, you've always been too fanciful. What on earth would a Chinaman want with you?"

Pidgeon shrugs. "I don't know. I just don't know. But he gave me quite a turn, I can tell you. And now, this matter of Lovejoy's daughter…"

"Her murder? You can't think they're connected?"

Pidgeon leans forward, taps the table for Hunt's attention. "McBride said Lovejoy had received a threatening note. A

28

note that warned him of a terrible tragedy. What if it was from that Chinaman? Surely it's too much of a coincidence that I'm menaced by that blackguard in the same week as Lovejoy receives a threatening letter and his daughter is murdered?"

Hunt lets out a long breath, leans back against the sofa. Looking over his shoulder to where Cosgrove still stands, he says, "And you, Cosgrove, have you had any threatening letters?"

Cosgrove lights a cigar, a plume of smoke rising about his head. "Hunt, I'm a man of science. I'm always receiving ugly correspondence from the more godly people of this town. One glance and I throw the missive in the fire."

"Nothing in particular lately?"

"No, sir, not that I've noticed."

The others turn back, resume talking, but Cosgrove's gaze holds mine. For once, his eyes are not smiling. He looks troubled.

CHAPTER 4

It's dark by the time Amah Li Leen makes her way along Limehouse Causeway. With each step, she edges further away from the muddy stench of the water. On almost every corner, fish shops reek of rancid, burnt oil, the smoke adding to the smog from the chimney stacks, coating the already dark brick buildings in soot. Alleys she hopes she never need enter are heaped with kitchen waste, and as she walks along the cobbly courts, muck squishes under her shoes, but it's too gloomy to tell what she's treading upon. She passes many sailors, and dockworkers, mooching home or to one of the noisy taverns along the way. Two Malay men—there's no mistaking those high cheekbones, the neatly chiselled lips—huddle together by a baked-potato vendor. How surprised they'd be if Amah approached them, lifted her veil and exchanged a few words in their own language. Many foreign men wander these parts, but very few women—women not stuck in a bagnio or in a backroom of a public house at any rate.

Turning down a street to her left, she passes a row of dingy shops and pauses in front of one that's sandwiched between a tobacconist and a cobbler's. The glass in the shopfront window is too cloudy to see through and, in any case, is covered with a long curtain. The name Chan Chee is painted in white across the cheap panelling above the lintel. As Amah opens the heavy door to step inside, her nostrils are assailed by a mixture of body odour, incense and noodle soup.

The room is long with a low ceiling. Her heels click across

rough, untreated timber and cold air seeps through the cracks in the floor where it's not covered with rattan mats. Hats and coats line the walls that are yellowed with age and smoke. At a small table to the front of the room, two lascars eat their supper and, as Amah passes them by, they peer at her through the steam rising from their soup. But the four Chinese men playing mah-jong in the corner ignore her, puffing on their pipes, coils of grey smoke suspended on the still air about their heads. The tiles of their game clack upon the tabletop.

On the back wall is a scroll covered in Chinese calligraphy, but Amah can't read the black lines and slashes. Back in Makassar she'd learnt some Latin alphabet from the Christian missionary who played *pai gow* with her grandfather—each week he wagered his allowance of tobacco against her grandfather's rice wine. And then later, Amah's stepfather had paid a young man from Holland to teach her to read a little, write a few words. He was also the tutor to the Dutch residents' children, but she'd always found his lessons such a chore, especially when there was the chance of watching a ship newly arrived in the harbour, silks and birds and pale women in heavy gowns spilling from its decks.

Amah pushes open the door at the back of the room and peeps through into the kitchen. "Miriam?"

The kitchen's much cheerier than the room Amah closes the door upon. The walls are the shade of marigolds and the timber benches have the gleam of fresh straw. A pretty girl, slender and dark, tends to a pot of boiling broth, while Miriam, majestic in a gown of blue and white gingham trimmed with lace—totally unfitted for kitchen work, Amah would have thought—rolls and pushes at some dough on the kitchen table.

"Li Leen," she says, a smile lifting her cheeks, which are rosy from the fiery ovens. "Shed your coat, dear. You're just in time to help me make these *jiaozi*."

She pronounces it wrong, always does, with a long "ee" sound at the end. Amah has tried again and again to correct her, but it has never stuck. Probably in the same way that Amah can never master the word "boot", according to Heloise. Although how she manages to mispronounce such a simple word to the point that makes her daughter mock and laugh, she isn't sure. She mouths the word as she takes off her coat and drapes it over a chair.

"Where's Uncle Chee?" Amah asks as she ties an apron over her skirt.

Miriam covers the dough with a damp cloth, pushes a curl of fair hair from her forehead with the back of her hand. "My husband is an enigma, Li Leen. You know that. He could be down by the docks trading some gold for nutmeg or he could be watching a boxing match. I won't know until he arrives home later tonight, with or without his purse."

Amah searches her face for any sign of anger, but Miriam smiles.

"Don't worry, Li Leen. Either way, he will return with a bunch of peonies for me, and go to the markets before dawn so I can have a nice lie-in." She tugs the elbow of the girl at the stove, says, "Rosemary, say good evening to Auntie Leen."

Miriam's daughter has her mother's freckles and arched eyebrows, but her skin's darker, has the tone of honey. Amah can see traces of Rosemary's father too—in her hair with its blackbird sheen and her eyes the colour of apricot kernels. Rosemary pipes out a cheerful greeting to Amah as she pours her a cup of tea.

"Have you minced the pork for me yet, Rosemary?" Miriam sets the chives onto the board to chop. "I need enough for fifty dumplings." She pauses, her knife poised over the chives. Her blue eyes find Amah's. "Were you after Chee, Li Leen?"

Amah shakes her head. "No. I had a sudden yen for your dumplings."

Miriam smiles again, and her cheeks flush darker. "Oh. That's nice to hear."

32

Amah pulls the bowl of pork to herself, adds some of the chives. She's embarrassed by Miriam's response. It's not often she has the time or inclination to regret the way she'd behaved in the past. What's that saying she used to admire so much? Something about a tongue being like a sharp knife—it kills without drawing blood. But, at moments like this, she feels bad. Poor Miriam. Amah had been so hard on her when they'd first met. Chee had brought Miriam to Liverpool to visit her many years before, but Amah was unfriendly to the young, skinny thing. Unfriendly or wary? Amah can't remember. Chee had married a white girl. A *gweilo* from London. Maypole of a thing, Miriam was then, all gangly and pale, and Amah's unkindness had just heightened her clumsiness over the two days they had stayed with her.

But look at Miriam now. She's able to chat with Chee in a patois of English, Chinese and Malay. And her cooking— well, Amah knows she could never cook as well as Miriam does. She watches the other woman as she ladles noodles into a bowl of soup, sending Rosemary to deliver it to the table of Chinese men. And of course she owes a lot to Miriam now...

"Li Leen." Miriam's voice cuts into her thoughts. "Can you finish off the filling while I take these bowls out?"

Amah rubs the chives into the cold mince, seasoning it as she goes. When Miriam returns, she flattens and cuts out the dough, and between the two of them they fill the circles with deft fingers, pleating the edges until they have a tray of crescent-shaped dumplings.

Rosemary swings back into the kitchen. "Ma, did you tell Auntie Leen that Jakub is back?" She grins at Amah, pulls a chain and pendant out from under her bodice. "He brought this back for me." An oval locket, gold, only as big as a fingernail, teeters upon her fingertip. "He said it's to keep my love's lock of hair in."

"Get away with you," scolds Miriam, an uneasy smile on her face. She turns to drop the dumplings into boiling water, but her back stiffens, and Amah wonders if a lick of pink creeps up the back of her neck.

"No, your mother didn't tell me. It must be nice to have your big brother back. How long has he been in London?" asks Amah.

Rosemary gathers up a stack of cups to take out into the other room. "He's been here for nearly two weeks. And I hope he stays this time." She nudges the door open again, leaving Amah alone with Miriam.

They're silent. Miriam continues to lower and scoop dumplings from the pot while Amah washes the bowls and pans. It isn't until Miriam sets the platter of *jiaozi* between herself and Amah on the tabletop that she finally meets Amah's eye.

"You didn't tell me he was back?" Amah's head tilts to the side as she asks the question. "How long was he on the seas for? Three, four years?" But Amah knows exactly how long. Three years, eight months.

Miriam nods. "We haven't really seen much of him. I was meaning to have you over for supper one night when he was in."

Miriam's eyes drop to the table. She fidgets with saucers and, picking up a pair of chopsticks, she serves Amah and herself two dumplings each.

Amah picks up a bottle of soy sauce, asks, "Where did you get this from?"

"Chee bought a dozen bottles a week ago," says Miriam. "From the *Coromandel*. She's just sailed in from Canton. Same boat Jakub came in on."

"He's been in China?"

"Amongst other places." Miriam splashes a liberal amount of soy sauce across her dumplings. "I think he spent most of his time in America, actually."

Amah's chest hurts a little, like it's been smeared in chilli paste. Ridiculous. It's no surprise at all that the boy hadn't contacted her. Why would he?

34

She bites into the dumpling. It's everything she had antic-ipated. Tender, delicious. She closes her eyes.

The black figure by the apothecary's. Something familiar about the shoulders, the narrow back. Jakub?

But why hadn't he approached her, greeted her?

She looks up and finds Miriam staring.

"What's on your mind, Li Leen?"

Amah considers her—the faint lines that fan from her kind eyes, the permanent furrows that etch her forehead. What a cheerful mother she must be to her children—the three young ones, to Rosemary, to Jakub. Jakub. She's a much better mother than Amah has ever been. It's true. Heloise would agree. Has agreed. Threw it at her head many years before when she'd asked why she couldn't go live with her sweet Auntie Miriam.

But Jakub—Amah always thought they had a special connection.

"Nothing important, Miriam," she says. "I was just won-dering if I could sneak a bottle of this soy sauce into Agneau's kitchen. Do you have any spare?"

Miriam takes a bottle from the larder and places it in a basket as Amah finishes her last bite of dumpling. Amah had planned on staying the whole evening but her heart isn't in it anymore. She's just reaching for her bonnet when the door that leads to the back alley creaks open. Heavy footsteps tread down the short corridor towards them. A man's footsteps. Jakub's?

But no, it's Chee. As predicted, he's holding a bunch of flowers, but they're daisies rather than peonies. Amah knows he's a good seventeen years older than his wife, but really, despite several white strands in his hair and a bit of a round belly, he looks much the same as he did twenty-six years ago when he'd fetched her from Makassar. He beams at Amah, insists she sit back down, calls her his *kodok kecil*, his little frog, as he has done since she was little. Amah suspects he's imbibed in a little too much rum or rice wine with the sailors by the dock.

Along with the flowers, Chee hands his wife a hessian bag from which she brings out half a coconut. "*Masak* coco flummery thing I like, *silakan*?" he urges.

Amah and Chee chat over cups of jasmine tea, which he proudly pours from a white teapot in the shape of a resting camel, while Miriam prepares custard to go with whipped egg white and the coconut flesh that Rosemary shreds for her.

Chee tells them of a new boxer he'd bet on. "Won 15s, I did. I know he would win, because he is very angry young man. Very *marah*." He points at Amah. "Your Jia Li, he would like it."

Amah's smile is grim. "Her name is Heloise, now, Uncle, not Jia Li, and it's 'she' not 'he'." Although she concedes that he's probably correct about Heloise enjoying the boxing.

Chee waves his hand at her, repeats "Jia Li," before telling them of the newest vessel in dock.

By the time Miriam walks Amah to the front door of the shop, the night sky has taken on the gleam of an oyster shell. Miriam has tried to insist Chee accompany his niece home, but Amah's adamant. She'll be fine. A cab driver will be glad of the fare.

At the door, she turns around, nods towards the scroll on the back wall. "What does that say, Miriam?" she asks, pointing at the Chinese script. Something wise, perhaps. Like *Deep doubts, deep wisdom*, or the proverb that used to hang on the wall in her grandfather's sitting room in Makassar: *A man is never too old to learn*.

Miriam points at the scroll, her finger following the lines of ink. "If you want your dinner, don't offend the cook."

Light the colour of parchment glimmers past the edges of the drawing room curtains, marking Amah's way through the gentle mist that hangs in the air. She pulls the netting back from her face and glances up at the window. Heloise still has guests with her. A pleasant tinkling on the pianoforte reaches Amah's ears. Can't be Heloise playing then. Neither her brief time at a ladies' college or the expensive lessons she insisted upon taking a year beforehand had improved her skill. Now, if she just practised once in a while instead of gallivanting around town all the time... her lip twists to the side.

Amah passes the front door and continues around the corner in order to enter the house from the back. The fog's not bad, and yet the street seems darker than usual. She pauses. The rest of the street is asleep; no lights to illuminate the oak trees or the carriage that waits by the side of the road. She can just discern the faint movement of the two horses as they nod gently against their mouthpieces.

It takes her less than a second to realise what the problem is. The lamp post closest to the servant's entrance to Heloise's house isn't lit. Her eyes search the darkness, seek out further shifts in the shadows.

How very strange. They've never had problems with this lamp, not from a shortage of gas, and not from one of those explosions, thank heavens. She treads closer towards the lamp post, wishing her heels didn't click so loudly in the silence. A crunch under her left sole. Her right shoe scrapes something forward, something that tinkles. Glass. She peers up at the lamp post. The lamp's dome has been smashed, leaving a jagged saw of glass.

Amah frowns. Such a quiet street.

Dread creeps its sticky fingers up her spine.

Close at hand, hidden in the gloom, she senses something wicked. Something watching her. She feels it bursting to free itself, like a held breath. Its foulness suffuses the air, its charred eyes are upon her throat. She takes two steps backward. Swinging around, she just reaches the top of the six steps that lead down to the servant's door when she's knocked from behind.

Amah is thrown forward, wrenches her ankle on the second last step, clips her forehead hard against the door. She crumples to the ground. Groaning, she tries to sit upright. Her fingers find the fissure of skin that peels open above her brow, the hot blood gushing down the bridge of her nose, stinging her eyes. It's so dark. Too dark. She can't see a thing.

She tries to get up, find her bag, her knife, but cries out as pain judders up through her left leg from her ankle. Collapsing back, she's just about to try again when somebody lands on top of her, so heavily the breath grunts from her body.

She scrambles against him, strains with her fingers until her fingernails tear, thrashes her legs, her sprained ankle forgotten. But something isn't right. He's not moving—is as heavy as a sack of rice—apart from his head, that lolls damply against hers each time she tries to push him away. She hefts against his shoulders, shoving him aside, so that they lie crammed against each other in the confined space of the landing. She can smell the *nilam* oil, and something more gamey, raw; thinks she can feel its stickiness smeared across the skin at the base of her throat. Gagging, she pushes him away.

The servant door swings open. A lantern is held above her head, so bright she has to shield her eyes with her hand. She can't see who holds it.

She clambers into a seated position, crouches away from the body. His face is hidden from view, pressed against the tiled step, but the crown of his head faces her at an unnatural angle, almost reaches between his shoulder blades. The tartan tie she recognises, although the green stripes, and the blue, are soaked in gore the colour of cherry pulp.

McBride.

CHAPTER 5

It's chilly when I wake. I squint past the shadows of my room, see dawn's pearl light glimmer through a crack in the curtains. I burrow backwards into the bed, want to melt into the soft warmth of Hatterleigh's body, search out the hard. But all I find is cool linen, empty space.

Opening my eyes, I stare at the bed's velvet canopy — at sprigs of flowers coiled around golden artichokes.

He went home after the police were called and interviewed us in the drawing room. The only guests who still remained by that time were the Pidgeons and Hatterleigh. The others had left throughout the evening, thank heavens. I don't know when. I drank a great deal of champagne.

A headache taps at the base of my skull. My mouth is dry, sour. I roll over, press my face into the pillow where I've dribbled in my sleep. Poor Amah. By the time Bundle had drawn her into the kitchen, called me down to her, she'd managed to wipe some of the blood from her face and hands. But there was one crimson globule of *something* — my stomach squelches like it did last night — teetering from the damp strands of hair by her right ear. My eyes were drawn to it as she spoke, as she told me of the dead man on the back step of my house.

Hatterleigh was already there, gazing down at the man's body when I reached the back door.

"No, Heloise, you mustn't," he said, grabbing hold of my shoulders as I tried to push past.

I frowned up at him—his face was pale—and said, "Of course I must."

The man's body lay on its side across the landing, arms and feet splayed back. But it was almost as if his head was on a hinge, pressed right back, like no circus contortionist I'd ever seen. The light from Bundle's lamp cast a shadow of my hair, feather quivering aloft, across the wide pool of his blood—ruby dark and as still as a lake.

My bedroom door creeps open and Amah pokes her head around.

"Ah. Finally. You are awake."

She limps into my room, closely followed by Abigail, the new girl who helps out during the day. While Abigail kneels, stokes the fire back to life, Amah yanks the curtains open.

I groan, bury my head under one of my frilled pillows. "It's too early. Let me sleep."

I feel the mattress dip slightly as Amah sits next to me. She waits for Abigail to leave the room, close the door quietly behind her, before she says, "Well, it's all right for you. Poor Bundle went to bed very late and was up before sunrise trying to mop the blood from your back step."

"Bloody hell. The poor thing." Lifting the pillow, I clamp it under my head. "Pass me that glass of water, would you?" As I take the cold glass from Amah, I think of the two policemen that Pidgeon had summoned, of how one stomped his great heavy boot into that pool of blood while turning the corpse over. How the corpse's head refused to follow the rest of his body, his face lolling against the bottom step.

"Sliced almost clear off," the copper said.

That sobered me up quickly, or so I felt at the time. As I look back, though, the rest of the night is patchy, as inconsequential as a nightmare. My drawing room blanched of warmth as we sat across from each other—me, Hatterleigh, Isobel and her father—answering the policeman's questions as best we could, his pencil scratching our responses into his tattered notebook. Pidgeon repeated the story of how he knew McBride from their travelling days, but he didn't mention the break-in, or his friends, the Lovejoys. Isobel's eyes were bright, but she didn't cry. Her colour was high, almost feverish. I asked the policemen if they'd found a knife or anything on the road; would they question the neighbours to see if they'd noticed anything?

It's only now I remember Hatterleigh frowning at me, the slight shake of his head. But I ignored him, kept pressing the police constables for more. My mother was upstairs in her room washing off a man's gore. I was indignant. And I was scared. It was almost a relief when Hatterleigh decided to leave with the others. It gave me the opportunity to check on Amah throughout the long night.

And now I can see that Amah is already dressed, as neat as an oriental magpie, but I can tell she is not herself. The fine cut on her forehead is clean, half hidden in the hair of her left eyebrow. She picks at the embroidery on my bedspread, stares at a spot on the floor. Maybe she is thinking of all that blood. I can't help myself—I glance at her hands to see if any of his blood is captured beneath her fingernails. Of course, there isn't.

"His name was McBride," I tell her. "He was with us last night. Not for long though. A friend of Pidgeon's."

The police constable had only spoken briefly with Amah, before Hatterleigh cut the interview short, allowed me to guide the shaken woman to her rooms. So she missed out on much of what we learned, and I hope that maybe if she knows more, she'll be able to rest.

"Do the police know why he was killed like that?" There are dark smudges under Amah's eyes. Her face seems older.

I shake my head. "Surely he was mugged for his purse," I say, although now I remember he still had it in his pocket. I also think of what the others had spoken of, after McBride had left my gathering—of threatening letters, of Chinamen. I think of that little girl, savagely murdered just a few days ago. How her throat was cut too. I take another sip of water, close my eyes.

"I had a look outside this morning," Amah says. "There was a smooth, grey stone in the gutter. From the garden of the house two doors down—you know the one? It was almost covered in horse dung, but I think it might have been what the murderer used to smash the glass of the lamp. How else did it find its way onto the road?"

I watch her as she stands, winces against the pain in her twisted ankle. She moves to the window and gazes outside.

"So someone had it planned? You think McBride was ambushed?"

She shrugs.

I feel sick again, and it's not from my hangover. What if Amah had been just a minute earlier? Would I then have found two bodies huddled at my back door? Was McBride's death part of a robbery or was he specifically chosen to die?

From the window in her sitting room, Amah watches as Taff helps Heloise mount her brute of a horse. Of course, she looks handsome seated upon its glossy, muscled back—she wouldn't have it any other way, even if it is a risk to her life. Amah tuts.

A wave of fatigue flushes through her and she rubs her gritty eyes. She wishes that Heloise had left her alone last night when she was trying to sleep. Her heart lurched every time Heloise peeped into her room, letting some of the hall light in. How could Amah find her balance—breathe in, empty mind, empty mind, breathe out, right out— when the bedroom door creaked open every few minutes? How could she steady her racing thoughts? How was she to forget?

And now, with each thrum of her leg, the beat beat beat that throbs up from her ankle, she tries to shut out all thought of McBride. McBride and his head... the blood...

Despite her best efforts—her eyelids squashed tight, the

heels of her palms pressed against her eyeballs—flashes of memory illuminate the dark cavern of her mind.

The sea, kingfisher blue. The dirty, wide decks of the *Dukano*. The stench of burning coal that left her feeling giddy, the smokestack that coughed black clouds into the clear sky. And, of course, Mrs Preston. Jane.

Amah won't think of the last time she saw her. She won't.

But she does think of her smooth brown hair, parted in the middle, loosely pulled into a bun at the nape of her neck. Her thin fingers, almost impossibly long, with fingernails as smooth and pretty as pipi shells. Amah was with her when she first saw McBride. Amah disliked him, even then. But he was friends with Mr Preston—another foolish man—so there was no avoiding him. Just as her mind cannot avoid him now.

CHAPTER 6

It's early evening by the time I return from my ride in Hyde Park. I make sure to appear along Rotten Row at least three times a week in order to stoke the fire of my fame. I didn't take the phaeton this time, just Malani, a Hanoverian warmblood, my favourite horse. She's so tall and fine, I tower over the other women riding their ladylike ponies.

I slide from the saddle, rub my hand down the white blaze that marks Malani's nose and up again against the bristles. Taff acquired her for me from a soldier newly arrived back from India, who told him of Malani's bravery in battle, but also of her unpopularity there because her black coat was considered unlucky. But I've found the opposite to be true. Her inky sheen complements my own hair, which has a sable gloss, thanks to Amah soaking it in egg white, oil and honey every Sunday. Malani's assured gait calls attention to my new paletot, which is almost mannish, what with the row of military buttons down the front, although I make sure it fits snug over my breasts and accentuates my small waist. I feel almost regal seated upon Malani when I pass the cluster of people by the side of the road who wait to catch a glimpse of me. I angle my face to its best advantage, lift my chin. I pretend I don't notice this audience of mine, like I'm not aware they are there to see me, but of course I know they are. A man even wrote a letter to *The Times* complaining about them—about how they block the thoroughfare.

I leave the horse with Taff and let myself into the house.

Pulling the gloves from my fingers, I rub my chill hands together. I unpin my top hat, and from its rim I unwind the chiffon scarf that has the shimmer of a dragonfly's wing. I've taken to draping squares of silk or chiffon around my riding hats, and just today I had the pleasure of seeing both Lady Rowe and the Marchioness of Beste with scarves trailing their riding hats too, aping my new fashion. I grin into the hallway mirror. I'll wear the scarf for the rest of the week, see how many more women I can goad into copying me, and then I'll never wear it again.

Bundle comes out from the drawing room and gives a slight bow. "Guests for you, madam." He leaves the door ajar.

Sir Henry Pidgeon and another man are just about to take a seat when I enter the room, but rise when they see me. Pidgeon's friend groans a little with the exertion.

"Ah, Heloise, you are home," says Pidgeon, taking my hand. The lines on his face are more present than usual. He has obviously been as affected by McBride's grisly death as the rest of us, perhaps more. "May I present my friend, here, Mr Erasmus Lovejoy. Mr Lovejoy, Mrs Chancey."

Mr Lovejoy. It only takes me a moment to realise this must be the father of the poor little murdered girl. I shake his hand and his fingers are as dry as autumn leaves. "Please, call me Heloise."

I take the armchair opposite. Bundle has left the tea things ready on the table and, as I lean forward to lift the teapot, there's the sound of something bumping to the floor in the next room. I turn and stare at the painting of a peacock that covers the dividing wall, but there is no further noise. I smile at the men. "I hope the maid didn't knock over anything too valuable."

I hand Pidgeon his tea, who says, "Thank you, thank you. You must be wondering why we are here."

"Not at all," I murmur as I pass a cup of tea to Lovejoy, who takes it in both hands. His hands shake so hard, the cup rattles in the saucer. He places it back down on the table.

Lovejoy's wiry hair is unkempt, and white, but the dirty white of snow pushed to the gutter. Even his sideburns, that creep low on his cheeks, are bushy and white. His skin is pallid, and the creases in his face have a greyish tinge. He is not a handsome man, by any reckoning. In fact, he has a bad-tempered face. And he's old, much too old to have such young children, I would have thought.

"Heloise, you once told me of a man you sometimes work for," says Pidgeon. "Runs an investigation agency, or something." Poor Pidgeon. His watery blue eyes are bloodshot. But after last night I probably don't look too fresh either.

"Yes. Sir Thomas Avery."

"Ah, yes. Can you put me into contact with him?"

"Of course I can," I say, rising to my feet. "I will write his directions down."

When I return from my study, I sense that the two men have broken off from a hurried exchange. I don't immediately hand Pidgeon Sir Thomas's card because I'm curious as to why he wants to see him.

"Has Sir Henry told you of the terrible incident we had here last night?" I ask Lovejoy. I offer them the plate of almond macaroons before taking a seat.

Lovejoy looks as though I've startled him from a deep reverie. He mutters, "Yes, yes," as he takes a biscuit.

"That's partly why we'd like to have a word with Sir Thomas," says Pidgeon.

"Oh. You think it might be connected to…" I glance at Lovejoy, who's staring at the macaroon in his hand.

Pidgeon sits forward on the sofa. "Have you heard anything more of McBride's death? Did the police tell you people anything at all?"

I'm tired. I've had a difficult day trying to block memories of McBride's blood trickling down the back of the steps. I think back to earlier that morning, when the lead policeman returned to my house, interviewed us all over again. As he fired questions at us, he strolled around the drawing room, gazing into cabinets, staring up at my painting. Although he asked questions of both Amah and me, he looked to Bundle, the only other man in the room, to provide the answers. As he bowed to me on his way out, I thought a slight smirk twitched the policeman's lip, and couldn't help wondering if he had heard uncomplimentary things about my former relationship with Sergeant Bill Chapman. They were from different stations, but men do so gossip about such things. Or maybe he'd heard of my successful detecting, but couldn't bring himself to believe it of a woman.

"The police think it was most probably a botched robbery," I say, rubbing my temples.

Pidgeon's eyes widen. "How did they come to that conclusion?"

"I think that, maybe, he still had his purse and watch chain on him." I shrug. "But what else could it have been?"

The two men exchange looks.

Pidgeon slumps back into the cushions. "Yes, this is exactly what we were afraid of."

"Afraid of?"

He nods. "That the murders…" He glances at Lovejoy, shakes his head in apology. "That the murders might be related. That the murders might be part of a larger…" He places his hand over his mouth, leans his elbow on his knee.

"Of a larger…?" I prompt.

His eyes find mine. "Revenge plot."

"But revenge for what?"

"Sarawak."

"The riots you were talking of? All those years ago?"

He nods. "Yes. Unfortunately, when the Chinese *kungsi* attacked Kuching, we had to kill many of them just to defend ourselves." He steeples his fingers at the middle point of his forehead, presses his eyes shut. "It was very distressing." His hand drops and he gazes across at Heloise. "But, you see, if we hadn't, they might even have murdered my poor wife,

God rest her soul. Slaughtered her, cut her down with a sabre, like they did to poor Mrs Crookshank."

"Poor Mrs Crookshank," murmurs Lovejoy.

"Yes," says Pidgeon. "We lost several people that day. Wilkins and the Crookshanks escaped by their kitchen door, and were trying to run across to our house when two villains rushed out from the stable. Killed poor Crookshank with a spear, and sliced through Wilkins's arm. Mrs Crookshank slipped in the grass... She lay like that for six hours, weltering in her own blood, before the brutes allowed us to retrieve her body. She didn't survive more than an hour after that." His voice trails away.

"And you think one of these—*kungsi*, I think you called it—has come here to exact revenge?" I ask.

Pidgeon nods again. "A couple of days later, after we'd driven them off, they sent a message to Brooke—the sultan there, you know—that stated they'd avenge all their dead, even if they had to follow us to the ends of the earth."

"And now, one of those bastard Chinamen is after us!" Lovejoy's voice is hoarse, but loud. "One of those vicious, ungodly, grasping bastards murdered my girl." The macaroon crumbles from his clenched hand. I hope Amah doesn't walk past the open doorway anytime soon.

Pidgeon pats him on the knee. "Now, now, Lovejoy. This may not be the case. We must wait to see what Sir Thomas thinks."

Lovejoy wipes his hands down the sides of his trousers, up and down.

"What do the police say about Miss Margaret's death?" I ask, my voice soft.

"They think the murder was..." Pidgeon looks away from the other man, "was closer to home."

"Have you told them of your suspicions? About the Chinese man trying to break into your house?"

"We tried. But they were not receptive."

"And that's why you want to bring Sir Thomas in?"

"Yes." Pidgeon drawls out the word. "But something else…"

Bundle stands in the doorway, announces, "Mr Cosgrove."

I feel a dip in my stomach. I sit straighter, wish I'd taken time to neaten my hair, pinch colour into my cheeks.

"Heloise. Please excuse my sudden intrusion," he says, handing his gloves and hat to the butler. He's wearing a handsome navy coat, set firmly across his broad shoulders, and grey trousers with a diagonal stripe. His necktie is held in place by a stickpin of gold, studded with a blue stone, so deep and pure, that it brings out the colour of his own eyes.

"Ah, Pidgeon," he says, taking Pidgeon's outstretched hand, "your man said I'd find you here."

He catches sight of Lovejoy, frowns. "Lovejoy, sir, you here too?" He takes a seat on a chair by the end of the sofa, next to Lovejoy. "I was sorry to hear of your daughter."

Lovejoy grasps Cosgrove's hand, says, "Terrible business, Cosgrove. It's been terrible." His bottom lip jerks.

Cosgrove's frown deepens, the sides of his mouth draw down. "Have the police found out anything yet?"

Lovejoy waves his hand. "Nothing. Nothing at all. They've ransacked the house, mucked around in the outhouse, the garden. They've even emptied the pond, in search for the… the…" His lips jerk again.

"The weapon," says Pidgeon.

"They think someone in the house did it," Lovejoy says, barely louder than a whisper.

"That's why we're here," explains Pidgeon. "We've come to ask Heloise of the private detective she sometimes works with."

"You think the police won't find the culprit?" asks Cosgrove.

"It's not so much that." Pidgeon looks to Lovejoy, whose chin has sunk to his chest. "We believe they're searching in the wrong quarter."

Light raindrops tap the window glass. A man calls for a cab out on the street.

"You're thinking of McBride's death? Of that Chinese fellow you saw. That these murders might be connected to Sarawak?" says Cosgrove.

"Indeed." Pidgeon's hound face is apologetic.

Cosgrove stares at the two men, then nods, once, as though he's made up his mind. Reaching into the inner pocket of his coat, he pulls forth a folded piece of paper. "I found this amongst my mail this morning."

He smooths out a scrap of cheap paper on the tabletop, revealing the words: *Your blood be our profit*. Under the words is a symbol, of a triangular shape, that resembles a child's drawing of a roof. The words are a scrawl, scratched into the thin paper.

I lower myself to my knees, my skirts billowing as I lean on the table to have a better look. The nib pen has been pressed against the paper savagely enough to make a tiny tear at the right-hand corner of the triangle.

I tap my fingertip near the edge of the paper, and say, "What's that peculiar mark smeared across the symbol?" It's a rusty colour, has the deep hue of an autumn maple leaf. I snatch my hand back into my lap, my eyes widening as I stare at Cosgrove. His face is grim. "It's not…"

He nods. "I think it might be blood. Or, at the very least, it's supposed to appear to be."

Cosgrove looks at Lovejoy, who's gawping at the letter, mouth open. "McBride mentioned something about a threatening message you received, Lovejoy. Did yours resemble this note, sir?"

Lovejoy shakes his head slowly, before turning it into a nod. "No. But yes. I don't know."

"Is it possible to see the letter you received?"

Lovejoy shakes his head again. "I threw it in the fire. Thought it was just an empty threat from a coachman I'd recently let go."

"Did it also have a smear of blood on it?" I ask.

"No, I don't think so. But it had lain in the mud for some

time before I opened it. I found it by the doors that lead onto the back patio. It was the same illegible scribble though."

"What did it say?"

Lovejoy shrugs. "I can't exactly remember. Something along the lines that I'd be sorry, or repentant." He pinches the bridge of his nose, and his shoulders lift on a sob.

"Did it have this symbol at the bottom?" asks Cosgrove.

Lovejoy swallows hard. "I think it did, Cosgrove. I think it did. I took it for an 'A'. I thought it stood for 'anonymous'."

Pidgeon is even paler than before. He licks his dry lips. "Cosgrove, you recognise that symbol, don't you?"

Cosgrove's face is serious, looks almost feline. "It's the sign of the *kungsi* gang that attacked us."

"But how do you know?" Lovejoy's gaze swings from Cosgrove to Pidgeon.

"They wrote it on the wall of the house we were staying in when we were in Kuching. During the riot," Pidgeon's voice cracks. "You must remember that, Lovejoy."

Lovejoy presses his eyes shut. "Ah, yes. They wrote it in Crookshank's blood. I remember."

Pidgeon's eyes catch mine. "I'm very sorry, Heloise, that you have had to listen to this."

Cosgrove folds the letter up, pushes it back down into his pocket. "Heloise is a sensible woman, Pidgeon. We don't need to tiptoe around her."

I'm so gratified by his words I almost grin.

Amah Li Leen stands back, before taking one more swift look through the peephole. The drawing room's empty. Heloise has ushered her guests into the hallway. Amah's fingertips tingle with heightened nerves as she replaces a small oil painting over the peephole. Usually she stops to admire the painting—of dark, roiling waves under an apricot sky. It reminds her of Makassar, of its heat and colour. But this time she's too troubled by what she has just seen and heard in the other room.

Lovejoy.

She picks up the coal scuttle she'd dropped to the ground when she first saw him through the peephole. Gathering up the scattered coal, she carries it to the fireplace. She'd come in to start the fire, warm up the room for their supper, but now she can't do anything but stare into the empty, scorched grate. Lovejoy looks so much older than when she saw him last. But, of course, that was more than twenty-five years ago. He's still an ugly man though. Inside and out, no doubt.

She sinks into one of the bentwood chairs that circle the parlour table. Heloise would be surprised to see her so shaken, but the distant past is a nightmare that Amah only ever reluctantly revisits.

The door opens, and Abigail puts her head around. "I'm about to go home. Do you need help starting that fire, Amah?"

Amah stands up, wipes down the front of her skirt. "Yes, you do it. And then fill the coal scuttle, will you? Bring it back here. You're a big, strong girl."

She likes this young woman, even if she does trip over her, it seems, all around the house. Amah admires how she gets on with the job, doesn't whinge, doesn't cavil at the cleaning, the scrubbing. Not like the last miss they had in to help out during the day, who dragged her steps as she polished the banisters, and refused to clean the chamber pots properly. Abigail didn't quibble at Amah being Asian either, didn't back out of the house, saying, "No fucking way am I working with a damned chink," like the footman Bundle was thinking of hiring. Abigail said she'd worked with a family who had servants from India, who even had foreigners as guests sometimes.

As Abigail stokes the fire, Amah neatens the crystal decanters of alcohol on the sideboard. She heard some of their conversation through the air vents high in the wall. Pidgeon—yes, she remembers him well, too, from that voyage a quarter of a century ago—was terrified of some *kungsi* gang they came across in Sarawak. He said one of them was here, in London, to exact revenge, starting with Lovejoy's child. Sounded like nonsense to Amah.

But... a loitering Chinese man. And threatening letters. Amah thinks of how she saw Jakub standing on the corner—it was Jakub, wasn't it? She also thinks of Miriam's words, about him being back in London.

Could it be Jakub who Pidgeon had interrupted at his house? It's not like there are a multitude of Chinamen in London, after all. But why would he be stalking these men from Amah's past? Jakub couldn't have anything to do with that Sarawak business. He wasn't even born then.

Amah feels a swoop of fear in her belly. Was it Jakub who had lain in wait for McBride? Is that why she'd seen him so close to their house? Was it her beloved boy who'd cut the man's throat?

CHAPTER 7

The sip of whisky warms my chest as I stare up at my portrait above the fireplace in the drawing room. I'm still feeling rather pleased with Cosgrove's words. If only Hatterleigh could be that matter-of-fact with me. I know in some ways he is proud of my sleuthing, but, most of the time, he cannot help but try to dissuade me from such unpleasantness. Like last night, when he tried to steer me away from questioning the police, and that glint of concern in his eye when we discussed my last case. Of course, it is Hatterleigh's wish to protect me that maintains my life of comfort. When I think of this, I struggle between a preening complacency and feeling like there's a stone around my neck.

"Madam," says Bundle.

"Yes, Bundle. Supper ready?"

The butler nods. "Yes, it is. However, it's on another subject I'd like to speak with you."

I feel a flicker of concern when I see the troubled look on Bundle's usually bland, handsome face. Even that time I'd arrived home, blood smeared across the bodice of my dress, or when I'd turned up arm in arm with a vagrant, Bundle never so much as lifted an eyebrow.

"What is it?"

He leads the way into the hallway, to the mahogany display cabinet that stands against the wall between the drawing room and the parlour. He lifts the glass top so we can gaze down upon the curios collected upon the felt overlay.

"I had Abigail dust these today," he says. "That's when I noticed…"

My eyes take in the ivory netsukes from Japan — the glossy rabbit with flowing ears, the hunched man clutching a large fish to his chest. And the less polite netsukes, that are rather rare and precious — engorged men with spreadeagled women, who have wide smiles, their heads flung back. A woman with her intricately carved tongue poked into another's *chatte*. God, I wonder what Abigail thinks when she's dusting them. My two favourite netsukes stand in the top left-hand corner. A tiny, hardwood snake, as black as ebony, coiled upon itself. I'd bought it at an auction, because Amah was born in the Chinese year of the snake, but she wouldn't keep it, insisted it stayed in my display cabinet. Beside it is a tiger — my Chinese sign — yellowed with age, jaw snarled, front paw ready to strike.

"Has something been stolen?" I ask Bundle, looking over the pieces of dress jewellery made from cinnabar, the brass oxen, the jade Buddha.

My eyes snag on a long gap at the bottom of the felt overlay. I place my fingers on the empty space, stare up at Bundle.

"What was here?" Even as I ask, I know the answer.

A *kris*. A short sword, maybe a foot long, its keen blade a series of curves, with an intricate pattern engraved upon the iron and garnets peppered along its handle.

"That fancy knife, madam," says Bundle.

I frown. Who among my guests would swipe the *kris*? Surely if a guest or servant were after something to sell, they'd choose an easier item, like silver or my jewellery.

"How long has it been missing?"

"I saw it there just yesterday, when I polished the cabinet." His voice is as deep as usual, but I think I discern a hint of a tremor. "I wonder if, perhaps, it was taken from here last night?"

Last night.

I look in horror at Bundle.

"You think it was used to murder McBride?" The pool of blood, glistening in the moonlight.

Bundle nods.

"But who…?" Who would take the *kris*? Who would want to kill McBride? "That means…"

Bundle nods again. "If I am correct, it means that someone—someone in this house last night—took the knife to use on McBride."

I think of McBride's head, wet, hinged backward. The damage to his throat. Amah had once told me that the *kris* has a wavy blade in order to sever as many blood vessels as possible. So the victim bleeds out quickly. The end is more certain.

I lean upon the display cabinet, my other hand clamped across my stomach. "Where's Amah?

"She went out about twenty minutes ago. She did not leave word on where she was going."

Amah's Uncle Chee is seated at a table in the corner of his own eating house, bent over a bowl of soup. He has the *Singapore Chronicle* spread before him, open at the shipping news.

She's come to see Miriam, to find out more of Jakub, but she takes a seat across from her uncle.

"You want soup?" He speaks to her in their own dialect, a mix between Malay and Makassarese. "Miriam made me some *sayur asam*. It's good." He slurps from his spoon and grins. "Not as good as your mother's, of course. But it's impossible to find tamarind here."

He ladles some soup into a small rice bowl, slides it across the table to her.

Amah stirs the *sayur asam*, watching the chopped tomato rise in the steaming soup, disappear again. She looks over at the customers grouped around the largest table, sipping tea, their voices low and urgent. Chinese sailors, in faded trousers, tattered shoes. Each has a long plait that ropes low to the seat of his trousers. Chee, although of the same blood, wears his hair short.

He shrugs. "More sailors stranded here."

"They didn't get paid?" asks Amah.

"I don't know about that. They were promised work on a voyage home, but when they got here, the company backed out. Happens all the time."

This time Amah notices the slumped shoulders of the young one nearest her, the flushed cheeks of the middle-aged man next to him. "Where will they go?"

"There are two lodging houses nearby. There's also a Chinese missionary, and the Strangers' Home."

Amah thinks back to that first evening, many, many years before, when they stepped off the ship onto Toxteth wharf in Liverpool. How chill the air was, how barren the dock. Nobody was there to greet them, no venders with food, no touts offering somewhere to stay. Certainly there was no Chinese missionary or Strangers' Home to go to. She turns back to Chee. "Not as grim as when we arrived, then."

He grunts in agreement, points at her bowl with his spoon and says, "Eat."

"Is Miriam here?" she asks, sipping her soup. "I wanted to ask her where I can find Jakub." The soup is good. But Chee is right. It's not as tasty as her mother's *sayur asam*. A bit too much vinegar, maybe?

Chee makes a sucking noise at the side of his mouth. His eyes harden. Amah has never seen him look more like her grandfather—his father. "Who knows where that boy is."

"So Miriam doesn't know either?"

"She's worried about him. I hate it when he makes her worry." Chee's spoon clatters against the bowl. "He's only ever thought of himself, that boy. Never others."

"He's not a boy, Uncle Chee. He's a young man."

"He still acts like a boy. I wonder sometimes if it would have been different if he was brought up in the old country."

"Makassar?"

"No! China."

Amah's mouth twists. "Uncle Chee, you've never been to the old country. How would you know?"

"I just know it." Chee's hand curls into a fist on the tabletop. "If someone strong like my father had him in hand…"

"He would have run away like we all did," answers Amah, her voice dry.

Chee meets her eye. He waves his hand, relaxes, but his mouth is still pursed in an unsatisfied line.

"But, really, Uncle Chee, do you have any idea where I can find Jakub?" she asks.

He frowns at her, takes another mouthful of soup. "Why do you want to find him so much?"

Amah's eyes drop from his. She can't tell him the truth — neither of the reasons she wants to see him. First, that she's a little hurt that Jakub hasn't sought her out after so long away. Second, that she's worried for the young man. She wants to make sure he's not involved with these murders, that he's not the Chinese man the others are talking about.

But she knows she can't get away with telling a falsehood to her uncle. This is the same man who'd caught her out when she'd smuggled the baby cuscus, with its gamey, soft fur, and its eyes as round and glossy as buttons, into her grandfather's house, and hidden it amongst her mother's bed cushions. Another time he'd caught her watching the little boy next door, laughing as he pissed on the smoked fish drying in the sun. Amah can still feel the flick of his hard finger to her ear, the residual warmth after the sting. She almost lifts her hand to her left ear with the memory.

Amah's voice is low as she says, "Uncle Chee, you know I'm always interested in what Jakub is up to."

He stares at her for a few moments. "That boy, he's very suspicious, you know." He shakes his head from side to side, makes the sucking noise again. "He should have trained to be a lawyer." He laughs, but it's not a happy sound.

"What do you mean, Uncle?"

"He found out that Miriam is not his real Ma."

Amah gapes at him. "But how does he know this?"

"I am not sure." Chee shrugs. "He asked me many questions, but I thought he was just curious about his heritage."

"Like what?"

"What boat we came in on. What year it was. Then, just before he left for the East, he told Miriam he knew the truth, that she's not his real mother."

"Why didn't you tell me?"

"Miriam thought it best not to worry you with it. She was very upset. She loves that boy. She's always been a good mother to him."

Amah hugs her arms to herself. Anxiety threads her chest tight. "Yes, she has."

"So, what do we do now, *kodok kecil*?"

Although her chest hurts, she manages to smile sadly at Chee. "Why do you always call me 'little frog', Uncle?"

He throws his head back, thinks for a moment. He smiles as he recalls the past. "I think it's because when you were small you wouldn't leave your mother's skirts. You used to peep out at me like a frog under a husk."

Another lifetime. She's almost forgotten that little girl.

"So, Li Leen, what should we do about Jakub, do you think?" he asks.

The young Chinese man at the big table hunches over and starts to cry. The man next to him clasps a hand on his shoulder, makes soothing sounds.

Amah's mouth twists to the side again. "Tell him the truth, I suppose."

As Amah trudges along the road in search of a cab, she thinks back to those first few days on the *Dukano* as they crossed the Java Sea. The pictures in her head are sepia, bright yet unclear.

Besides her mistress, Mrs Preston, there were four other families making their way to Surabaya. One end of the deck was crammed with crates containing pet dogs and birds, and furniture that couldn't fit in the hold. Three women, their pale skin gleaming in the heat, slumped to the ground, faint. After that, all the white people stayed in their cabins until the sun was low and a breeze picked up. Late at night, the servant boys slept on the floor of the saloon. Amah was never sure where the other servants slept, but Mrs Preston let her sleep in the small room where her mistress's baggage was kept.

The other ladies were Dutch and, in the evenings, they languished about on deck-chairs dressed in kebayas and sarongs, like their servant girls. But not Mrs Preston. She was British. She always dressed in a blouse that buttoned to her throat and a dark skirt that billowed to the ground. That is how Amah learnt to dress the way she did. Only if it was so steamy that even Amah felt trapped in her skin, would Mrs Preston unbutton the top few buttons of her blouse.

Amah shakes her head, even smiles, when she thinks of how insolent she was when she was first in Mrs Preston's service. If Amah had a servant that acted like she did then, she would slap the servant's face until her cheek was as red as a dragon fruit. But Mrs Preston was kind, and sickly from a fever she'd picked up in Nieuw Guinea. And, of course, Amah had recently lost her mother. She was lonely. And foolish. It didn't take her long to soften. Mrs Preston treated her like her child, really. Or sister. Combed her hair after Amah did hers, taught her English words. Of course, now, Amah realises that Mrs Preston was probably just bored and starved of company, but by the time the Dutch families left the boat in Java and the *Dukano* had arrived in Sarawak, not two weeks later, Amah couldn't be pried from her mistress's side.

CHAPTER 8

Cosgrove stands in the doorway letting the cold night air in.

"Come, Heloise," he urges. "The others are waiting in the carriage."

I've been fretting about the *kris*. Amah still hasn't returned home, and Bundle has gone to the police station for me, to report the *kris's* disappearance.

"Cosgrove, something terrible has happened," I say to him, ushering him in so I can close the door. "Bundle found that a *kris* is missing from that cabinet there." I gesture further down the hallway. "You know, one of those jewelled Malay knives? He thinks it's only been missing since McBride was murdered."

I'm sure Cosgrove's blue eyes darken as I speak. "Is he sure?" He looks from me to the cabinet.

I nod. "Cosgrove, that means…"

He stares at me. "Someone from this house that evening must have taken it."

"Exactly."

"The police. Have you told them?"

"Bundle is there at this moment."

"Good."

He bows his head, frowning at the floor as he thinks. "Could it have been taken by one of your servants?"

I've wondered this myself, but most of my staff are of long-standing, and if Abigail wanted to steal something, surely she'd take something more easily fenced. I shake my head. "I really don't think so."

"Well, I guess we can each expect a call from the police soon, making enquiries about that *kris*."

How absurd. I feel mortified, as a hostess, that something as ghastly and inopportune as a murder has happened on my premises; that it has become an annoyance to my guests.

Cosgrove smiles at the stricken look on my face. "At least we can forget about it all tonight, though, Heloise. I overheard Hatterleigh say he was going to the Billinghams' ball tonight, so Milly thought it would be a nice idea if you came out with us. What do you say?"

A night at the theatre. It does sound enjoyable. Better than being alone, maudlin by the fireplace. But I feel a frisson of irritation that I've only been invited because they know I'm not otherwise engaged with Hatterleigh. I could cancel on Hatterleigh if I so desired, couldn't I?

I'm already pinning my hat to my hair when I ask, "But how do you know I do not have other plans?"

His lips curl into a smile, crinkling his eyes. "Well, I suppose I was hoping you did not."

I cast about for my purse and fur, in order to avoid his eye.

Crammed into the corner of the carriage is poor Isobel, who's laughing that Milly's ribbons are poking her in the eye. Next to Milly is the chubby gentleman she'd played cards with at my soiree. As Cosgrove helps me climb into the carriage, I see that I have to sit next to the tall young man, the one who was licking his lips over me the other night.

Cosgrove squeezes in next to me. "Do you remember Thatcher and Webb?"

Thatcher greets me cheerily. His cheeks are as rosy and round as apples. I glance up at Webb, to my right. Although he's not licking his lips this time, they're as wet and unattractive as I remember. His hair hangs unfashionably long and recedes from his large forehead.

"Charmed," he murmurs. His eyes gleam with what he, no doubt, thinks is a "knowing look".

"We're going to the Grecian," Milly tells me, her voice raised above the crunch of the carriage wheels. "To watch their pantomime."

"I did a season at the Grecian." The words are surprised from me. I'm usually very careful about what I reveal of my past, but really, I don't think I need to worry about this lot.

"But that's wonderful," says Isobel. "Tell us of it!"

As we trundle along the roads to Shoreditch, I regale them with stories of ponies that hauled spangled coaches onto the stage, of how the actors had to avoid stepping in the manure in their silk slippers. Of the time Dick Whittington's "cat" caught alight and streaked through the audience, screaming, and when poor Harlequin fell down the trapdoor, mid sonnet, and broke her hip.

"The last part I played there was as an Arabian princess in *Aladdin*," I say, just as our carriage pulls into the side of the road outside the theatre.

I'm the last to alight, and as Cosgrove takes my hand to help me climb down, he smiles, and says, "You'd be the perfect Arabian princess, madam," but my pleasure at his remark is spoiled by Webb's accompanying leer. I turn, roll my eyes, and Isobel presses her lips together, suppressing a grin.

Disappointingly, Cosgrove walks ahead, with Milly and Isobel on either side, while I'm left flanked by the younger men. Just as we enter the theatre, Isobel runs back to me, links her arm in mine.

Cosgrove pays a shilling each for us to have seats in the boxes, which are up two flights of steps. The theatre is quite full, and we're a little late in taking our seats towards the back. A milkmaid and a shepherd are singing something nonsensical yet witty, going by the laughter of the audience. Rather than disturb the patrons already seated, Cosgrove and Webb, both tall men, decide to stand at the back of the box until there's a break in the performance. The others edge into their seats, and I follow, taking the one closest to the aisle.

I'm just settling the taffeta skirts of my gown—olive green, but with a lovely burnished finish—about my knees when I feel a tap on my shoulder. A slight figure kneels by my side.

"Heloise, dear, it *is* you." Kitty, a stage hand I know from when I worked here, clutches my wrist. "You're not up for a bit of a romp again, are you? We're in a bit of a tight spot."

"What is it?"

"Well, poor Madge—remember her? Small thing, wears a different wig every day?—well, she's got somethin' wrong with her innards. Started clutching her sides and spewing. Had to call for the doctor, we did. But now we're without a Red Riding Hood."

I stare at Kitty for a moment, conscious of Isobel listening in beside me.

"But…" I haven't taken to the stage in over two years now. I glance along the row at my companions. I don't want to appear foolish; or, more to the point, cheapen myself in their eyes. "Surely someone else can cover for her."

Kitty shakes her head. "Everyone's performing tonight. Even Jasper, the prompt."

Isobel nudges me. "Go on, Heloise. If you don't, I will!"

Cosgrove appears in the aisle behind Kitty. "Is there a problem, Heloise?"

I laugh up at him, lightly, but I watch for his reaction as I say, "Kitty here wants me to take a part in the pantomime. But, of course, it is impossible."

"But Heloise," Kitty beseeches me, "they've finally allowed me to take to the stage. I'm to be the Wolf, but if there's no Red Riding Hood…"

I stare into her anxious eyes, and relent a little. "What will I wear, though? I won't fit into Madge's costume. I'm far taller than her." More buxom, too, from memory.

A wide smile lifts Kitty's face. "All you need is the red

cape, Heloise. Anyone will recognise you from that. You'll do it then?"

Isobel and Milly giggle behind me, pinch my arm, whisper, "Go! Go!" Excitement bubbles in my chest. I can't deny I'm drawn to the prospect. The exhilaration of being on stage, shining brighter than the limelight. The chance to show off my acting abilities to my friends; my talent for drawing the eye with an expression or word.

I get to my feet and say to Kitty, "Of course I'll help you." As I pass Cosgrove, who looks amused, I widen my eyes, as if I don't know what I've gotten myself into, but really, in my head, I'm already applying greasepaint to my face, wondering what lines I might have to learn.

"You don't have to say anything on stage," says Kitty, as she shoves a goblin from the seat in front of the dressing room mirror. "We're just part of the general ensemble of fairy tale characters."

She's already tugged the gown from my body, and now lathers pale cream across my face, pats it out across my forehead.

"Who was that delicious man you were with?" she asks. "The last I saw of you, you were with that ugly farmer type. A lord or something."

I rub pink circles onto my cheeks. "That's Maurice Cosgrove. Just a friend."

"Nice friend," she says, winking in the mirror at me.

I grin, but can't wink back in case I smudge the black paste I've applied to my eyelashes, which now have the thick curl of chrysanthemum petals.

After I've swapped my gown for layers of frilly petticoat and a red cloak, and Kitty dons her wolf suit—which includes a full head mask of whiskery brown fur and gleaming yellow eyes—we join the others by the side of the stage. Kitty tells me that all I have to do is run from her once in a while, a game of hide-and-seek. As we wait in the wings, I'm jostled on one side by Mother Goose, who's bearded and fat, and on my other side, I think, by Sleeping Beauty. Kitty bumps into my shoulder three times, half-blind in her mask.

The fairy council flitters from the stage and Kitty pushes me forward, whispers, "We're on."

I follow Rapunzel, careful not to step on her trailing hair, golden as buttered corn, sweeping wisps of dust along with it.

For one moment I'm so dazzled by the monstrous pomp on stage, I pause, so that Mother Goose runs into me, swears under his breath. Stage lights glitter, and tall mirrors line the back of the stage, multiplying the colourful crowd of fairy tale characters. We must be a magnificent sight from the stalls and boxes—the golden crowns, the elves' green collars, the sparkling crystal chips on the Fairy Godmother's dress. Up close, though, the splendour is marred by the smell of dust, body odour and fresh paint.

Cinderella joins us, but not in a horse-drawn carriage, as I've seen countless times before. She's lowered in a basket that is attached to a billowing, golden orb that's supposed to be a hot air balloon. The audience gasp and clap. I almost do myself.

From what I've gathered so far, the fairies are mourning the loss of a precious gem from which they get their magical powers, and the Frog Prince tells us that we've been gathered to find a hero who will find it for them. I position myself towards the front of the stage. I won't peer into the boxes for Cosgrove and the others, but I'm sure their eyes are on me. I play my part by ducking behind a prince in order to hide from the Wolf, and I'm having so much fun, I wish I was cast as the hero. If only I knew the lines.

A trapdoor, not two metres in front of me, drops open and Puss in Boots springs into the air, and lands with a smart flourish at the front of the stage. In a pretty contralto voice, Puss in Boots sings of the power of *le chat*, of the cunning pussy, and while some of the audience laugh, many just nod along with the song, oblivious to the wordplay.

Puss in Boots has a lovely cascade of chestnut hair under her tricorne, and her legs... Oh god, I wish I was wearing tights like that too, showing off the length and curve of my limbs. I start to feel a steady tick of irritation that she's in the spotlight, and I'm hidden beneath this ghastly cloak.

Just as Puss in Boots hums her last note, Kitty slams into me from behind. I squeal, as my part requires, and pretend to run away. Hansel and Gretel are ahead of me, holding hands, and as I surge forward, I collide with their locked hands, somersault over. I land in a flurry of petticoats, and the red riding hood falls from my shoulders. Pain ricochets from my buttocks, but it's worth the laugh from the audience. For one moment, everyone's watching me, not that stupid Puss in Boots.

CHAPTER 9

The morning air is so cold I wrench the divan a little closer to the fireplace in the parlour and lie upon it, bunching the cushions beneath my head. I actually feel quite fresh, apart from the bruise on my bum. No headache, not too weary. I didn't drink too much in the end, being caught up with the pantomime.

I'm enjoying a new book, one by Braddon. I'm up to the part where Eleanor marries Monckton but only so she can keep investigating her father's death. What a pity she has to leave off her gallivanting. Of course, Eleanor really does love Monckton, she just has to keep secrets from him. Secrets. Secrets seem to be a necessary part of a woman's existence if she is to live a whole life, it would seem. My life is so full of them, it's sometimes difficult to prise the real from the make-believe.

Abigail brings me a cup of steaming chocolate mid-morning, and a slice of lamb pie for lunch. She must've enjoyed some of it herself, too, in the kitchen, for I see crumbs of pastry caught in the downy rabbit fur on her lip.

"Madam, may I ask you, but where is Amah from exactly?" she asks me as she clears the tray.

I sit up straighter in the divan, rearrange the cushions. "Well, she's Chinese." I peep up at her face. She doesn't seem put out. It'd be a nuisance to have to find a new housemaid so soon again.

"Yes, I know that, madam. But is she from China?"

I shake my head. "Ah, no. She's from the Malaya area."

"She speaks very good English," Abigail says, but really it's a question. She's by the door, and I let her go without further comment. Amah's business is hers to tell, not mine.

For the rest of the afternoon I read and doze. The room has darkened by the time I get to the end of the novel and I angle the pages so that the light from the fire illuminates the words. I close the book and rest it against my breast. What a pity Eleanor had to sink into the vapours as well as her husband's arms, in the end. But there was such a fuss about Braddon's last book, I'm not surprised she's thrown conservative sop to the critics.

Rain lashes against the glass, so heavily the world outside is a blur. Standing, I clasp my dressing gown closer around my body, sink my nose into the swansdown ruffle. I make my way to the window and place my hand against the chill glass. The wind whistles its way through the gaps at the edges of the window frames. The street is empty apart from a slight figure making his way along the footpath and a brown brougham parked across the way. The horses are drenched, but there's no sign of the coachman.

Bundle enters the parlour with the evening paper. He pulls a small table to the fireplace and flattens out the wet sheets of newspaper to dry.

"I'm sorry, madam," he says. "The paperboy did his best."

I look back out the window. Horizontal sheets of rain drive the young man back down the street, and floods of water gush against his heels. "The poor thing."

I wonder how much longer his route is, if he has somewhere dry to bed down later. I remember one night when a couple of us took refuge from weather such as this under a bush in Kew Gardens because it was too late to sneak into the Palm House. What a miserable night that was. I shiver and rub my hands up and down my arms. I'm confident—absolutely resolute, in fact—that I will not be caught out like that ever again.

Taking a seat on the edge of the divan, I peer down at the

front page, careful not to smudge my fingers or clothing on the damp ink. A picture of a fine house, its many windows blotted black with rainwater, takes up half the page, under the words, *Second Murder at St Chad's Lodge*.

A second crime has been committed, brother to the hideous wickedness so recently delivered upon the Lovejoy family of Stoke Newington. We may well remember the heinous murder of young Margaret Lovejoy, poor creature, found lifeless in the water closet. This crime, quite without parallel in our criminal records, has been repeated upon the father, one Erasmus Timothy Lovejoy. As far as we understand the story, Mr Lovejoy was locking the side gate to his property, after loosing the watchdog from its pen. The murderer or murderess had stolen upon him, either secretly or brazenly, we cannot say. Taking out some sort of blade, cunning and razor-sharp, the culprit had cut Mr Lovejoy's throat to the very vertebrae, and then thrust him face down into the horses' water trough.

My eyes run through the rest of the article, in which the reporter issues instructions on how the police should investigate the murder, and finishes with: *We must all do our part to assist the police in finding who is guilty for these foul deeds.*

Bloody hell. Lovejoy. The same grey gentleman I met just yesterday. Squishing my bottom lip between my fingers, I stare into space, remembering his trembling hands, his confused state.

I wrench the front page from the rest and leap to my feet so quickly I bang my knee against the table, knocking the rest of the newspaper to the floor. Hobbling into the hallway, I ask Abigail, who's straightening a bouquet of hyacinth in a crystal vase, "Abigail, have you seen Amah today?"

She tosses her head towards the top of the house. "Up in her room, I expect. She'd be mad to be out in this gale."

I hurry up the two flights of stairs, and I'm quite winded by the time I rap on Amah's door. I push it open, nearly knocking her in the nose.

"What is it, Heloise?" she asks, looking past me in alarm.

"Look at this." I take a seat at the round table in Amah's sitting room, spread the front page flat across the table, accidentally sweeping the silk embroidery she's been working upon onto the floor. But even as she reads, squinting down at the small print, I say, "Lovejoy. He was here just yesterday. He's the father of that child that was murdered."

Amah pulls a chair out next to mine, lowers herself slowly. She picks up the shawl she is embroidering for me, places it on the back of her chair, but it slips to the floor again under the weight of its lace border.

"Was his throat cut too?" she asks.

"Yes. The same as the girl. It says his head was almost severed altogether. Just like McBride."

I notice the colour has faded from Amah's face.

She presses her eyes together for a moment, then frowns. "Why? Why?"

"Nobody knows." I'm puzzled by Amah's reaction. I've seen her amongst the mayhem of murder, the blood, the stench. Usually she doesn't turn a hair. I wonder if the poor thing is still upset by the other night, if she has been thinking of how close she was to being a victim herself? After all, Amah usually has the upper hand in these situations — Amah and her bitey little switchblade. "But surely his death has to be connected to McBride's. They're so similar."

Amah stands up so abruptly, the chair totters behind her. She hurries to the window and, pressing her forehead to the glass, she gazes up and down the street.

I join her. "What are you looking for?"

She just shakes her head, the crease between her brows more pronounced.

I become still, then draw back behind the curtains. A chill draught ripples across my skin, which has nothing to do with the storm. Amah's watching for the killer. She thinks he might be outside.

I frown. But why would McBride's murderer return here?

A green carriage nudges in behind the brougham across the road. A man climbs down into the street, lands in a puddle. He covers his head with what looks like a magazine. As he darts across to my house, the brougham's door swings open, releasing another man who follows the first.

The rapping on the front door is so loud, so persistent, we can hear it from two levels up. I run to the top of the stairs, lean on the newel as Bundle opens the door. The voices are too low, too hurried, for me to hear clearly, though, over the rush of rain slapping against the doorstep.

Bundle shuts the door. It's quiet again, so I know he hasn't allowed the men to enter. I hurry down the stairs and, pausing on the first landing, lean over the banister until I can see Bundle's shadow. "Who was it, Bundle?"

He takes a step forward so I can see him. "Reporters, Mrs Chancey."

My shoulders relax a little. Have they heard of my turn at the Grecian last night? Maybe they've come to ask me of the crowds in Hyde Park. How very forward to hunt me down in my home. I smile. Rather pleasing, though.

"Apparently there has been another murder. Lovejoy, I believe they said," says Bundle, his deep voice as smooth, as toneless as usual. "They seem to think it is connected with the murder committed here two nights ago. Said the methods were similar."

I stare into his steady, grey eyes and then glance up at Amah who stands on the landing above. Her arms are crossed, and she shakes her head.

"Better stay in tonight, Heloise."

CHAPTER 10

I think I will never get to sleep. The heavy rain that drums against the bedroom windows cannot mute my heartbeat, which throbs against my ribs. I lie on my back, fling my right arm above my head—how I usually find my way to sleep. But nothing.

How on earth am I going to get rid of those reporters? The last time I peeked out the window, the carriages were still there, biding their time, like a couple of damned debt collectors. What the hell will the neighbours think? The police the other night, and now blasted reporters. I've nothing to tell them of McBride. Didn't even meet him. I slide onto my left side, then the right. Feeling feverish against the banked-up pillows, I fling two across the floor.

And I can't involve the others. The reporters must not find out about my friends—of who they are—or the Pidgeons and Cosgrove may never attend my soirees again.

And Hatterleigh. He wouldn't like this sort of publicity at all.

I lie on my back again, stare over at the closed curtains. Who did Amah think she'd seen out there when she gazed at the street? The same person who left McBride on my back doorstep? Lovejoy's murderer? Why would he be lurking here?

I think again of the pooled blood on the doorstep, its shiny depths. As black as ink. Of drawing the ink into a well, dipping my pen in it... I wrench awake, clutch my throat.

The rest of the night is much the same. I feel like I haven't slept at all, yet I wake to fragments of dreams, of draping myself over Hatterleigh's broad back; of arguing with Amah until I feel a scream buzz in my eardrums. Worst—that I'm back in that room in Liverpool, the musty stench of mouse droppings, mould dappling the walls. My fingers are numb with cold, my jaw frozen shut. I weep and weep, heaving from my chest.

When I wake, the blankets have slipped off the bed and goosebumps pimple my arms. The grate is heaped with ash, barren of comforting amber embers.

"You're awake early," says Abigail, as she lumbers into the room, carrying the coal scuttle.

I sit up, watch her as she yanks the curtains open. "I don't think I really slept." Overnight, the rain has settled down to a light patter against the fogged windows.

After Abigail's conjured up a brisk, cheerful blaze, she leaves the room, saying, "I'll bring up your breakfast directly."

I lean over the side of the bed, pull the pillows back up beside me. There's a tautness across my forehead, almost a headache, from lack of sleep. I'll wager there are dark smudges under my eyes, too. My skin will be puffy. I'm no longer feeling anxious, just grumpy. What the hell did that man have to be murdered on my doorstep for? What on earth is happening?

I press my eyes shut. *Think of something else. Think of something pleasant.*

I remember I'm seeing Hatterleigh later this evening. We're going to Motts, and although it's a treat to look forward to, I feel a sliver of irritation that I'm not well rested for it. That I won't look my best.

Think of something pleasant…

Rolling over, I gaze towards my dressing room. I have a new Worth gown—French silk and the pretty lilac shade of a flowering betony. It has a wonderful array of frills, too, but the bow on the back, the rectangle pleats at the waist, make it look more like a walking dress than something I can wear to a dance.

I sit up, layer the pillows behind my back. So maybe I'll wear the ivory taffeta gown again, the one with moss green trim. I don't think Hatterleigh has seen me in it yet.

Amah comes into my room carrying my breakfast tray. She places it on the dressing table. "Heloise, can I dress your hair as soon as possible, please? I need to go out this morning."

I swing my legs over the side of the bed. "Where do you need to get to in such a hurry?" I take a seat at the dresser and tilt my head to the side, appraising my face in the mirror. I don't look tired at all. My eyes are a little bright, but that's not a bad thing.

"I'm going to visit Miriam," Amah says, hairpins clamped between her front teeth as she pulls the plait from my hair.

"Again? So soon?"

She shrugs, brushing my hair in long, smooth tugs. My head yanks back, but I know it'd be a waste of breath to complain.

I watch my mother's serious face in the mirror. Of course, her hair is neatly drawn back into a low bun, and she is already dressed in her customary black skirt and white blouse. I'm pleased to see that she has clasped the collar together with the ivory cameo brooch I gave her. But I wonder if I can discern extra shadows under her eyes, if the lines of her face seem a bit more accentuated.

"I sent a missive to Pidgeon last night," I tell her. "Asking him what he knows of Lovejoy's death. Or if there's any more news on McBride. I think the reporters must be right. They must be connected somehow."

Amah's dark eyes find mine. "And the little girl?"

I shrug, shake my head. "I don't know."

Amah presses my hair neat, pins small flowers into the braid.

"What are you doing today, Heloise?"

I take a sip of my coffee, pull a face when I realise it's not sugared yet. "If the weather settles down I might go for a ride in the park. Tonight I will be out with Hatterleigh."

Amah nods, but her eyes are fixed on the curls she's arranging in my hair.

I remember that I have a gift of perfumed soap for Aunt Miriam and as soon as Amah pats my hair neat one last time I hurry into my dressing room, find the package at the bottom of the shelves that house my hats.

"Give these to my aunt, will you?" I say, placing the fragrant package into Amah's hands. "I bought them from a sweet little shop on Tottenham Court Road. The woman said they were from France. Made with lavender."

Gazing at my vast assortment of hats, I remember my young cousin, Rosemary, swooning over my straw bonnet, the one with the cluster of silk rose buds across its curved brim. I take it from its shelf, but hesitate a moment. It's not as if Rosemary expects me to give it to her. I really love its velvet ribbons and it's a bit of a wrench to give away, but I really love Rosemary too.

I hand it over to Amah. "And give this to Rosemary. She admired it when we had morning tea last month."

Amah puts my offerings on top of the chest of drawers. "And what will you wear today?" She rummages through the top drawer, brings out a chemise and bloomers. "You're staying in, aren't you?"

I stare at her. "Maybe a ride; seeing Hatterleigh tonight," I tell her again, wondering where her mind is at. "I really wanted to wear the new gown from Worth, but it's still drizzling, and I don't want it to become ruined."

Amah glances at me and sniffs. "That purple thing? Be good if it was ruined in the rain."

CHAPTER 11

Amah comes down the stairs, securing a woollen scarf around her neck. She tugs it a little way from her skin because, although necessarily warm, wool always makes her feel itchy.

Abigail peers through the sidelight by the front door. Looking over her shoulder at Amah, she says, "Four coaches now." She returns her gaze to the window. "And I can see at least five of those vermin reporters."

Amah reaches the bottom floor and turns towards the back of the house, passing Agneau in the kitchen, who's chopping chives with fine precision, a steaming cup of chocolate before him. She lowers the netting over her face and opens the back door. Cold air, as sharp as a knife, strafes her skin. She quickly pulls the door shut behind her, before Agneau can complain.

Bundle has done a fine job of cleaning the back steps, although, in the furthest left corner, right at the bottom, almost covered by a tendril of ivy, she can see the slightest smudge, as ruby red as pomegranate juice. But maybe she's only imagining it. She decides to not look too closely.

Coming out onto the side street, a man runs towards her, notebook in hand. He blocks her way. "Madam, madam, can you tell me anything of the horror that happened here three nights ago?"

Over his shoulder she sees two more men approach. Across the road and three doors down, a young couple step from their house and stare at her, curious, and she recognises them from the other night—the two who had gazed so lovingly at each other, strolling arm in arm.

"Madam, tell us what happened," the reporter says, his voice more urgent as the others almost catch him up.

Amah lifts her veil, stares at him blankly. Shrugs. "Sir?"

The reporter gapes at her for a moment, his eyes roaming over her facial features. He jots something in his notebook, turning away from her.

Amah's mouth twists to the side as she pulls the veil back down.

She makes her way to Limehouse, to her Uncle Chee's. She gives Miriam the presents from Heloise, and asks after Jakub.

Miriam barely reacts to the presents and instead, looks worried. "We haven't seen him. He might be at that Strangers' Home. Down West India Road. Near St Andrews."

Amah's not sure how far it is, so she summons a cab, which drops her in front of a handsome two-storey building with at least twenty arched windows across its façade. She climbs the shallow steps to the portico and pushes the heavy swing door open.

The commotion in the expansive hall reminds her of the market bazaar in Makassar after a large ship had come in. Men cluster around neat rows of benches and tables, which are spread across the vast floor space. Lascars, and maybe a number of Cingalese, in soft tunics with bandanas swathed around their heads, are seated at the back of the room, as close to the fire as possible. More are slumped against the wall, arms crossed, waiting. Seated at the tables closest to the entrance are three groups of Chinese men, dressed in robes that hang to their shins. They appear to be arguing, but on closer inspection, Amah sees that the occupants of one table are in the middle of a noisy game of cards, while the men gathered at the remaining two tables seem to be trading clothing, nuts and pipes.

Glancing around for an office of some sort, at which she can enquire after Jakub, she's surprised to see three Indian women standing by an open doorway that leads into another hall that smells of roasting meat and boiled cabbage. Their saris—spangled blue, carnation pink, the off-white of an elephant tusk—wink from beneath their heavy overcoats. The woman in blue has a white baby cradled in her arms, while the woman in the pink sari wears sandals, her toes bare to the cold weather.

A sudden icy draught brings forth two men through the swing doors. They're taller than anybody Amah has ever seen, with skin as dark as mulberries. They're dressed in drab suits, battered bowler hats on their heads. They walk straight through the hall, disappear into a room to the right.

"Zanzibaris," says a voice at her elbow. "A ship just came in from Africa. Can I help you at all?"

A man, only as tall as she is, smiles at her. His hair is like ash, streaks of white and steel grey, and his skin is so pale she can see the spidery red veins that travel across his cheeks.

"What is this place?" she asks.

"Ah. This is the Strangers' Home. We look after foreign seamen, mostly, who need somewhere to stay between voyages. Some of these men might be looking for more work, but unfortunately some are itinerant."

"And the women?" Amah nods towards the Indian women.

"Nannies, come to hear news of relatives," he says. "The one in the pink sari, she seeks a passage home. Are you after the same thing? Because there is also an excellent agency I can point you to that looks after women from… China?"

"Makassar."

"Ah. Let me introduce myself. Reverend John Cadogan. I was previously a missionary in China. I can speak a little of the language, but no Malay, alas."

"Mrs Chan," Amah responds. "I'm looking for my nephew. I was told I might find him here. Jakub Chan?"

"I'll have to look in the ledger, I'm afraid. We can house up to two hundred people here, you know. Sometimes more. It's very difficult to keep track." He smiles apologetically at her, as he guides her past the three Indian women. "If you'll just wait for me in the reading room, please. I believe luncheon is to be served soon in the dining hall, and it's bedlam around here then."

He leaves Amah in a plain room that smells of dust and something like dried leaves. Four sofas, the leather worn and creased, are arranged near the bookcases that line the walls. Only one of the bookcases—the one nearest the window that faces the road—has an assortment of reading material. The bottom shelves are heaped with old periodicals, and the three top shelves are lined with leather-bound books of different shades, each one with a gold cross engraved upon its spine. Amah takes down one with a moss-green cover, blows dust from the top, flips it open. She thinks it might be Chinese script she's looking at and, slipping it back onto the shelf, she pulls down another, this one with a red cover. The script is unfamiliar, the words long. She pushes the book back between the others just as Cadogan returns.

"Please, take a seat, Mrs Chan." He's holding a thick ledger, which he balances on his knees as he sits down.

Amah perches on the sofa's edge a couple of feet away from him.

Placing a pair of spectacles onto his nose, he opens the ledger. "When do you think he might have arrived?"

Amah thinks back to Miriam's words. "Within the last two weeks, perhaps?"

"That's a lot of names to go through," he says, flipping back through four pages of the large book. His finger presses its way down the names written in the three columns arranged on each page.

A man dressed in a tidy naval uniform, turban upon his head, enters the reading room, picks up a newspaper from the pile on the table in the middle of the room. He lights a pipe, and settles into a chair to read.

"Ah, I think we have him here." Cadogan shifts the ledger around so Amah can see. "There's his name." His voice drags at the end, as if he reads something troubling.

Next to *Chan, Jakub. Dormitory 34b* is an asterisk and the words: *3 nights/departed with one Sin Hok.*

"Do you know this Sin Hok?" Amah asks, pointing to the name.

Cadogan's brow lifts in surprise. "You read?"

Amah gives a short nod and repeats her question.

Cadogan frowns. "Actually, I do. To tell you the truth, he's quite an unsavoury character, which is why Arnold, my associate here, has made a note of it."

"Who is he?"

"A Chinese fellow. Recruits for a group who call themselves The Three Lotus. Came from Sarawak, I believe."

"The Three Lotus?" Amah has never heard of them. "What do they do?"

Cadogan takes off his glasses, polishes them with a handkerchief. "They originated as three *kungsi*, I believe. The Golden Lotus, The Iron Lotus and The Fragrant Lotus. Do you know about *kungsis*?"

Amah shakes her head, although it sounds familiar. The word flickers like a warning at the back of her brain, like a shaft of lightning in the distance.

"Originally, they were just a collection of Chinese groups —Hakka—who wanted to strengthen their trading powers against the Hokkien Chinese in areas such as Sarawak and Montrado, but they've since branched out. One such collection has settled here. The Three Lotus. They've caused a bit of strife around here lately. The gang leaves their mark on buildings with a sign that looks like a triangle."

"What sort of strife?"

He places his glasses back on his nose, glancing to the side at Amah. "Well, let us just say, they are not a good group for your nephew to become involved with. They've been associated with both extortion and violence. I believe this

Sin Hok is what they refer to as a *straw sandal*. He recruits for them."

Amah's chest is tight. Her breaths feel constricted. Why would Jakub want to join The Three Lotus when he could be at home with Miriam and the children?

"Where can I find this Sin Hok?"

Cadogan looks alarmed. "Madam, you cannot track down these men. It would be too dangerous."

"Of course I must," says Amah, her voice firm. Annoyed, even. "If I do not, who will?"

Cadogan spreads his fingers. "I do not know where they are situated, in any case."

"What of this Arnold? He might know?"

Another man in naval uniform enters the room, carrying a plate of food, and seats himself next to his compatriot.

"Arnold is not here today," says Cadogan. "He might be in this evening. I will ask him if he knows where to find this Sin Hok. But, madam, if I do provide you with his whereabouts, you must promise me that you will not search for him alone. Surely, there must be some gentleman you can take with you or you can send in your stead?"

Amah stares at Cadogan for a moment, at his earnest expression, at the cross pinned to his collar. She doesn't worship his god, so feels no compunction about lying to him. "Of course I will."

It was on that terrible day in Sarawak that Amah first learnt more of this god the British were so devoted to. Mrs Preston was to meet her husband in Kuching, and she took Amah and her Uncle Chee along with her. They travelled down the Sarawak River, until a group of native children waved them in from the banks. Several men on horseback cantered down the hill behind the children. One was Mr Preston. He was an ugly man, and his face was bad-tempered, like a sulky child's. As he ushered Mrs Preston onto the muddy banks, his voice was testy. Amah still can't understand how a nice lady like Mrs Preston was saddled with such a man. It was also the first time Amah saw McBride and Pidgeon. McBride, skin shiny and orange even from a distance, calling out to them, organising the local people to help them alight; Pidgeon, his long face, skin peeling from too much sun.

Amah only recognised a few English words back then, as the men greeted Mrs Preston and bowed over her hand. They took them to the village, with its newly constructed homes, neat and white.

Knowing they would be a while, she made her way to the bazaar by the water. There she found a familiar sight, for it wasn't so different from the markets of Makassar, just smaller. The local Iban sold leafy greens and nuts, while two Indian traders dealt in spices from other islands and colourful saris. One old woman, Chinese, Amah could tell, sold broken pieces of porcelain. As she ran her fingers over the sharp edges of a chipped teacup, she could smell the cardamom on the old woman's breath from the betel nut she chewed, the red cud wrapped in sirih leaf.

On the outskirts of this little town, she spied a simple bamboo shack with a cross on its highest gable, a cross like the one on Mrs Preston's bedside table. Amah hesitated in the doorway, peering into the shadows. At the furthest end of the room, hanging on the wall, was a statue of a thin man, almost naked. His arms were flung from his sides, but as she tiptoed closer she saw that his hands and feet were nailed to the wood and blood seeped from his wounds. He reminded her of the fish the cook prepared in her grandfather's kitchen, damaged and limp on the timber cutting board. What worship of agony was this? She glanced around, wondering where the flecks of gold were, the incense, the food offerings.

It was then that Amah heard the bell ringing, pealing across the village, urgently calling to those who were not safely inside. Women and children screamed, men shouted to each other in a mix of languages, none of which made sense to her.

CHAPTER 12

I flip through the newest issue of *Journal des Demoiselles* again, pausing at the print of a woman dressed in a white satin gown trimmed with stick-candy pink. A corsage of roses runs at an angle across the skirt, and three roses dot the bodice. Amah would hate it. And she'd be right. Looking at it again, I realise it's a bit too much. I turn over a couple more pages until I find the other gown I admired. The skirt's upper flounce is in the shape of orchid petals, but now it reminds me too much of a child's fairy costume. I toss the journal down onto my dressing table.

I consider myself in the full-length mirror, admiring my new dress, cerulean blue with smart navy bows down the middle.

"I rather like this one, but I'm not sure of this white collar," I say to my dressmaker, Mrs Shelby. I tilt my head to the side, cover the collar with my hand. "Is it too late to have it removed?"

"Of course not, madam."

My face relaxes back into a smile. "Good. Help me out of it and you can take it back with you. What was your other idea again, Mrs Shelby?"

She struggles up from where she's kneeling. "There. That hem should do it." Her chubby face is red from the exertion, and she's a little puffed. "I was saying we should increase the number of flounces on your dresses. Use lace to make them frilly."

Flicking again through the pictures in the journal, I note the neatness of the gowns, the severe lines despite the billowing skirts. Of course, the evening gowns are more embellished, but maybe Mrs Shelby is right—maybe my day dresses could be prettified too. I picture myself riding in the park, in a dress like spun sugar, despite the dirt and pollution. Yes. And what would it matter if the dress became filthy after one wear? Hatterleigh would pay for more. It'll be amusing to see who has the funds to keep up with me.

Mrs Shelby helps me get dressed again and then gathers up her sewing basket and gowns. As she leaves the room, my gaze jags on the letter that lies upon my bed. I unfold it to read again. A reply from Pidgeon. He writes of his shock at Lovejoy's death, and of how he will meet with Hunt and Cosgrove to discuss this threat that presses upon them.

Clearly he is in accordance with the reporters and thinks the cases are all connected.

The sound of male voices rises to the second floor. By the time I reach the top of the stairs, I only catch a glimpse of Bundle's back as he ushers someone into the drawing room. When he returns, he looks up at me, says, "Sir Thomas, Mrs Chancey. With an Inspector Hatch."

I pull a face at him, and smooth my hair back from my forehead as I step down the stairs. An inspector. What does he want with me?

"Ah, Mrs Chancey." Sir Thomas takes my hand in his. "How wonderful to see you again. Please, let me introduce Inspector Hatch, here."

Hatch shakes my hand. "Detective Inspector," he corrects Sir Thomas. His voice is low, serious, but a pleasant smile hovers about his lips. He's a very pale man, and his side whiskers, as coarse as straw, are almost as impressive as Sir Thomas's. The cloth of his suit is of good quality, but worn, and the leather of his boots has been polished, yet does not shine. He's much taller than Sir Thomas but seems at ease in my drawing room, so much so that he ushers us to the sofas, asks us to sit around the table where Bundle sets out glasses of sherry. It's like he's the bloody host. I tuck my grin away for later.

Hatch plucks his trousers at the knees and takes a seat himself, opposite us.

"Mrs Chancey, Sir Thomas here says that you might be able to assist me in a case."

I sit straighter. "What kind of case, sir?"

Hatch sits with his legs wide and, for a moment, he frowns and leans forward, elbows resting on his knees. "Have you been following the Lovejoy murders in the papers, madam?"

I sit back, bewildered. "Of course." Do I mention that I met the man himself just two days ago? Or no?

"Tell me. What do you know about the affair?"

"What I've read in *The Times*." I look from Hatch to Sir Thomas. "About the poor girl murdered in the lavatory. Her throat was cut." My hand finds its way to my own throat. "And then her father was murdered yesterday. In the same manner." I don't know whether to tell him of what I know. Of what Pidgeon and Cosgrove have discussed.

Hatch leans back and nods. "Yes. Well, we have our suspicions on what might have gone on, but we have yet to prove anything." He takes a notebook from his breast pocket and stares at it absent-mindedly. "The thing is, for a number of reasons, we were quite sure we knew who'd murdered Margaret Lovejoy, but then her father was killed. His murder has given me pause in my suspicions."

"Who did you suspect?"

"The nursemaid."

"The nursemaid?"

"Mmm. Nurse Marie Brown." The Detective Inspector's mouth makes an almost girlish pucker with the noise. "Yes. She shared a room with Margaret and the younger child. And Margaret's bed was not slept upon. It seemed obvious, really."

"But why would she murder the little girl? A girl in her care?" I ask, incredulous.

"Exactly what I wondered. In fact, just before we found out about Lovejoy's death, I'd sent two constables to pick the nursemaid up for further interviewing. When I first spoke to her, I could tell she was keeping something from me."

"Was there anyone else you suspected, Hatch?" asks Sir Thomas.

He shakes his head, but frowns. "Not really. But now I wonder…"

"Tell us of the others in the Lovejoy household."

"Well, there's Mrs Lovejoy, of course. She's Lovejoy's second wife. And there's Emily—she's fifteen years old—and Joshua, who's sixteen years old, I believe. They're Lovejoy's children to his first wife. There is also Cyril—the second Mrs Lovejoy's child, you understand—maybe three or four years old, who is in the care of the nursemaid. Of course, there are the servants, but I've counted them out by reason of alibis or lack of motive."

"And you don't believe the nursemaid guilty any longer?" I ask.

"No. No, I'm no longer totally convinced, Mrs Chancey."

"Do you think an outsider is to blame?" I ask. It looks like Pidgeon and Cosgrove might be right after all.

"Oh, no. I think it's definitely an inside job. I think the jimmied drawing room door was just a ruse. I think someone in the house definitely committed these murders."

"I have to be frank with you, Detective Inspector." I decide the only thing I can do is tell him of what I know. Sound him out. If I'm to help him in this case, he needs to know all the facts. "I happened to meet Lovejoy just a couple of days ago. He was with a good friend of mine and they were incredibly worried about some threatening letters they'd received. Something to do with their time in Sarawak? And a Chinese gang? They believed that a man named McBride and Margaret Lovejoy were murdered in revenge."

The Detective Inspector is still frowning, but smiles at me too, like I'm a gullible child that's disappointed him. "Of course

I've heard all this before. Both Mr Lovejoy and Pidgeon have told me of this fantasy of theirs. You must see how ludicrous it is, Mrs Chancey." He looks from me to Sir Thomas, like he's questioning Sir Thomas's wisdom in bringing him to me. "Another detective, a very sensible fellow, is following up on the McBride murder. I do not have time to be distracted by such things, like the reporters—who may as well be men of fiction— who wait outside your home at this very moment."

He leans towards me again, and his eyes gleam like a terrier set on a rat. "Mrs Chancey, I will share with you why I think the Lovejoy murders are domestic." He holds up a finger. "One. The guard dog—and I've been assured it's quite vicious—was roaming the garden in each instance. That surely counts out a stranger." He holds up another finger. "Two. How on earth did an intruder break in through the drawing room, pass numerous servants and family members to steal away one little girl? The logistics are preposterous, in fact. And Three." He pauses, his three fingers rapping the tabletop. "According to the linen list, the cook's wrapper is missing. I believe this wrapper—which was something like a dressing gown, with long sleeves, mind you, and a skirt low to the floor—has been discarded because someone was wearing it when they murdered Margaret Lovejoy and it was covered in the girl's blood."

"You don't think the cook did it?" asks Sir Thomas.

"No. She stayed at her brother's house that night. And, really, why would she? But anyone, especially the nursemaid, with her comings and goings to the kitchen and servants' quarters, could have requisitioned it for the evening."

"The household seems to be mostly full of womenfolk," I say. "Would a female be capable of Lovejoy's murder?"

Hatch's face is stern as he says, "With a sharp enough knife, or razor even, a child could have sliced Lovejoy's throat, let alone the girl's. And the women to be found in that household are robust, believe me. We've had any number of letters from the public accusing the men who found the body, but I just do not believe the Lovejoys' drunkard gardener found his way into the house, let alone the night-soil man."

I take a sip of my sherry. Really, he does sound quite convincing. His story is surely more plausible than that of Chinese marauders seeking vengeance in London?

"In what capacity would I assist?" I ask.

"I'd like you to go into the household, find out what mysteries lie abed, secrets I cannot unearth myself. Apparently Mrs Lovejoy doesn't wholly trust the children with the nursemaid anymore, so I've decided the best thing is if you can go in as the interim nursemaid. We've arranged the paperwork with the agency already."

I feel a sense of dread creep upon me. I'd been very tempted up to this point. I pick up the decanter on the table between us to pour more sherry as an excuse to think on Hatch's offer. Nanny? To someone else's children? Hadn't I chosen this life, as precarious and improper as it might be, in order to avoid the drudgery of the nursery room?

"Of course, your position as nursemaid will just be a smokescreen. Really you will be there as my spy." Hatch catches my eye on the word "spy" as I hand him his sherry. A spy. Like Eleanor in Braddon's novel, or Fouché's spies they once whispered of in Paris. For a moment, Hatch has succeeded in making the work sound exciting, perilous even, but really… it will be a toil.

A sharp rap on the front door catches my attention and I approach the window to see who it might be. Another reporter by the looks of it. There are now four carriages parked on our narrow street. Bastards. I roll my eyes. It won't help matters that they've seen a police detective enter my house.

Rubbing my tongue across that tiny chip in my front tooth, I look over my shoulder to the others. Sir Thomas's eyebrows are raised, waiting for my answer, but I can tell from his bland expression he's not fussed whether I take the work or not. Hatch, on the other hand, nods his head once at me, as if urging on a child in a running race.

Glancing back out the window, I realise that if I am to take Hatch up on his offer, at least I'd be away from the attention of these newspaper men. Although, no doubt the Lovejoys' home is surrounded by reporters as well. And, anyway, it cannot be. I'm to see Hatterleigh tonight, in any case, and my new lilac gown is waiting for me upstairs. Hatterleigh's also promised to take me to Brighton early next week, so I just won't be available.

"I'm very sorry to have wasted your time," I say, finally, turning back to the men. "Unfortunately, I really am not able to help you in this case, at this time." As I say the words, I feel a twinge of regret. Maybe I'm missing out on an adventure. "But I can suggest someone else for the role."

The cab drops me at an address in Tottenham Court Road, where the shopfront's window is emblazoned with the words *Bower's Servants' Registry Office*.

The offices themselves are very plain. Prospective domestic servants form a long line along the unpolished timber flooring, while others lounge upon wooden benches that hug the walls. There's nothing for it—I have to wait in line too. The man in front of me turns to the side and blows his nose into his lapel, while two women near the top of the queue quarrel loudly about who's more suited to a scullery position. I wish I'd sent Taff or even Abigail on this errand.

I wonder how Bundle had hired Abigail. Through the newspaper, through an agency such as this? Or had she approached us? I glance at the sheets of paper pasted to the wall beside me, and note the neat copperplate handwriting and sketched likenesses.

"Lists, they be," whispers the woman behind me. I turn to her and smile. Not a woman, after all. I don't think she could be a day over twelve years old really. "Black list of all them who've been bad servants."

I'm surprised. I look again at the poster nearest to me and read, *Max Brownley. Formerly of service at the Hare and Rabbit Inn. Roughly five foot, eight inches. Brown hair, beard, missing little finger, left hand. Stole barrel of rum, one turkey and a guest's pair of riding boots*. And then, *Paulie Sawyer, also known as Pete Sawyer. Dark hair, considered handsome. Takes liberties with young ladies of the house*. Next to this statement is a penned likeness, in which he doesn't look that handsome at all. Under this is, *Fiona Lucy Coyne. Roughly five foot, ten inches. Brown hair, smallpox scars. Extremely rude, lives above her station. Lazy*. Well. Good on her.

These lists remind me of the directory that used to be available in London, that recorded the particular charms of each fancy bird. I'm glad it's not around anymore. I don't need my "ruby tips" and "pleasing grove" described to all the leering pigs in town.

By the time I reach the stout woman at the front desk, my feet feel pinched in my new shoes, and I've received numerous looks from women staring balefully at my taffeta gown.

"What kind of position are you applying for?" the woman asks as she looks up from her ledger. She's short-sighted and narrows her eyes to peer doubtfully at my smart hat, and the onyx and emerald earrings that hang from my earlobes. "I apologise madam. I mistook you. Usually our clientele write to us of what servants they need and we send them a selection. How may I help you?"

"I was after one Bethany Bird. I've heard she's an excellent nursemaid. I was directed here."

"Excuse me a moment, madam. I will just enquire." She waddles to the back of the office and pulls a drawer out from a filing cabinet. After a search that only lasts a matter of moments, she returns to me, reading from a card in her hand. "Wet nurse. Has been in a new position for three months so far. I'm sorry, it seems you've missed out on her." Her eyes move to my stomach, trying to gauge how many months I might be.

I glance at the card that lies slack in her hand on the counter. An address in Finsbury. Simple.

CHAPTER 13

"What do you think, Heloise?" Hatterleigh asks.

It's quite late in the evening; an evening I'd expected to enjoy. Yet, I have to force a smile. I can't get drunk quick enough.

Instead of Motts, Hatterleigh has brought me to the top of Haymarket to a dance hall he has heard of. We had to walk past numerous oyster shops and gin palaces until we found the bar he was after. The shopfront was plain enough, covered in black curtaining, a cold fowl perched on a platter in the window. Squeezing past men squatted in the gutter and women dancing the polka on the pavement, their eyes bright from cheap brandy, I almost had to shield my eyes from the glare of gaslight that greeted us as we entered the smoky room.

"I heard a couple of fellows talking about this place at the Billinghams' ball the other night," he shouts to me over the din from the brass band in the corner of the room.

I take two more gulps of my gin and water. My elbow's jostled by a shrieking woman as she's carried to the dance floor by two men, and some of my drink slops down the front of my new gown. My mouth twists to the side, like Amah's does. I polish off the rest of my gin.

Hatterleigh orders me another drink and then stands close, his toe tapping to the music, his hand warm on my back. He's rarely so intimate with me in public. He's watching the crowd bob and weave around us with a smile, and his nose is already turning puce from the cognac he has secreted in his coat pocket. He won't drink the common brandy they serve here—says it's ruinous to one's health.

And I realise something. While I am with Hatterleigh in order to experience the more refined side of life, he is with me in order to transgress the dark. What irks me about these evenings is that I feel familiar, almost comfortable, in these surroundings, yet soiled at the same time.

The sound of a drum roll barrels across the room, silencing the musicians and even hushing most of the clientele. A man snatches off his top hat and waves it in the air, whooping, while two pretty ladybirds near me clap their hands and balance on their toes. Everyone is straining to see the back of the room.

Four women, dressed in ivory frills and silk petticoats, take to the stage. They laugh and bow to the crowd, turn to the men of the band, the closest one indicating with a wave of her hand that it's time to begin. Without further preamble, the tune bounds upon the air, a rat-tat of feverish melody. The women heave up their skirts, exposing their lean, long legs encased in black stockings. The higher they lift their petticoats, the more milky thigh can be seen above the stockings. They sashay a slippered foot to the right, then to the left. They bow low, poking their pert bottoms to the back of the stage, and the crowd roar and clap with approval.

I haven't seen cancan dancers since Paris. I squeeze through the crowd so I can watch them more closely, craning up onto my tiptoes to see the women swish and twirl across the stage. If there is one thing I wish I'd learnt at a young age, it's dancing, so I too could have been a cancan dancer in some Parisian bistro.

The women sail across the stage, peeling back their chemises to shouts of delight from the audience, revealing pert breasts. A man steps in front of me, and I'm crammed in on either side, so I can only really see the dancer on the end, a tall woman with Titian hair. With each hop, the huge ostrich feathers that embellish her hat bounce in time with her full breasts.

The dancers link arms and, with a swivel of their hips, they kick their legs up in unison, and I can feel my eyes widen, even as a woman behind me gasps. I push forward, and then, yes, mid-kick, I see that I wasn't imagining it—a sliver of red hair flashes at me from between her legs. Confirming their scandalous behaviour, the dancers turn and flip their skirts up to show their bare arses, finishing on an almost deafening crescendo of music. I turn my head and search the crowd for Hatterleigh, and when I catch his eye, I grin. He smiles back at me, salutes me with his hip flask.

Later, in my bedroom, I stand facing the warmth of the fireplace. I've shed my crinoline and gown, and I reach my fingertips down and draw my slip up over my thighs, feel the silk feather against my skin. I pause a moment, my slip ruched above my hips, bend forward as if inspecting a blemish on the shiny skin of my shin. I know Hatterleigh's eyes are on my behind, which I jut out a little, wondering if beneath the apple shape of my bottom he can see some of the core.

I let my slip fall to the floor, but keep on my chemise. The linen is almost translucent, and it's open at the front so that with each movement my breasts sway, allowing him a fleeting glimpse. I reach for a large tome I've left ready on the mantelpiece and take a seat next to him on the chaise longue. I swing my legs over his, nuzzle closer so that my naked quim presses against his thigh. He puts his arm around me, his thumb caressing my back, and asks me what's in the book.

I open it against my bare thighs and peel back its pages until I come to a gouache print. "A friend of mine sent me these little paintings from India. I keep them safe in the pages of this book." I lift the picture away from the pages so Hatterleigh can see it better. The paper is fine and brittle, the fresh colours painted upon it giving it weight. Pretty branches with pink buds reach across a wall the colour of lemon, and a hill, celadon green, rests in the background. In the foreground is a man, dark and bejewelled, who stares ahead, while one of his hands holds a naked woman by the waist, her legs parted over his thigh while the fingers of his other hand toy with her nipple. The woman is arched all the way back until her hands and long black hair reach the ground, in ecstasy, in supplication.

"This is a painting depicting the secret pleasures of a famous prince, apparently." I let Hatterleigh look at the print a little longer before tucking it back into the pages of the book. "My friend is translating a Hindu text. A book of love."

I flip through to the next print. A woman reclines on cushions, clothed in a little yellow top and a full red skirt, below which her naked limbs are spread, revealing her neat *chatte*. The prince is poised above her. He has a cloth crown on his head and wears a smart jacket, but he's without trousers, so that the hood of his long prick is poised against her.

We laugh at the next one, of a naked couple, he on his back, she balanced above him facing his toes. She has gold bands around her upper arms, and pretty necklaces around her neck and a nose ring. I turn the picture over. The artist has scrawled the words, *The Wheel*, on the back.

As I leaf through the book for the next print, Hatterleigh's hand snakes inside the opening of my chemise. He cups my breast, strokes its curve. His thumb rubs my nipple in small swirls, presses its tip. I can feel a loosening in my limbs, between my legs.

"Oh my. I don't think I could do this one," I say, peering closely at the picture before us. She's facing away from him, so he has full access to her breasts, which I like, but her legs are curled right up behind him, tucked beneath his bent legs where he crouches behind her.

"Yes, you would have to be quite the little circus acrobat to perform some of these postures," he says. He waits for me to find the next one and his eyes trace the position of a couple joined together on a plush carpet, her leg slung over his shoulder.

"*Split Bamboo,*" I read from the bottom of the picture. I pull at the top of his trousers, feel my way to his cock. He's hard, becomes more erect the more I stroke.

"This is the one, I think, that we can try." The woman rests back on a sofa. The prince has his arms about her as he presses his way in between her legs, which are hooked over the crooks of his arms. Her breasts are high and firm as he leans into her. "It's called *The Flower.*"

Hatterleigh kneels onto the floor and I straddle him. He brushes back my chemise with his lips and takes my breast in his mouth. He nudges his cock into me and I gaze at the picture of the woman, the flower, who's draped in chains of gold, who stares patiently into the distance.

His arm weighs heavy across my belly and I fling it off, playfully. "Too sweaty." We've made our way to my bed. My limbs feel syrupy, and my mind billows close to sleep.

I roll onto my side towards him. "When will we leave for Brighton?" I murmur against his arm, and then peck his skin with a kiss. I love going to Brighton. The restaurants, the sea, the people. And Hatterleigh's always a bit more relaxed there too. It's our place.

"Ah, yes, about that…" He takes my hand and presses a kiss into my palm. "I don't think I can make it after all. Why don't you ask Isobel or that Milly lass to accompany you?"

I open my eyes. "Why can't you come?"

"My wife. She's been confined. I've had word that I really should head back into the country as soon as possible."

My insides frost over like a pond's surface chilling to ice. Although I want to snatch my hand from his, I will my body to stay relaxed. "How domestic," I drawl. I smile so that my voice is light too. "God, how many brats is that now? Four? Five?"

I know it's three.

He laughs. "I'm not a rabbit."

I stay pressed against him for a count of thirty seconds.

Then I roll onto my back. I fling my arm over my eyes, like I'm preparing for sleep, but my stomach has that terrible tightness I get when I'm irritated. I hate little reminders like this that our relationship is merely a fleeting amusement for Hatterleigh. I feel that familiar pang of jealousy when I think of his wife. Not that I'm envious of their marriage, but it just makes me want to grit my teeth when I think of how easy her life has been, and always will be. I bet she's never had to sponge her fanny clean from a bucket that's already been used by numerous others; or been so hungry she's eaten someone else's leftovers. And I sure as hell know she's never had to worry about money or about what will become of her in old age.

Which is all absolutely ridiculous, because I have accrued enough wealth to not have to worry either, and I don't want to be tied down to one blasted man anyway. If I really wanted Hatterleigh to stay by my side, I'm positive I could do it. I could! And not in a sneaky way, like that Tracey Greenfield who trapped Sir Neville with her belly full of arms and legs. I turn onto my side away from him and stare into the shadows. Not that that's an option for me, anyway.

Don't be such a sook, I chastise myself as I sit up and swing my legs off the bed.

"Where are you going?" He tries to catch my hand but I snatch it away with a bright smile.

"I have to take these pins out of my hair, or else they'll stab my head all night and I won't be able to sleep."

I drape a linen cloth across the plush seat of my dressing-table stool because I'm damp between the legs. I can see Hatterleigh in the reflection of the mirror as he plumps up the pillows behind himself and sits up against the bedhead.

My skin glistens in the lamplight and I can feel his eyes on my naked back as I pull my hair loose. I think of when I saw Bethany Bird earlier in the afternoon, after I'd tracked her down in Finsbury. She really did look happy as she fed that fat little baby. It was many years ago we were tails together, but when Bethany had become pregnant, she'd been talked into a life of good by the missionary who took her in. She wasn't allowed to keep her child, but she managed to find a new vocation as a nursemaid. And sometimes, between engagements, she helped me out with Sir Thomas's cases.

"But how do you still have milk, Beth? Have you had another child?" I watched the baby's pink lips suck at her nipple and knead her full breast with its plump fist.

She laughed at me as she rocked in the wooden chair by the kitchen fire. Apart from her snaggled bottom teeth, she looked like a Raphael Madonna. Always did. Sometimes that's exactly what the punters liked, especially those bastard God-bothering ones. "No, Heloise. But by keeping up this work, near babies, I can keep my milk in stock."

"But when you're away from babies?"

"Well then I have to milk myself. Something like a cow. It's nothing different from a Charlie giving them a good tug, though," she whispered to me, looking around to make sure the other servants couldn't overhear.

"So you can take on the Lovejoy position, after all?" I urged her. "The money is good, Beth. Probably the same as you'd make here in six months."

She looked doubtful. "But I like my place here, Heloise. I'm not sure I'm up to a bit of your carousing for Sir Thomas again. I nearly lost my hair that last time we tricked those fellows at that dance hall."

I cast my mind back. Ah, that's right. The amorous adventures of a gentleman we were watching on behalf of his wife. He'd become suspicious, and drunkenly fallen upon Bethany, ripping the wig from her head, along with a substantial amount of her hair. I pulled a face. "Well, it grew back, didn't it?" I teased.

I badgered her until she capitulated, and she promised that in the morning she would tell her mistress that her mother had become terribly ill and that she had to return to her home for a week.

But now, as I stare into the mirror, I think about how this is no longer necessary. I'll send Taff around first thing, to deliver Beth the message that she will not be needed at the Lovejoys' anymore. I will go.

Let Hatterleigh gallivant off into the countryside to be by his stupid wife's side. I might as well keep busy with what I enjoy.

I brush my hair, and with each stroke my breasts lift and jiggle. I catch Hatterleigh's eye as he watches. "That actually works out well, you going into Yorkshire. Sir Thomas came by today and offered me some interesting work. I won't need to turn him down, after all."

Hatterleigh frowns. "What work?"

"Oh, didn't I tell you? He came around here earlier today with the Detective Inspector who's investigating the Lovejoy murders. They want my help."

Hatterleigh's frown deepens. "But that's absurd. You'd be better to take one of your friends to Brighton."

I pout as I braid my hair into a loose plait. "No. That sounds just too boring. I will definitely take up Sir Thomas's offer."

Hatterleigh climbs out of bed and pulls on his trousers. My lips curl into a slight smile. He doesn't want to argue without his breeches on.

"But, Heloise, dear, there's a murderer at work. It will be far more dangerous than you are used to."

I twist in my chair and stare at him. What the hell does he know of what I'm used to? But then, I am a bit mollified that he's worried about my welfare too.

"And what do they expect you to do?" He sits down on the side of the bed again to pull on his shirt.

"I'm to pose as the nursemaid."

Hatterleigh's eyebrows could not rise any higher. "Nurse-maid! No, Heloise. I forbid it. I can't have you doing menial work in another gentleman's house. What if people were to find out?"

I glare at him for a couple of seconds, then turn slowly

back to the mirror. So, being in the vicinity of a murderer is slightly worrying, but the fact that I'll be posing as a servant seriously offends his senses. The sooner he rushes to his damned wife's side, the better.

I dab some cream across my face and rub it vigorously into my skin. "Sir, you needn't worry about your name or my welfare. I have always, and will always, take fine care of both."

CHAPTER 14

Squeezing through the omnibus door, I wonder if this is going to be the first of many times I regret taking on this case. If only I hadn't bloody quarrelled with Hatterleigh! But Hatch was right. The new nursemaid cannot be seen to arrive in a hansom cab or, heaven forbid, her own carriage.

I wedge myself between a pretty mother who has a little boy dressed top to toe in royal blue velvet draped across her lap, and a young man whose top hat is so tall it almost brushes the ceiling. Luckily my skirts are not as voluminous as usual, as I've dressed more in accordance with what is due of a nursemaid. I think.

As the omnibus trundles along, I can only see outside through the window behind the old woman seated opposite me. The window has been reduced to a sliver of glass because it's pasted over with advertisements for silverware, whisky, matches. With each sway of the coach, the old lady's basket inches across the floor against my toes and a peculiar stench wafts from her red coat. I spear her basket with my umbrella and nudge it back towards her.

I curse Hatterleigh again. I'd much rather be at home, or shopping for ribbons and pretty knick-knacks. I'd especially prefer to be in Brighton. Maybe I should've just gone there with Milly or Isobel after all. I cross my arms and stare balefully ahead as two more passengers cram themselves amongst us.

Last night, Hatterleigh left in a bit of a humph, but it's not the first time, or last, we've had words. He'll be back.

But Amah... my hands drop to my lap and I fiddle with the seams of my gloves as I think of her. She's so preoccupied with something, I don't know what. She's been staying out til late, forgets to dress my hair, and she didn't even make one rude remark about my purple dress. When I'd told her of this latest caper, I'd expected her to cavil, perhaps be a little scornful, as she usually is. However, she'd just paused in her embroidery, and nodded slowly. "That might be best."

As she helped me pack a small valise, I asked her, "Why do you say that? That it might be for the best?"

She folded my Spanish shawl—although made from the finest wool, it's of a sober hue, suited to a nanny—over and over until it was a tight little square. "I wonder if it might be a bit unsafe here, after... you know..."

"You mean McBride's death?"

She nodded as her hand hovered, undecided, over my glove drawer.

Maybe she didn't hear me properly before. "But, Amah, I'm going to the Lovejoys' house. Where there have been *two* murders."

She sucked her tongue against her teeth, waved her hand. "I have a feeling whoever is doing this murdering, is finished with that household." Placing two warm nightdresses onto the bed, she asked, "How will you explain your presence there?"

"I'm to be the new nursemaid."

Amah gaped at me, her eyes almost as round as when she's furious. And then she'd laughed, holding her sides, until she was reduced to a series of coughs. "You're going to look after children?"

Even now, I smile at the memory. I mean, at the time I pretended to be offended at her mockery, but really, I can see why she was so amused. It is laughable. Heloise Chancey, *paon de nuit*, reduced to wiping the nose of a brat named Cyril.

"Your stop, miss," calls the conductor from behind the

coach as it lurches to a halt. "Stoke Newington. Just before the toll gate, we are, just like you said."

As he pulls free my valise, I ask, "Which direction is Lordship Road?"

He nods to the road that branches from the one we are standing on. "That's it there, miss."

I walk towards the street, lugging that heavy valise so that it bumps against my skirts with each step, making my crinoline swing like a pendulum. The air is so cold my breath puffs out before me, reminding me of how much I'd savour a cigarette.

The dwellings along Lordship Rd are more spacious than what I am used to seeing so close into town. Large houses, slick with modernity, are surrounded by expansive gardens peppered with oak and elm trees.

"Excuse me." I stop by a woman who holds a tray of puddings slung from her neck. Her apron is filthy, and she has a jaunty ostrich feather sticking out from her bonnet. "Can you direct me to St Chad's Lodge?"

"Over there, it be," she says, pointing down the road, to the right. "The house near the corner, under that there walnut tree."

I thank her and walk in the direction she's indicated. Along the left-hand side of the road, new terrace houses are going up and, as I pass a group of four men who are puffing away on their pipes as they stir up barrows of cement, I hear a low whistle. I act as though I didn't hear it, but not before I see one of them murmur something to the others with a smirk.

As I walk, I can feel their eyes inch across my body. Somehow it doesn't feel the same as when I ride in the park. The spectators who line the park lanes to watch me are there to enjoy themselves, and I'm displaying my plumage for their admiration. I've crafted the artifice. It's a performance. Here, I'm just walking, damn it. Times like this... it feels different. It slithers under my skin, trembles there self-consciously, reminds me of a dark night long ago.

Usually my reaction depends on my mood. In a good humour, I'll be jaunty, say thank you, catch their eye with my bold one. I'll be just disdainful enough that usually their gaze will drop away. But if I'm cranky, I've been known to do worse.

But here I'm posing as a local nanny. It might be necessary to pass them, again and again. So, no rude gestures.

Finally, I come to stand outside the Lovejoy house. Two coaches are parked by the side of the road, the horses languid, their heads dipped. A gaggle of reporters—five or six maybe—stand around under a large oak, stomping their feet against the cold. When they see me hovering, they make a start across the road and call out, but I duck through the gate, trot down the front path. St Chad's Lodge is a handsome house with a pillared front door and a fine arched window above it on the second floor. I almost approach the front door, but remember my station and move to the back. I tap at the servants' door and, upon no response, I rap on it louder. A thin woman, wearing a mob cap and apron, opens the door.

"Yes?"

"I'm the new nursemaid."

"Oh, yes, yes. The missus said you was coming. I'm the cook." Many of her teeth are missing so that her bottom jaw appears to be not unlike a piano keyboard. She stands back against the wall to allow me to enter. "I'll just let the missus know." She hurries before me down the hallway, calling out to someone named Ruth. "Hurry up and tell Mrs Lovejoy that the new nursemaid has come."

As we reach the kitchen, a girl, slight with a mop of curly hair, pops her head around the doorway. Her shy eyes sweep over me and she gulps a "Yes, Cook," and scuttles away.

"Poor Ruth has so much to do now. And the missus. We used to have a housekeeper, we did, but she left soon after... Well. I'll make you a cup of tea, shall I? You must be thirsty. How far did you have to come, dear?" The cook sets about the stove-top, without really needing an answer from me. "I've made a lovey batch of scones too. But we won't eat them until the family have had their fill first. I was going to make a second batch, just for us, but…"

"That will do, Cook," says a deep voice from the hallway. "I'll see to the new nursemaid from here."

The voice belongs to a tall woman, dressed all in black, from the netting over her hair to the ribboned hem of her skirt. She's heavyset yet handsome, and her thick eyebrows are so straight and long they almost meet in the middle. It's only when she turns to the side that I realise that her skirts billow wide because she is with child.

She beckons to me. "What do we call you?" she asks as she leads the way.

"Louise, madam." We pause in the draughty entrance hall, from which four rooms open. "Louise Casey." I look to the back of the house and wonder which of the two rooms is the drawing room—the room that had its doors jimmied open, and where Lovejoy had found the note.

"We will call you Nurse Louise then, if that suits." She nods to the rooms on each side of us at the front of the house. "That is the sitting room, where the family usually gathers, and this one here is… was Mr Lovejoy's study." She swallows and purses her lips tight for a moment. Now that I am closer to her, I can see that the rims of her eyes are as red as raw beef, that her eyelids are puffy. "Please pay attention. There are thirteen rooms in this house, and I won't have time to repeat all of this to you." Pointing to the back of the house, she says, "That room there to the right is the dining room, and there to the left is the drawing room where we entertain guests. However, as there is plenty of space in the nursery, it will not be necessary for you to use any of these rooms down here."

"Yes, madam," I say. I nearly bob a curtsy but stop myself in time.

Lifting her skirts, Mrs Lovejoy climbs the stairs, slowly,

as though a great weight pulls her back. "I'll show you upstairs."

"Was this house once a church?" I ask, as my hand runs across the smooth timber of the handrail. "St Chad's?"

"No. It's the name of the cathedral in the town my husband... my late husband, was born in."

Once we reach the landing, she points to the end of the hallway at the left side of the house. "My rooms." Turning to the right, she says, "The children's rooms are here. At the end there is Joshua's room—he's a young man now, you won't be called upon to care for him—and next to his room, there, is Emily's."

"Do I care for her, madam?"

Mrs Lovejoy stares at me for so long I wonder if she's confused. But then, as she exhales, I smell the spirits on her breath. Gin? Brandy? Something stronger than mere sherry or ratafia, in any case.

She turns and goes to Emily's door and knocks. "Emily. Emily, the new nursemaid is here. Can you please come out and meet her?"

I hear something shift behind the door, but the girl doesn't reply or come to the door.

Mrs Lovejoy sighs. "She never listens to me. Their mother was Mr Lovejoy's first wife, you know. Emily is just turned fifteen, so she should be under your care too, but I fear she might be difficult to persuade." She walks past me and opens the door to the room across the corridor. "And this is the nursery."

The room is richly appointed, with crisp new wallpaper featuring small posies of flowers, while the curtains that cover the three sets of windows are of a more concentrated floral pattern. Any number of expensive toys are scattered across the Wilton carpet. A crib stands by the middle window, silk brocade draped prettily over its sides. Three dolls lie side by side in the crib, staring stonily at the ceiling.

Mrs Lovejoy moves to another door, tucked behind a set

of table and chairs. She opens it slowly to reveal a plain room with three single beds arranged against the walls.

"This is where you will sleep." Her stern face relaxes. She must've been truly beautiful, once. "And this is Cyril. He's having his afternoon nap."

I gaze at the little thing—at the long, long lashes that rest against his flushed cheeks, at how his blond hair catches the light, turns to gold. Really, how much trouble can a sweet little mite like this give me?

Mrs Lovejoy closes the door again and looks me over. "Well, you appear to be neat enough, so I don't suppose I'll need to order more nurse uniforms, after all. Are all your dresses like that one?"

"Yes, madam. I have brought two more with me."

Her eyebrows rise. "So many? Good enough. Please keep a list of your linen, so it doesn't go missing with the laundry. Our laundry woman sometimes misplaces things." She frowns for a moment, her hand resting on the nursery door. Maybe she is thinking of the missing wrapper. Maybe she wonders if it's drenched in her daughter's blood.

"What are Master Cyril's movements? Does he need to follow a strict routine?" I ask.

Her dark eyes find mine again. The cold expression returns to her face. "Nurse Marie will tell you what you need to know."

"But... where will I find her, madam?" I thought she'd been dismissed.

"She is staying in the housekeeper's room for the time being. She will help you with the children, but you must always keep an eye on her." Her voice drags on the last few words.

CHAPTER 15

"Where can I find Nurse Marie?" I ask Cook, as Cyril, the little beast, wails and squirms in my arms.

"She's just behind the kitchen, to your left. In old Mrs Forbes's room, she is." The cook holds my elbow for a second and says, "Let herself go, she has, poor thing. Ever since... well. I'll bring you both a nice cup of tea."

I carry the boy to where Cook points and, although I try to knock lightly, Cyril boots the door, then howls even louder that he's hurt his toes.

The door swings open. A sallow young woman holds her arms out to the boy, folds his plump little body to hers. She buries her face into his neck, her bony fingers squeezing his shoulders.

I think she might be crying, from the grimace on her face, but when she opens her eyes again, they're dry. "Cyril, turtle dove, why all this noise?" she coos to him, wiping the sweaty locks from his forehead. She takes a seat by the bed, settles him onto her lap.

"Her!" he says, one stubby finger pointing at me. "Her. I thought her a monster."

"Well, that's hardly fair," I say, my hands on my waist. "All I wanted to do was get you dressed into a warm jacket so you didn't freeze to death."

"She wouldn't sing me a song," he whispers to Nurse Marie, his beady blue eyes on me.

I take a seat on the bed. "I only sing songs for good boys."

He looks like he might take the bait, but then plugs his thumb into his mouth and leans back against Nurse Marie's chest.

"I'm the new nursemaid, in case you haven't guessed." I smile at Marie, to show I'm friendly, that I'm not here to trump anyone.

She doesn't reply. She looks exhausted. Her wide mouth droops, and her fringe is so long, strands teeter upon her eyelashes. There are dark smudges beneath her eyes, which are as red as Mrs Lovejoy's. I wonder if her dress—grey with a navy pinstripe—is the uniform Mrs Lovejoy spoke of. The cuffs are a little frayed and one of the faux tortoiseshell buttons is missing from her bodice.

The air is chilly, for there's no fireplace in here, and I wish I had my shawl. Nurse Marie doesn't seem to notice, though, as she pats Cyril's small hand.

Cook rustles in with two cups of tea, which she places on a small side table. Balanced on the saucers' rims are slabs of butter cake. Cook takes one and gives it to the boy. "And one special piece for Master Cyril."

Cyril scowls at her in lieu of saying thank you.

I take a sip of my tea. "Marie, might you come upstairs and help me? With Cyril? I don't know when he eats or what he does before bedtime?" It certainly looks like she misses the boy. Maybe she can come back to the nursery and resume her work; Mrs Lovejoy seemed happy enough with that. That'll give me a chance to observe her further for the Detective Inspector, and free up my time to do a bit of detecting around the house. And god knows I don't want to be left alone with the little brat for too long.

Cyril twists around in her lap and squeezes the nanny's sunken cheeks with his sticky fingers. "Yes, Nursie. Come upstairs. I don't like her." He leaves cake crumbs smeared on her skin.

After we finish our tea, Nurse Marie carries Cyril up to the nursery. I'm not sure how she does it—her arms are as thin as twigs. They look like they might snap. Surely too frail to overpower a man of Lovejoy's stature.

As we walk along the hallway, I pause to look at the pictures that adorn the walls. Between a painting of two swans in a rococo frame and a portrait of a man standing by a bull is a photograph of the whole family. At the back of the group is the nursemaid, holding the hand of a toddler while cradling the other child in her arms. Mr and Mrs Lovejoy are seated to the fore, two young people behind them, their hands resting on the parents' shoulders. Next on the wall is a large photograph of Mr Lovejoy—those snowy sideburns, the hard eyes—and above that, in a large gilt frame, is a painting of the boy himself, Cyril. Just outside the door to the nursery is a painting of a little girl, who has Cyril's flaxen hair and the pretty eyes of a kitten.

"What a sweet thing," I say. "Who is this?"

Nurse Marie turns slowly towards me, Cyril still clasped to her chest. Her eyes wander over the girl's features and her lip trembles.

"That's Meggie," Cyril says. "Emily said she's gone to heaven to be with Emily's mother."

"Emily? Your sister, Emily?" Half-sister. The daughter of the first Mrs Lovejoy.

Cyril nods. "Meggie wouldn't like you either."

I go to say something acerbic to the boy but catch the reproachful look Nurse Marie gives me.

The next two hours are taken up with the tedium of preparing a child for bed. I watch on, half-hearted in my attempts to help feed and bathe him, which Cyril also seems content with, apart from taking the opportunity to splash soap onto the apron I had the foresight to put on.

"Can you please ask Cook for Cyril's warm milk?" Nurse Marie asks me, as she settles down to read to the boy.

"Of course." I'm glad to escape. I trip down the stairs and make my way to the kitchen, where I ask Cook for the nightcap.

Cook's so busy bustling around the stove as she explains to Ruth how to turn the overripe peaches into chutney that I take the chance to slip back into the corridor. Light pours from the sitting room doorway at the front of the hall, and the gaslight chandelier still shines in the dining room, but to my right the drawing room is shrouded in shadow. There's just sufficient light for me to make out the shape of the furniture as I creep towards the French doors at the back of the room. I want to have a closer look at the jimmied door Hatch mentioned.

As I fiddle with the handle of the first set of doors, my eyes adjust to the gleam of moonlight that shines through the glass. The handle seems to be sturdy enough, as I wrench it up and down. I move onto the second lot of doors. This time I can discern a slight looseness in the handle's swing. I shift to the side to allow for the light from the dining room to illuminate the door and, bending down, I think that maybe I can see scratches in the white paint. I'm just rubbing my fingers against the grooves when the light in the doorway is blocked. Two figures, still and quiet, gaze in at me.

I draw back. "Oh my. You did startle me."

"What are you doing?" The voice is male and quite deep, yet I can tell he's still young.

Well, I've already acted guilty, so I'll pretend to be a goose. I bob a curtsy and say, "I really must apologise. I'm the new nursemaid, Nurse Louise. Maybe your mother has told you of me. I'm just waiting for dear Cyril's milk and, being of a very careful disposition, I really felt it necessary to check that all the doors and windows are secure."

They stand back for me to pass into the hallway.

"You must be Master Joshua and Miss Emily," I say, clapping my hands together. "Your mother has told me of you. She says that I shall have the pleasure of Emily's company in the nursery from time to time."

Although tall, Joshua actually looks younger than his sixteen years. A rather foolish smile is fixed on his moon-face, and his hair is unfashionably straight, flops over his forehead. But his sister is another story. She's almost as tall as he is; I have to look up at her. She's well-padded and her shoulders are broad. Her face is as pasty as a currant bun, with terrible pimples dug deep into her cheeks, several already bursting into white-peaked pustules. The expression on her face is contemptuous. Maybe a little grouchy.

"She's our stepmother," she replies. "And I am too old to need your service. I am perfectly fine in the company of my brother."

Cook calls to me from the kitchen. "Nurse, the milk is ready."

Emily's lip lifts in a sneer. "You'd better fetch up precious Cyril's milk then."

I nod and turn to go, but decide to ask one more thing, see if I can rattle this odd duo. "Those doors in the drawing room. I think I read in the newspaper that it was through them that the… um… culprit crept into the house?"

They just stare at me, the vacuous smile still on Joshua's face while an angry flush creeps up Emily's thick neck.

CHAPTER 16

"Nurse Marie, Cyril will be fine for the night with Nurse Louise. You may return to the housekeeper's room." Mrs Lovejoy doesn't lighten the words with a smile as she leaves the nursery.

Cyril is fast asleep, tucked up in his bed, looking as deceivingly cherubic as when I first laid eyes on him.

Nurse Marie's eyes lower as she gathers up Cyril's plate and cup to return to the kitchen. I feel a pinch of unease.

"But, Nurse, what if he is to wake in the middle of the night?" I ask her.

She pauses by the door and frowns at me. "Surely you know how to settle a child back to sleep?"

My eyes widen. "Of course I do," I lie. "I just mean because he so obviously adores you, yet has taken an uncommon dislike to me. He will no doubt kick up a ruckus."

She shrugs. "If cuddling and soothing doesn't help, there's some gripe water in the cabinet. That always manages to settle him straight back to sleep."

As she closes the door, I move to the cabinet she'd indicated and inspect what it holds. Behind a brown jar labelled with handwritten instructions and an assortment of pins and ointments, I find the clear glass bottle of Woodward's Gripe Water. Unscrewing the lid, I sniff the contents and smile with surprise. Smells just like the spirituous tipple we girls sipped before a night entertaining the gents. I lift the bottle to my lips and take a small swig. I smack my lips together. "No wonder it sends the little mite straight off to sleep." I replace the medicine and close the cabinet door.

Unlike the housekeeper's room, the nursery has a cheerful fire to keep the cold night air at bay. Leaving the bedroom door ajar so I can hear if the boy stirs, I settle into the armchair by the fireplace and open Darwin's heavy tome I have towed all the way here, tucked amongst my spare clothing. I've been especially keen to read this ever since the others'—well, Cosgrove's really—enthusiasm about it the other night at my house. That night when… Suddenly I see Amah's hands covered in blood that darkens at the creases of her fingers. McBride slumped across the steps. Is that how Lovejoy had looked? Head wrenched back at that ungodly angle? And young Margaret, the very first sorry victim?

I press my finger to the page and force myself to focus upon Darwin's response to those who object to his notion of Natural Selection. It only half manages to keep my attention. I gaze at the nursery door where I'd last seen Nurse Marie and I think of how Hatch had her in his sights as the little girl's murderer. Are her tears the effects of guilt? Really? That broken woman, who so obviously adores the objectionable Cyril? I can't picture it.

As I read of imported hive bees supplanting Australian native bees and the missel thrush's ascendency over the song thrush in Scotland, I listen for the sounds of the house bedding itself down for the evening. On the lower level, the servants rattle windows shut, bolt doors with a clack. Mrs Lovejoy retired long ago, and not long after nine o'clock I hear voices in the corridor as Joshua and Emily make their way to their rooms. The floor creaks as they pause outside the closed door of the nursery and their shadows dim the bottom of the doorway. I hold my breath but all I can hear is the crackle of the fire, the distant bark of a dog. My heartbeat quickens. I'm just wondering if I should open the door, ask them if they're in need of something, when they finally move on. One door after the other clicks shut further down the hall. What very unnerving children they are.

By the time the clock down below chimes eleven, the house is quiet. I think everyone has gone to sleep. I wait a half-hour longer, impatiently reading through Darwin's ideas on organisms' struggle for existence, before I place the book on the nursery table and go into the bedroom, where I don a nightgown and a warm dressing gown. It'll be much easier to tip-toe through the house without my wide skirts on. And if someone catches me, I can say I couldn't sleep, that I've come in search of a warm drink. I riffle through my valise for the silk reticule that houses my small pleasures—a silver case containing my rolled cigarettes, a flask of cognac and tissue-wrapped caramels. And there, tucked into a special pocket of the reticule, is my pistol. Glancing across the room, I can see that Cyril is still fast asleep. He's only stirred the once, turning onto his side to face the wall. He'll be fine. I won't be too long.

The nursery has sufficient light from the fireplace, so I decide to take the oil lamp with me. Turning it down low, I carry it into the hallway, first checking both left and right, to make sure all the bedroom doors are shut, that there are no glimmers from underneath. I'm pretty swift on my feet as I move down the stairs. Only one step creaks, five from the top. I'll try to remember that for later.

I move straight to the French doors in the drawing room that I was looking at when I was disturbed by Emily and Joshua earlier. The handle turns but is locked and, yes, I was right, there are scratches on the door jamb. How peculiar. If someone had broken in, the marks would be on the outside. I must see if the door…

I stand tall. Was that a creak from the staircase?

I rush into the corridor. I must get myself to the kitchen before I'm caught nosying around. But as I cross the hall, I can't see an answering light making its way down the stairs. I tuck myself behind the kitchen door and wait. The silence feels like it might engulf me and I bite my lip to stop from giggling.

I can't hear a thing.

Peeping into the hallway, I almost jump as that damned clock chimes midnight, each deep peal quivering under my skin. I wait impatiently for the chimes to finish, for the house to settle into silence again. It's time.

I creep down the long corridor towards the servants' door. On the left is the housekeeper's room, and I wonder if Marie is still awake. Either way, she's probably trapped in the same nightmare, poor thing. I assume the last room, narrow and squashed behind the kitchen, might house Cook and Ruth. Pausing, my ear to the door, I'm quite sure I can hear a whistling snore.

I cast around for a hook or ribbon that might hold the key to the back door, but no, like many other households, the housekeeper, master or mistress of the house must have them to hand. Of course, there is no master here anymore, nor housekeeper; maybe Cook is now in charge of them. Not that it matters. I bring out a nail file and special pin that have helped me many times before. Inserting the file into the lock, I hitch it upward, feeling for the bolt. The silver grates so noisily against the lock plate, I waggle the nail file slowly, slowly, until I feel it release the stump. I pause for a moment, can feel sweat beads prickle my upper lip. When I'm sure I haven't disturbed anyone in the house, I insert the pin, turning it in the groove, and push on the spring, until the lock clicks open. Again I pause. Bedsprings squeak in Cook's room. I hold my breath. Nothing. Just the distant tick of the grandfather clock. Turning the handle, I open the door and step outside.

It's a bright, cloudless night. Cold, I shiver and I pull my robe tight across my chest. I place a stone at the door to keep it ajar, and then move swiftly across the grass to the drawing room doors. The ground near the doors is turned to sod, it needs new grass seeds sown. Rubbing the toe of my slipper against the dirt, I imagine Mr Lovejoy finding the nasty letter, trodden into the mud.

I hold the lamp up against the handle. Yes. The scratches are deeper on this side. Really gouged into the wood. I can even see the chip that'd been chiselled out in order to pry the latch open.

My eye catches a glint in the door's glass.

I swing around, but there's nothing behind me. I stare into the gloom. It's difficult to see past the glare of the lamp, so I extinguish the light and gaze again into the darkness. I don't blink for so long, my eyes dry against the cold air. Turning back, I hold my hand to the glass, peer into the drawing room, through to the corridor. Nothing.

Maybe I should just go straight back inside. Back into the warmth of the nursery. And I've been away a little while now; Cyril might be awake.

But what I really want is to breathe some tobacco smoke deep into my lungs — more so than ever, now. At least it'll serve to steady these stupid nerves of mine. I look above to where the nursery windows are. I couldn't smoke in there. If I were caught, then I'd certainly be turned away, and what good would that be to Hatch?

My eyes sweep across the yard, trying to find a discreet spot. I know, from Cook, that the servants' outhouse is further down in the back corner, under the two skeletal oak trees that loom black against a sky as shiny as a silver plate. Closer to hand, down a short path, is the family's outhouse. But Mrs Lovejoy's rooms look down on this side of the yard, so, leaving the lamp by the back door, I move off to my right towards the gardener's shed. I pass the pretty garden I have already seen from the nursery window — the neat row of hedges that meet in the middle to form a circle around a stone water feature. I walk very slowly to lessen the crunch of gravel under foot, lighting a cigarette as I go. I take cover under the spindly tree behind the shed.

The smoke lifts like fog as I stand against the wall of the

shed. I can feel the bricks' rough surface catch upon the wool of my dressing gown. The house and surroundings are in shadow and, as I draw on my cigarette again, I hear a flutter above me. An owl. His tawny feathers are almost invisible amongst the dry leaves, but his yellow eyes gleam in the darkness. It looks down on me, then scratches away under its wing with its beak. I draw deeply on my cigarette again and watch the nursery window, the only one with open curtains and the welcoming glow of the hearth. My fingers are cold against my lips as I lift the cigarette to my mouth. I shiver again. Time to go back in.

I'm grinding the cigarette end into the dirt when I hear light footsteps tap across the gravel. Pressing myself to the side of the shed, I draw my arms and body in as much as possible, my reticule clutched under my chin. Nobody's going to take a stab at my throat. I slip my hand down into the reticule until my fingers touch the pistol's ivory handle.

The footsteps halt for a moment, somewhere near the shrubs, then pick up again, until they're tabbing across dry leaves, closer. Closer. So close, I can hear breathing, strained and quick.

Above me the owl rustles from the tree branch, the flap of its wings drowning out my intruder.

By the time I peep around the corner of the shed, the bulky shape that lunges for me is so low to the ground, I'm taken by surprise. I fall back, scraping my hand against the brick wall.

The dog takes a vicious snap at my leg and growls. He barks at me twice, so loudly I'm afraid he'll wake everyone up. His teeth flash in the moonlight, and I decide it may be a good thing if someone wakes and rescues me. Better to be tossed out of the house for smoking than to be mauled by this brute.

I snake my hand into the top of my reticule, my fingers brushing against the pistol handle. Digging further, I feel the rustle of tissue paper and draw out a small square. I toss the caramel to the ground and the dog draws back, as if wary of a strike. He sniffs at the sweet. After a few seconds of snuffling, he wolfs it down. He looks back up at me, expectant.

He is a stout thing and darker than the night. His beady eyes mirror the sky.

"Well, that shut you up." I try to keep my voice steady, soothing. "I forgot there was an ugly creature like you around."

I throw another caramel. After gobbling it up, he steps closer to me, sniffs at my dressing gown. Maybe he smells Cyril or Cook.

The third caramel I offer on the flat of my fingers, and he slobbers against my skin, seeking out any residual sugar.

"Not so vicious, after all." I turn my hand over so he can sniff my scent. When I think he's ready, I run my hand over his brow, tickle behind his ear. "What's your name then?"

I glance up, thinking it's time to go back inside. And that's when I see it.

Someone at the nursery window. Gazing down on me.

CHAPTER 17

When Amah presses her forehead to the window, she can gaze up at the night sky above the tall buildings across the way. The sky's not black, squid-ink black, like how she remembers the Makassar sky. It's more like the metallic underside of an empty mussel shell, as barren, as cold.

That man of god at the Strangers' Home, when he spoke of the *kungsi*, Amah didn't remember at first, but now she does. That day in Sarawak. That's what they had called the group of Chinese that rioted through Kuching, brandishing poles and spears. They set fire to the new houses, destroyed the markets, cut down as many white people as they could catch. Amah saw all this from the doorway of the prayer hut with the cross over its gable.

Strong hands grasped her by the upper arms. "You cannot stay here," said Uncle Chee. "They will surely burn this place down too. Come with me."

Crouched low, they ran across the edge of the village, ducking behind huts and carts when they could. She was peeping out from behind the stables when she saw a group of white people run from the back of a house. She recognised Preston, but not the other couple. They raced for the next house, which was larger, towards a blond man with a neat beard, who beckoned from the front doorway, but before they could reach it, two of these *kungsi*, black plaits snaking down their backs, burst from the front of the stable. The first one clubbed the woman over the head, as the other swung his *kris* low and far, slicing the air until it found purchase against Preston's shoulder. He then swung the *kris* in an arc so that its blade left a crimson cleft in the other gentleman's throat. A loud crack pierced Amah's ears, then another, and the two *kungsi* fell to the ground. From a window, she could see Pidgeon as he lowered a shotgun, his mouth agape, lengthening his long, foolish face.

CHAPTER 18

I take a swig of cognac and gaze down into the yard from the nursery window. I think I see the shape of the dog seated by the shed door, scratching behind its ear, but all else is still cloaked in darkness.

When I saw the face in the nursery window, I nearly stumbled over the dog. By the time I'd righted myself, the face was gone. I ran to the back door. At best, someone was checking on me; at worst—oh god—Cyril might have been attacked. On my watch.

I rushed two steps at a time up the staircase to the nursery, practising my story of a visit to the lavatory, but when I burst into the room there was nobody there. I checked the bedroom. Cyril was lying on his back, still slumbering, his chubby hands curled by his sides. Alone.

My fingers follow the engraving of ferns and leaves on the silver flask as I take another sip. Who was the dark figure in the window? Backlit by the fireplace, it was hard to tell.

Mrs Lovejoy? Surely not. If it had been her, surely she would have stayed to remonstrate with me for leaving the boy. Nurse Marie? If she'd come to check on us, I was quite certain she would've remained by the boy's side until I returned. And where was she now, in any case? She wouldn't have had time to flit back to her room. I would've passed her when I came dashing back in.

I shove my flask back into my bag and tiptoe across to the

nursery door. I open it a few inches and peer into the corridor. It's so dark I can't even discern where the other rooms are, let alone the staircase.

Could the nursery's visitor have been Emily, or even Joshua? I think of his smile, of the blank look in his eyes, and my skin crawls. I pull a face as I shut the door again. I examine the handle and, although there's a keyhole, there is no key with which to lock it. I cast around for a chair to jam under the handle, but I can see that they're too short.

I position a footstool by the door, so I might at least hear it creak across the floor if someone tries to enter, and then shut the curtains. I take a seat on the medallion armchair by the doll's house and pull out my flask again.

I'm dreaming of my old friend Tilly, of how she's dyed her hair yellow, when I'm woken by a cold, prodding finger. Right in the middle of my forehead.

"Where's Nurse Marie?" Poke. Poke.

I wave Cyril's hand away and roll over in the nanny's bed, but he climbs up behind me, presses his wet lips to my ear. "Where's Nurse Marie? Where's my breakfast?"

I open my eyes and look over my shoulder at the little boy. His buttery curls are tousled, and snot crusts his nostrils, but really, he's an attractive little thing. I don't know how he could be Mr Lovejoy's son. "I don't know. It's freezing, though. Why don't you climb in here with me until she comes?" I lift the blanket for him.

He shakes his head and, as he takes a step back, I grab him by his chubby arms and pull him to me. I wrap my arms around him until I reach his sides, and I tickle and tickle, until he's squealing and trying to writhe out of my tight hold. Finally, he lies back against me, spent, and we are both smiling, warm under the blankets.

"Your feet are like icicles, Cyril." He shoves them against my shins again, and that's how Nurse Marie finds us, scuffling around my bed.

"Cyril." Her voice is sharp as she calls him. She doesn't make eye contact with me. "I have your egg and milk here. Hurry out to the table, please."

The boy scampers off and I lie in bed a minute more. I lift the curtain a little away from the window above me and the sky has the grey glare of dawn. Dawn. I'm much more likely to see first light after a night out dancing than to wake to it like this. In fact, I think I feel a bit sick in the stomach from waking so early.

I drag myself from bed and dress.

Nurse Marie is feeding Cyril, but I can see from the breakfast tray that there is no tea for me. I feel a tick of irritation. Silly woman. If only she knew I was here on Hatch's behalf to find alternative suspects to her.

"I had a bad night, Nurse Marie," I say, moving to the nursery door. "I might go to the kitchen and have a nice cup of tea. I'm sure I can leave Cyril in your capable hands."

The nurse nods, gently stroking Cyril's hair back from his forehead as he chews on a piece of toast.

As soon as I enter the kitchen, Cook hands me an apron and directs me to wash the dishes. "Nothing for it," she says. "Poor Ruth is unwell, and I can't do it all by myself. You leave that Nurse Marie with the children and help me prepare the family's breakfast."

I pour myself a cup of tea and add three teaspoons of sugar and a generous dash of cream. "What do you mean by 'children', Cook?" I ask. "Nurse Marie only seems to watch over Cyril." I'm not sure if it was a slip of the tongue—if Cook is mistakenly counting in poor Margaret—or if she means the older children too.

Cook looks at me over a bowl of egg yolks. "Ha. She's supposed to care for Miss Emily too, but that girl has always been obstinate when it comes to the new nurses." She pours the eggs into a saucepan and hands me the bowl to wash. "Ever since her mother died, that is."

In a dark corner of the kitchen, between the kitchen

sideboard and the doorway to the scullery, is a family photo much like the one upstairs, but this one is lighter, over-exposed. I peer at it closer. "Is that the first Mrs Lovejoy?"

Cook bustles over to stand next to me. "Yes, that's her. Pretty thing, wasn't she. She was already poorly by then." She jabs a thin finger, its nail chewed down to the quick, at a figure in the background, standing between two children— Joshua and Emily, I presume—and whispers, "And that's Mrs Lovejoy as she was then. Mrs Lovejoy now, I mean. When she was the nanny."

"Mrs Lovejoy was their nursemaid?"

Cook returns to the stove and nods as she whisks the eggs. "Looked after them as their poor mother faded away, she did."

"I'm surprised the nursemaid is even in the family photos, actually."

There's a shrewd cast to Cook's eye. "By my reckoning, that was Mr Lovejoy's doing. Now, you get on with those dishes, or I'll never have breakfast ready by the time the family wakes."

In the scullery, I pick up a small skillet and gingerly dip it in the tub. I hope the soapy water and scrubbing doesn't roughen my hands.

I poke my head around the doorway and say, "I wonder why Mrs Lovejoy still allows that photograph to hang here. I wouldn't think she'd want the reminder."

The cook shrugs. "She's not down here much. I daresay she's forgotten about it. Or maybe the master insisted. Like he did with the one upstairs."

I mull over her words for a few moments. "So, after the first Mrs Lovejoy died, Mr Lovejoy married the nursemaid?" I infuse my voice with wonder, as though I find the whole thing terribly romantic.

"That he did." Cook glances up, watches the door. She yanks back her cap so that her hair, which is the dirty yellow of aged lacework, falls onto her forehead, and whispers,

"This Mrs Lovejoy took his first wife's place faster than it took the funeral wreaths to wilt."

I form my mouth in an amazed "Oh".

Cook's mouth twists to the side in a satisfied smile as she nods sagely at the cooking eggs. "Had her hooks into him earlier than that, though, by my reckoning."

Inspecting some bacon fat that's been burnt onto the bottom of a pan, I wonder if I dare ask for more gossip. "Did he always… you know… with the servants?" I ask, standing in the doorway.

Cook nods and lowers her voice again. "Oh yes, I think he did. That man had unnatural urges. Not that he ever tried anything on me, mind you," she says, thumping a knob of dough onto the table. "But some of the younger servants… well, if he were still alive, I'd tell you to take care, believe me."

Pursing my lips, I scour the pan with all my might, but the mark seems to be seared on, so I just place it alongside the other drying dishes.

She presses her shoulder against mine as she drops a spoon into the tub. "Liked to be a buttered bun, he did."

"Even up 'til his death?" I ask, damp hands on my hips.

She gives me a meaningful look, a sly smile on her cheerful face. "Well, it wasn't with little Ruth. I kept a sharp eye on her. Promised her mother, I did, that I'd take care of her. Mrs Forbes—you know, the last housekeeper—she was an old Tartar, she was. He'd have had to have been a very, very brave man to slide a hand up her skirts, as they say. And, like I said, it wasn't with me."

Which leaves Nurse Marie. I think of her sallow face, and her thin, brittle hands and arms. I know it takes all types, but I just can't imagine it.

"You can't mean Nurse Marie?" I say, surprised.

"She doesn't look all that comely at the moment, to be sure. But she used to keep herself quite nice. Almost pretty, she was. Always wore her hair with a nice braid through it, pinned at the back with a lovely tortoiseshell comb. And she wore her uniform with pride, she did. Not like now." Cook shakes her head as she collects the clean skillet.

Nurse Marie. Playing away with the master. I wonder if Hatch knows of this.

I wander out from the scullery and, with my thumb, I bend my middle fingernail downward. My nails are already softening from all the scrubbing and I grimace at the greasy stench of suet on my skin.

Cook stares down at the dollops of lamb kidney on the kitchen table. "Master Joshua does enjoy his devilled kidneys, but I'm not sure I have time to prepare them." She glances over at me. "I don't suppose you know how to cook 'em?"

My eyes widen in alarm. Besides having no culinary skills, I'm not even really sure of how devilled kidneys are supposed to taste because I usually avoid them. I remember when I was small, Amah used to fry the bloodshot meat with soy sauce if she managed to procure some from an incoming ship. I rather enjoyed it like that, but I hardly think that's how Cook wants it prepared.

She sees the doubt on my face and tuts, staring down at the meat again. "Well, I'll throw them on. You watch I don't burn 'em."

I make Cyril my excuse for escaping the house for an hour or two in order to meet up with Detective Inspector Hatch, telling Nurse Marie and Cook I'm taking him for a walk, that I think his cheeks need more colour in them. For a moment Nurse Marie looked like she might join us, but I told her to take the opportunity to rest. She looks like she hasn't slept in weeks. When I returned to the nursery this morning, I found her weeping by the doll's crib, holding the doll with chestnut ringlets. I patted her on the shoulder and, although I expected her to, she didn't shrug me away.

"I miss little Margaret so much," she said, a tear teetering over her nostril, ready to mingle with the snot on her upper lip. Her hair was pulled unevenly into a bun and she was still in the same dress, the grey one with the navy pinstripe. She probably slept in it. In fact, there was a sour smell that wafted from her, and I wondered just how many days she'd lived in that dress.

Her fingers ran over the lacework of the doll's dress. "So much loss."

I patted her shoulder again and murmured how sorry I was. I nearly asked her what she thought had happened to poor Margaret, but I decided she was still too fragile. I'd wait until she was more comfortable with my presence.

Cyril tugs on my hand as we make our way to Church Street. Only one reporter remains to brave the cold, and we trot past him, ignoring his barrage of questions. "What's your name then, miss? Who's this little fellow? Are you Cyril, my little man?" Cyril looks up at his name, but I place a hand over his ear and press him to my skirts, urge him to move more quickly.

We pass the building site, but the workmen from the other day don't seem to be there, maybe because it looks like it might rain.

"Which way to the park, Cyril?"

We turn right onto the main street of the village, Cyril still pulling me along. I've arranged to meet Hatch at the gates to Abney Park. Hopefully we can find a discreet bench somewhere we can sit while Cyril chases rabbits or whatever children do at the park.

On the first corner is a little teashop and across the road is a grand building that seems to be a school of some sort. A line of ten or so girls stream from the side of the building, and with a twist in my heart, I think of another school, far from this one. We pass the open door of an inn and I can smell the malty aroma of spilt ale that has seeped into the floorboards. Next to the inn is a little rag-and-bone shop, its dark corners crammed with jars of beads, boxes of utensils and baskets of worn clothing.

Of the many shops along Church Street there is only one

that catches Cyril's attention. The bakery has a pretty pink and white awning, and Cyril leaves smudges on the glass as he gazes at the sweets in the window.

"If you're a good boy, I will purchase you some on the way home."

He stares up at me and I wonder if he's going to have a tantrum, but on seeing that I'm resolute, he relents. "Good boy. On way home," he repeats.

The entrance to Abney Park is flanked by rather grand pillars. The interesting designs etched into the stonework are almost like something that belong in the museum. Reading the signage on the gate, I see that, actually, the park is part of a cemetery. I glance down at Cyril who's hitching up the back of his pants. I wonder if he knows what a cemetery is.

Standing by one of the further pillars is a woman selling dog collars, and two women walk past, shopping baskets swinging from their arms.

"Mrs Chancey." Hatch approaches us from inside the gates.

"Nurse Louise," I correct him, as I take his hand in greeting, nodding my head down towards the boy.

"Of course." His eyes are watering from the chill in the air. He leads us through the gates. "There's a park bench not far from here. The boy can have a run around while we talk."

He points out Abney House for us, a very handsome residence, and makes his way down a path that runs off to the left. We walk under the shade of tall elm trees that almost block out the overcast sky.

Reaching a small clearing on the banks of a small pond, he says, "We can take a seat beneath that tree over there."

As we sit down on the bench, Cyril stands by my side furthest away from Hatch and glares at him suspiciously. "Why don't you run over there, Cyril, and see if there is an eel in the water?" I say to him.

"What's an eel?" The boy's eyes reluctantly leave Hatch's face and find mine.

"It's like a long fish. Haven't you ever eaten eel?"

He shakes his head. His nose is running again, but I know I don't have a handkerchief in my bag.

"Off you go."

As he trudges off, I turn to the Detective Inspector. "Well, I've had a busy time of it. I'm quite exhausted already."

Hatch lifts his hat for a moment and pushes his straw-coloured hair back from his forehead. "Tell me."

I pick some cedar leaves from the bench beside me and rub the sprigs between my fingers. "Very late last night when I stole out into the garden to have a closer look at the drawing room door, I met the vicious dog. I'd entirely forgotten about him." I sniff the leaf's fragrance on my fingertips.

Hatch looks alarmed. "It didn't hurt you?" His eyes take in my hands, my arms.

A young couple stroll by and take up position next to Cyril by the side of the pond. They peer into its depths with the boy and seem to be asking him a question.

"No. He gave me a terrible fright, but really, I don't think he's as ferocious as you've been led to believe." I watch as the couple bid Cyril farewell and move on.

"Meaning…"

"Meaning, I'm not so sure he would be a real deterrent to an intruder. If someone came from outside to murder Lovejoy and Margaret, I think it's possible he or she could find their way past the dog."

Hatch casts his eyes to the sky and thinks for a moment. "All right. And what did you think of the drawing room doors?"

Cyril races across the grass towards us. "Nursie, Nursie. Ducks. See ducks!" He flings his arm out and points at three brown ducks that swim into view. "Bread, Nursie. Bread." I assure Cyril I have no bread, even proving my point by opening up my reticule for him to scrutinise. "Now go on and play."

As the boy runs back to the pond, I say to Hatch, "I suppose you noticed there were scratches on the inside of the door, as well as on the outside?"

Cyril crouches low, and leans out towards the boldest duck that paddles up to him.

Hatch nods. "Yes. Leading me to believe, one way or another, Margaret's murderer was trying to trip us up."

"One way or another?"

"Yes. I mean, if it was someone in the household, they've tried to make it look like an outsider broke in, but if it's an outsider who did break in, they've muddied the water by scratching up the inside."

I nod. "I see."

Cyril searches amongst the brush beneath the trees and finds a long stick. He drags it into the middle of the clearing and, lifting it above his head, he swings it down so it thumps the ground, again and again.

"What is that strange little creature doing?"

Hatch smiles. "Being a boy. My mother said when I was young I used to go into the garden and thump the tree with a plank of wood."

"But why?"

He shrugs, still smiling. "I don't know." He turns to me again. "And what other news have you for me? Any idea what happened to the Cook's wrapper?"

"No, I still need to ask her about it, although she gave me some excellent gossip this morning." I tilt my head to him as I ask, "I suppose you know the present Mrs Lovejoy was originally the children's nursemaid when the first Mrs Lovejoy was still alive?"

"Yes, that was made clear to us from the beginning."

"You might already have surmised this, but, according to the cook, even before the first Mrs Lovejoy died, Mr Lovejoy and the second Mrs Lovejoy were having…" I pause. I'm not sure how to put it delicately for the Detective Inspector. "That Mr Lovejoy and the second Mrs Lovejoy were already… romantic."

"Ha. Romantic. Is that what it's called?"

I grin at him. "Cook said he enjoyed being a 'buttered bun'."

Hatch's eyebrow hooks up. "Was there anybody lately he was being a buttered bun with?"

"Well, the cook said it wasn't with her and it wasn't with Ruth. And she said the old housekeeper was a dragon, who Mr Lovejoy would never have approached." I take my eyes off Cyril to look up at Hatch. "Which really only leaves..."

"Nursemaid Marie." He claps his hands together. "I knew there was something there that they were keeping from me. I should have known."

I shrug. "Mr Lovejoy liked his nursemaids, evidently."

"Have you asked her about it?"

"No." I frown. "She's... a little unhinged, I think. With grief." For the first time, it occurs to me that she has had a double loss: her ward, Margaret, and her lover, Mr Lovejoy. No wonder she isn't coping.

"I think you'd better question her next," Hatch says. He slaps his hand down onto the bench. "If only we could find that wrapper. We searched the gardens thoroughly and never found it, and no fires were alight in the grates overnight, so I don't believe it was burnt to cinders. At least not before the police were summoned." Hatch lifts his hat again to wipe back his hair. His face is troubled. "I'm afraid we don't have much time left, though, Mrs Chancey. Maybe two or three days at most."

"Why is that?"

"Have you read the latest newspapers?"

I shake my head. "No, I haven't had access to them."

A young woman leads a little girl towards the pond. The tiny thing has pretty flaxen hair that falls to the small of her back and she wears a velvet dress the shade of a violet, under a navy overcoat. Cyril drops his stick and steps closer to watch the girl as the woman hands her something.

"There's a lot of anger that the murder hasn't been solved yet. People have been writing letters. Journalists," his thin lips tighten on the word, "have been whipping the public into a frenzy of discontent. I'm afraid the Superintendent has told me that come Sunday, I will be moved to another case. And if it comes to that, I wouldn't be surprised if Nurse Marie is charged." He brushes off the back of his coat as he stands.

The girl tosses bits of bread to the ducks that waddle in the water at her feet. The woman offers a crust to Cyril, too, but he shakes his head and keeps staring at the girl. From here, I can see his bottom lip turn down. I can see how sad he looks as he gazes at her.

CHAPTER 19

Amah reaches her fingers into the blue and white porcelain jar and brings out a piece of pickled ginger. The flesh is soft and fragrant between her fingertips and juice runs down the side of her hand. With her tongue, she catches the drip before it reaches her wrist.

Why is Jakub punishing her? What does he have to do with these men who are turning up murdered? How would he even know about them, and why does he care?

Sucking the syrup from the ginger, she thinks back to what Uncle Chee had told her. That Jakub has somehow found out that Miriam isn't his mother.

She bites off some ginger and stares down at the fibrous threads of its flesh, wondering just how much Jakub had managed to find out. She fails to taste the sweet, her appetite fading, and she tosses the remaining bit of ginger into the fireplace.

Wiping her sticky fingers on a handkerchief, she replaces the jar's lid. She will have to search for him again. Striding over to the window of her sitting room, she looks out onto the cold, grey day. She presses her palm to the glass's chilly surface, and when she lifts her hand away, she leaves smudgy fingerprints.

As she ties the woollen scarf around her throat, loosening it again, she watches her reflection in the mirror. Her eyes are bloodshot, her face puffy. Her skirt is loose, for she has had trouble eating the last few days. She hasn't been sleeping well either. Ever since Heloise left for Stoke Newington, Amah has been frozen, unable to decide what to do. The same questions swirl in her mind, in a loop, only to be repeated again when she arrives at a dead end. Where is Jakub? Who are the Chinese men he's befriended? Is he in some sort of terrible plight because of them?

But no, she knows if he is in trouble, it has something to do with the past. The questions clack in her brain like tacky notes of an old piano, until the tune makes her think she's losing her mind.

She barely notices Abigail dusting the sidetable in the corridor, and only manages a small nod as Bundle bids her farewell from the kitchen doorway, her mind is so taken up with what she must do.

She walks until her boots pinch her toes and then summons a cab, which deposits her outside the Strangers' Home, where she finds Cadogan working over a ledger in the office. She asks him if she can speak to Arnold, the gentleman he'd told her about the last time they met.

"Laid up in bed, poor fellow," he says. "But I managed to ask him some questions on your behalf, nevertheless."

After Amah assures him she has a coachman outside ready to accompany her, he directs her to an address two streets away. "You'll find various rooming houses there, especially set up for the Asian seamen who find themselves between voyages. Arnold believes your best bet is one behind a shop that has the name Kung above its door, and another run by a man by the name of Ghosh."

As Amah turns to leave, Cadogan warns her of the street. His smile's pleasant as he speaks. Fond, even. "You might find the air a little more pungent than usual and, I know I can say this to you, you must be careful you are not swindled by the characters you will find down there. They sell all sorts of potions and tokens. The Oriental Hindu or Mussulman is nothing more than a grown-up child, after all, who believes in the influence of his jinns and spirits over firm facts."

Amah's gaze finds the gold cross that glints from his collar and she holds her eyes steady to stop herself from casting them to the ceiling.

But when she follows his directions, she finds the road quite quiet. A beggar sits on the doorstep of a narrow building, his head resting between his legs, a mangy dog by his side. She pops into a shop on the corner that she knows her uncle frequents on occasion to procure the pills he takes for indigestion. The shop smells of earth, joss stick smoke and tea. The walls are covered with red and black Chinese scrolls and tablets. She studies the small pots of spices and the bottles of soy. On the counter are colourful jars of ginger and condiments and a small heap of spinach, dirt still clumped at its roots. She asks Shing, the proprietor, where she might find Kung's shop and, after checking with another man, they point the way to the far end of the street.

When she reaches Kung's, the shutters are up and barred. She bangs on the front door, but doesn't receive a response. Just as she's losing heart, she notices a group of lascars trot through a doorway further down the road. She hurries across and manages to peer into a large room packed with row upon row of bedding. Sagging sheets, like yellowing sails that can find no wind, serve as curtains to sequester the space. Three sailors dressed in uniform are seated on their mattresses, leaning back against the wall, while on the other side of the room is a youth, asleep, his rolled-up prayer mat by his side.

A dark man, his belly pushing out the front of his tunic, steps forward, blocks her view of the room. "How may I help you?"

"Is your name Ghosh?" she asks, pushing back her veil.

His brown eyes take in her face, her western attire, find their way back to her face. "Yes, that is me."

"I'm searching for my nephew," she says. "His name is Jakub Chee."

"What ship did he come in on?"

Amah stares at him. She can't think. What did Miriam say? A word that reminded her of "caramel", or "carnival". "Coronation"? "I can't recall. But it didn't come in in the last few days. Maybe two, three, weeks ago? He's been staying at the Strangers' Home. They said he might have moved here. With a man called Sin Hok."

Ghosh's chin lifts, his lips lengthen into an unhappy line. "Sin Hok?"

She nods. "Yes." Lowering her voice, she glances over her shoulder to make sure nobody else listens. "They say this Sin Hok is with a gang. A gang called something to do with the lotus."

Ghosh snorts through his wide nostrils. "He dreams!" He considers Amah for a moment more and then shrugs. "Follow me."

He leads her through the front room, which smells of sawdust and mould, to a partitioned area at the back. A Chinese man, hair as black as tar, moustache as bristly as a shoe brush, lies flat on his back, tied to the bed with metres and metres of rope. His face glistens and his perspiration has seeped into the mattress, leaving a silhouette of sweat that looks like his shadow. His eyes are closed, but he murmurs something, tosses his head.

"Here is your fearsome Sin Hok," says Ghosh.

"What is wrong with him?" Amah feels her heart peak, her blood chill. Is Jakub somewhere, unconscious like this? Or did he do this to the man?

"Too much bhang. Too much gin. Who knows." Ghosh ushers her from Sin Hok's bedside, leads her back to the front step. "Smashed up Kung's shop. That's why it's shut up. Smashed up Kung too, actually. Lucky Sin Hok hadn't found the knife by then."

"The knife?"

"Yes. Came out onto the road, swinging it around, eyes red as the devil, shouting that he was going to murder someone. Took quite a few men to subdue him. Delirious, of course. Kung wouldn't have him back, so we tied him up here. We just have to wait for him to come around." He looks thoughtful as he pushes the door shut. "Of course, sometimes they never do."

Amah steps down onto the pavement, looking right and left. She doesn't know where to go from here in her search for Jakub. She wanders towards Limehouse Causeway and, as she comes closer, the beggar slides on his bottom down three steps until he can almost touch her skirts as she passes.

"Lady, look." He holds out his hand, which is encased in fingerless gloves, the weave unravelling at the edges. "Precious. Luck."

She peers at the object that lies in his palm. It's no bigger than a farthing, made from polished stone the colour of cypress bark. It takes her a few moments to see that the charm is in the shape of a fish.

The beggar says something in a language she can't understand, then repeats the word, "Luck."

Amah wants to back away from the beggar's odour and his filthy fingernails that are as packed with dirt as a pipe is with tobacco. She wants to back away from the empty promise the charm offers. But she hesitates. Is she really in the position to refuse an amulet that promises good fortune?

She takes out a shilling from her bag and offers it to the man, but he shakes his head, holds up two fingers. Amah shrugs, turns to continue on her way, but he catches hold of her sleeve. She yanks her arm back and glares at him. His eyes are tired, bleary as a dead snapper. His brown skin has a sallow tinge. Amah rummages in her purse again, takes out a few more pennies, leaving enough for her bus fare home. She holds the coins out to the man, who almost smiles, nods, drops the charm into her outstretched hand. He settles back onto the steps next to his dog, and Amah tucks the charm into her pocket, thinking of how she will hide it in one of Heloise's bed pillows. That girl needs all the luck she can get to pass through this life.

*

As she trudges along, Amah wonders why the boy is punishing her like this. Has she not been punished enough in this world?

She knows, though, that on that day long ago in Kuching she was fortunate. She survived. She can't recall how they straggled back to the boat, this time with many of the Sarawak survivors with them, about ten British citizens in all.

On the *Dukano*, the gentlemen took to sleeping in the saloon. She remembers Pidgeon being there, and that ugly Lovejoy, McBride with his loud voice. Amah's not sure where the servants found to sleep then—maybe on the deck? There were only two British women left, her Mrs Preston and Mrs Pidgeon. The other one who was knocked over the head, she died, after lying in the sun for many hours. From her position behind the stables, Amah saw another *kungsi* man approach her. The white men bellowed at him from the window, but he just leant over her body, poured a little water in her mouth. He shook his head, like she was a mistake or something.

Mr Preston died too. He held on for a few days, but there was no doctor on board, and the heat was unbearable. As Amah held Mrs Preston's hand while she wept, she thought about how it was for the best. It would be just her and Amah now.

CHAPTER 20

Nurse Marie has been reading a boring old book to Cyril about the moral improvement of a spoilt little boy. I can see how this might be of benefit to Cyril, but damned if I'm going to sit through it too. I tuck him into bed and tell him of the book I'm reading, full of stories of exciting animals and exotic places, but I'm not very far into Darwin's work before he complains that it's boring.

"Don't be silly, Cyril," I say. "It's very interesting." As I read that "the vigorous, the healthy, and the happy survive and multiply," I feel a tweak of remorse. I'm not sure about McBride and Lovejoy, but certainly this statement can't be true of poor Cyril's sister.

Earlier this evening, just after Mrs Lovejoy's visit to her son, Nurse Marie had brought us up a tray of supper. I was pleasantly surprised, because this time she'd included a plate and cup for me, although now that I think about it, Cook probably arranged it that way.

As Nurse Marie prepared some soup for Cyril, the boy, the tip of his tongue lodged between his lips with concentration, set my bowl and spoon next to his at the nursery table. He pulled another chair close and patted it. "This is for Meggie. She really likes soup. Much more than I do."

Although my heart ached for the little beast, the pain etched onto Nurse Marie's face was frightening. She covered her eyes with her hand and fled the room.

"Nursie Marie smells funny, Nursie," said Cyril. He held a piece of bread up to me. "Butter?"

I now smile at the little boy as he lies in bed, his cheeks flushed, his eyes drowsy. "Fair enough. Let me tell you another story then."

I share with him a tale Amah used to tell me. A story of a golden eel caught by a fisherman—a magic eel that promised the fisherman a lifetime of riches. The fisherman took the eel home and his wife mistakenly cooked it up for their supper. That very night they conceived a child. A girl, who caused all sorts of terrible catastrophes.

When I was younger, I used to think of this tale often, wondering if my mother looked at me strangely, closely, as she told me that story. I wondered if she ate eel the night she conceived me.

"Cook, Mrs Lovejoy said to ask you if you had anything spare I could throw over my shoulders to stay warm while I'm tending Cyril." I'm lying. I don't know any other way to broach the subject of the wrapper.

"You mean a shawl or something?" She wipes a strand of hair out of her face with the back of her hand. She unties the apron from her waist. There are weary bags under her eyes.

"Yes, something I can wrap myself in?"

Cook takes a seat at the kitchen table, gestures for me to sit too. She pours us each a cup of tea. "All I can think of is the spare blankets in the linen cupboard. I did have a very nice wrapper. Very handy. Made of a nice, crisp linen it was, just right to slip over my dress when the air has a chill to it in the early morning."

"Oh, I wouldn't take yours," I say, sipping the tea, which has gone a little cool.

"Couldn't if you wanted to," she says. "Missing, it is. Missing since... Well. Maybe old Mrs Warren did just lose it in the laundry, but she's sure she didn't—right indignant she was—and I have to say, she has always been reliable.

But then, she has her daughter-in-law working with her now. Maybe she mislaid it."

"How long has it been gone?"

Her eyes dart to the doorway to make sure nobody is listening, but I know there's nobody around. The family retired a good half an hour ago and Nurse Marie has already locked herself into the housekeeper's room. "Since the night Miss Margaret... You know," she whispers, shaking her head. She takes a handkerchief tucked into her cuff and blots her mouth. "Horrible it was. Horrible. And poor little Ruth — she found the body."

"Oh dear, how terrible for her."

Cook nods, eyes wide. A ruddy flush clouds her cheeks. "Nearly swooned, she did. Lucky the nightsoil man was nearby. He caught her, he did, brought her up to the back door."

"So..." I pause. I want to bring the conversation back around to the wrapper. "So your wrapper has been missing since that night? I wonder why."

Cook leans in closer across the wide table and whispers again, "The police think the murderer wore it to save his own clothes from blood." She shakes her head at me, eyes wide. "My wrapper. Used in such a devilish manner. I will never get over it."

"Don't tell me the intruder crept into your bedroom in order to collect the wrapper," I say, a shocked note to my voice. "How frightening." I peer around, as though I'm searching for a prowler to jump out at us.

"No, Nurse Louise, I'd left it on that hook over there." She nods towards a row of five hooks by the kitchen door. An umbrella hangs on one, while an overcoat, faded to the shade of a mushroom, hangs on another.

"So, really, anyone could have taken it?"

She nods slowly.

It's my turn to whisper. "Do you have any ideas?"

Cook clamps her handkerchief to her mouth and shakes her head. But her eyes tell me that she does.

I'll wait. She'll tell me in her own time. She might become suspicious if I push her.

Taking another sip of my tea, which is as good as flavoured milk by now, I say to her, "I haven't seen Emily again. She hasn't visited the nursery at all. I was going to ask her to join us for a walk tomorrow. What do you think?"

"Ah. I don't know about that one. I know Nurse Marie gave up on her all together."

"Always been trouble to the nanny, has she, Cook?"

The cook frowns for a moment, squinting her eyes as she thinks back. "She's always been a quiet thing. Well, the whole household was quiet back when the first Mrs Lovejoy was sickly. I will say this for the present Mrs Lovejoy—Nurse Kate as we knew her then—she brought some life back into the house. Ooh, she was so managing and forthright, it fair drove the housekeeper up the wall." A small smile lifts her lips. "That's right. Miss Emily adored Nurse Kate back then. You keeping up, Nurse? I'm talking about the present Mrs Lovejoy, when she was just the children's nursemaid. Miss Emily followed her around everywhere."

"And Master Joshua?"

"Oh, he's always followed Miss Emily around. Still does." Her mouth settles into an unhappy line. "I remember once I made a nice teacake for Mrs Lovejoy when she was ill, and Miss Emily came in and told me I shouldn't spoil her mother, that she was just putting on airs. Got that from Nurse Kate she did. She was too young to even know that sort of language. Another time, when Mrs Lovejoy was being taken away to visit a special sanatorium, Miss Emily wouldn't even kiss her goodbye. Broke her heart, it did. Miss Emily learnt that behaviour from the nurse, no doubt about it. And there was nothing the poor lady could do, because of course Nurse Kate had Mr Lovejoy on side too, by then."

"Are they still close? Emily and the new Mrs Lovejoy?"

"Well." She gives me a knowing look. "If you ask me, Miss Emily's now old enough to realise the games Mrs Lovejoy played with them all. As soon as the first Mrs Lovejoy died, Nurse Kate employed a new nanny for the children and married their father. Mighty cold she is to the older children now, especially after the new two came along."

"Margaret and Cyril?"

The cook nods. "It wasn't a pretty sight, I can tell you. The parents fair doting on the younger two, while Miss Emily and Master Joshua went about their own business with hardly a spare shirt between themselves."

I think of the paintings on the walls upstairs, lovely homages to the youngest two. How there are no pictures of the older children, except for the group photograph. I feel an unexpected pang of sympathy. No wonder Emily and Joshua are so odd.

The clock in the sitting room chimes the half-hour.

I pick up my reticule from the kitchen chair next to me. "I might just visit the lavatory before I return to the nursery."

"Well, I'm for bed." She picks up her apron and rummages in its pocket. "Here's the key to the back door. When you've finished, just drop it in that jug there, on the kitchen stand. I'll collect it in the morning. Don't forget to lock the back door, mind. Especially after..." She pulls a face at me, then shuffles off to her room.

A light fog hangs in the night air, muffling the lamp's glow, and I waste a few matches lighting my cigarette. I'm hiding again behind the garden shed and the dog has joined me once more. He sits at my feet, panting, hoping for another caramel, no doubt.

I pinch a stray bit of tobacco from my tongue and mull over what Cook has told me about Emily and her brother. Of how close the girl was to Mrs Lovejoy when she was her nanny. Of how their relationship has changed. I must find an excuse to talk with the girl, before Hatch's time runs out.

Once I've finished with my smoke, I step out from behind the shed and gaze up at the nursery window. I left the curtains closed this time, but was that a slight quiver of the curtains? A splinter of light?

Like a breath against the back of my neck, I feel a shift in the air behind me. The shed door creaks open, the sound in tune with my tense muscles as I turn. A black figure, swathed in grey fog, steps from the shed.

"That's a dirty habit for a young woman." His voice grates.

"Sir, you startled me." I hold the lamp up to his face and hope the dog will defend me if need be. But then I remember that the dog was of no assistance to either the master or Margaret. I grasp the shape of my pistol in my silk bag. "What are you doing here?"

He's hatless and has an unusually large head, and his long nose is so crooked it looks like a knob of ginger above his bushy moustache and beard.

"I'm Crossley, the gardener," he says. "Who you be?" He lurches one step towards me and that's when I see that he's very drunk. His eyes have that unsteady look about them, his lips are wet and loose.

"I'm Nurse Louise. The new nursemaid."

He leers, throwing his head back, but the movement pulls him off balance and he trips backward a few steps, lands against the brick wall of the shed. The dog pounces for him, in play or to threaten him, I'm not sure.

"Agh, git away with you, Rufus," he growls at the dog. Then he looks back at me. "Met the faithful mongrel, have you?"

"I did. Last night." I lift my lamp to see him better. "I didn't realise you lived here?"

"I don't," he said, rubbing his finger beneath his nose. "But sometimes I doss down here, when I've had a few too many ales at the inn. You want to join me?" His two front teeth are either missing or rotten black. I can't tell in the gloom.

"I'll be fine sleeping in the house," I assure him.

I go to turn away but am caught short by his next words.

"You wouldn't catch me sleeping in there with that lot. And don't you go listening to their gossip about me," he says. "Women! Always rabbiting away about something, they are."

"What gossip?"

"Those women. That there scrawny cook and her mouse of a scullery maid. They'll have you believe all sorts of things."

"Things like what?"

He folds his arms and his words slur. "That I had something to do with the child's murder, and her father's murder. Found the master, I did." He shakes his head.

"After…?"

"Yer. Head near sliced off, it were." He nudges the dog with the toe of his boot. "He was there too, wasn't yer, yer mangy mongrel? Sitting by the master's body, supping on his blood, he was."

My eyes fall to the dog, resting at our feet. Definitely not such a loyal hound, after all. I look back up at the gardener. It's a bit of a coincidence, him being so close by for each murder. I also remember Hatch saying something about it—something to do with the newspapers, and letters to the editor that accused the gardener and another fellow who found the bodies for the murders. However, Hatch did insist he'd cleared all the servants.

I think it is time that I return to the house, nevertheless. I'd feel more assured if I had my pistol in hand, but then I'd have to put down the lamp, and at the moment I want to keep an eye on Crossley.

"Who do you think killed the poor girl and her father, then?"

He presses a finger to the side of his nose and taps it. "All's I know is I wouldn't be so eager to go back into that house, if I was you."

I take a step towards him. "What do you mean?" Closer up I can see a line of dribble that glistens in his beard like a snail's trail. And he stinks of stale piss.

"Clearing out the house, they are," he says, glancing up at

the windows of the top floor. "You watch. Next it'll be that fat Mrs Lovejoy and then it'll be her wee white prince."

I close the back door behind me with a firm click and turn the key.

A prickle of fear slinks across the back of my neck. I'm not quite sure if it's from my encounter with the repugnant gardener or if it's his words that have affected me. Both probably. I shake my head and shoulders like that might dispel my foreboding.

I drop the key into the jug on the kitchen sideboard and make my way swiftly through the dark hall to the staircase.

My heart judders as a shadow billows from the bottom step. I can't help but gasp and, holding my lamp high, I quickly discern that it's Emily. "Oh, but you did give me a fright. What are you doing up so late in the evening?" I ask.

She has a blanket wrapped around herself and her feet are bare. Her hair hangs limp and, despite the lack of light, the terrible spots on her face blaze painfully from her pale skin. Her eyes seem almost black in the shadows of the night.

"Why were you talking with Crossley?"

"Ah. Was that you spying on me from the nursery window?" She doesn't answer, just continues to glare at me with those eyes as flat as stone, her wide lips turned down at the edges. Nerves jangle in my fingertips. She's just a girl, I tell myself. "Was it you watching me last night too?"

Still no answer.

I brush past her to climb the stairs, but angle myself so as to keep her in sight. "I am sorry I've missed your visits. Come see me again in the morning." I smile at her. I hope it's a welcoming smile and that the wariness I feel deep in my bones doesn't shine through. With each step up that stair case, I feel her eyes pull on my back like an anchor.

CHAPTER 21

"I want sugar in it." Cyril's high-pitched demand stirs me from the slight doze I've fallen into. He's talking to Nurse Marie in the nursery, over their breakfast. Rolling onto my back in the narrow bed, I pull the blanket up to cover my shoulder. I press the palm of my hand to my nose. It's as cold as freshly caught trout.

Nurse Marie murmurs something to the boy, to which he answers, his voice rising even more, "I want sugar in my milk."

Stifling a groan, I sit up. Only one or two more nights of this, hopefully. Pulling out a little mirror from my velveteen vanity pouch, I scrutinise my face for blemishes or lines. I wonder if it's dawn's gloom that causes the shadows under my eyes, or if they are there because I've been sleeping so poorly. Last night was yet another evening I'd lost sleep. Crossley's words haunted me as I tried to drift off, not to mention how Emily had made my flesh creep. Pressing my eyes together, I apply face cream, taking a moment to enjoy its rose fragrance. I dab a tiny amount of *parfum* behind my ears and then haul myself up to dress, swapping my nightdress for drawers and a chemise.

Picking up my corset, I loosen the lacing at the back because, really, my waist doesn't need to be so uncomfortably constricted for play with Cyril; there's no call for a nanny in Stoke Newington to be a fashion plate, after all. As I draw the steel busk across my chest, lifting my breasts into position before heaving the corset together, I think of what the gardener had said about someone clearing out the house—clearing it of people, presumably. And he didn't mean the servants were doing the clearing, either. He could only have meant the two older children.

I pull on one under-petticoat, wondering if I should put on another for warmth. Plonking down onto the side of the bed, I drag my stockings over my toes and wonder about Emily and her brother. I run my fingertip over a catch in the wool, thinking of how Cook claimed that Emily was very close with the second Mrs Lovejoy when she was still her Nurse Kate. Until the nurse turned the girl against her own mother.

Maybe Emily resented that now. Maybe Emily hated Mrs Lovejoy—and her father, even—for robbing her of time with her mother. And if Cook was right about the older children being treated poorly since their mother died, well, that could lead to all sorts of grievances. Jealousy even.

A tinkle of cutlery against crockery coming from the nursery catches my attention. I must hurry and help Nurse Marie.

I step into my crinoline and my mind returns to Emily and Joshua. Could that sort of jealousy lead to murder, though, as the gardener had hinted? Could Emily or Joshua really be that deranged? I think of Joshua's vacant stare, and of the malice that seems to ooze from his sister's skin as palpably as the pimples on her face. Maybe. After drawing my over-petticoat on—a plain one, no frills or stripes like I'd usually insist upon—I stare into space. Try to imagine them murdering their father. Anger driving them to incapacitate him in the garden, slice his throat. But what of their little sister? Pretty Margaret, the spoilt and loved younger daughter. Was that their first revenge upon their parents?

I know a lot about jealousy. It's as familiar to me as the smell of the back lanes of Liverpool. I know that it stabs deep and curls, heavy, in one's chest. I think again of that school in

Bath, of the neat girls reading French, of the ribbons in their hair, seagull white. And, yes, there's that ache in my heart.

But could I be driven to murder? I think if I had to live with the resentment every moment, of every day... I shake my head. Of course not. Although there's a flicker of doubt at the back of my mind as I pull my shoes on.

As I enter the nursery, I tie my apron around my waist. "What trouble are you giving Nurse Marie?" I ask Cyril.

"I don't like milk," he says, dunking a piece of his toast into the cup.

I start to say that it'll make him strong, but he doesn't care, and neither do I. "If you behave yourself we will..." What? I can't be sure of what he wants to do.

"Go for a walk again?"

I consider him. I wouldn't mind visiting one or two shops in the village. "We will see."

Dipping a linen towel in the washbasin, I wipe Cyril's mouth and hands. I look across to Nurse Marie, who's laying out Cyril's outfit for the day. "I met Mr Crossley last night. The gardener. Do you know him? He's a very strange man."

She shrugs, uninterested. "I haven't had much to do with him."

I stand close to her and, reaching for Cyril's breeches, I say, in a soft voice, "He said he wouldn't sleep in the house. He said he thinks the murderer will strike again, murder another Lovejoy." I watch her closely. "Made me tremble all night. I didn't get a wink of sleep."

A flash of fear is quickly replaced with a frown of annoyance. I wonder if more colour comes into her cheeks, but I can't be sure.

"How ridiculous." Nurse Marie unbuttons Cyril's shirt. "He's just saying that because the papers are reporting that he's the main suspect in..." She presses her lips together, shakes her head.

It's the first time we've actually spoken for more than one or two sentences to each other. She speaks softly, almost like a child—a sweet, sensitive child who's prone to tears.

I sit on a chair to allow the boy to step into his trousers. When has she had access to the newspaper? I watch as she finishes dressing Cyril and settles him onto the floor with his blocks. Pouring her a cup of tea, I call her to the table, urge her to sit.

"Rest awhile," I say. "He'll be all right."

She sips her tea and I notice her dress, although still grey with the pinstripe, is neatly buttoned at the wrists and doesn't smell musty any longer. Either she's washed and mended her uniform or has finally changed into the spare. Her hair is still a mess, though, falling about her narrow face, while the bun at the base of her neck looks like a wren's nest.

I prop my chin onto the heel of my hand and lean on the table. "I'm not sure if I can stay here, Nurse Marie."

Her eyes widen. "Why not? You've only been here three days."

I pull my face into an anxious expression. "I'm worried about what the gardener told me. I mean, the agency warned me of what had happened here, but they assured me they were committed by a mad person outside the household. And, of course, I was offered excellent wages for taking on the position, given the circumstances. But…" I shake my head.

"But, Nurse Louise, you must stay. I am waiting for my agency to find me a new position. In fact, I've even considered taking on work as a housemaid, I want to leave here so badly. But if I leave, and you leave…" Her eyes find Cyril, who's smashing a toy horse against a prostrate soldier figurine.

Mrs Lovejoy might have to actually spend time with her son, if that were the case. But what do I know of her grief? "Before… before what happened, did Mrs Lovejoy spend much time with the children?"

The nursemaid stares into her tea for so long I wonder if she didn't hear me.

"She absolutely doted on them," she says, eventually.

"She's with child right now, isn't she?" The nursemaid

nods. "How was she with Margaret and Cyril when they were babies?"

"I don't know. I've only been here about a year."

This surprises me. She's so attached to the boy, I imagined she'd been the family nursemaid for several years.

I narrow my eyes as though I'm remembering something. "I worked for a woman once who was a fine mother; cuddled and kissed the children. Insisted on doing everything, except for the nasty stuff. You know the type? But little Harry—the youngest—began to have terrible stomach troubles. The doctor was forever in the house. Turned out she was poisoning the little cherub. Added arsenic to his milk, the vicious thing. And she'd done it before. I didn't realise, but the family had already lost three young children." Hell, I'm too good at this lying game.

"Terrible," says Nurse Marie, placing her cup back onto the saucer. "Just terrible." Then her eyes catch mine and she stares at me, her mouth slack. "What are you saying? Why are you telling me this?"

I look towards Mrs Lovejoy's wing of the house. "Did you ever suspect that she might want to harm the children?"

Nurse Marie's eyes bulge and her lips gulp at air so that she resembles a fish. "I don't... I don't..." She can't finish the sentence. Her gaze drops from mine and she pushes the tea set into the middle of the table.

"But, Nurse Marie, if I am to stay, I need to know where I stand. If I'm safe." I reach across the table, entreating. "Do you have any idea what happened to Margaret and her father?"

The woman shakes her head, rapidly. "No. No, no."

"But you must have some thoughts on it, Nurse Marie."

She presses a napkin to her lips, and glances at the door. Her eyes wander towards the other side of the house—the side the two older Lovejoy children inhabit.

"Emily? Joshua?" I whisper to her, my eyes on Cyril to make sure he can't hear us.

"I don't know," she says. "I really don't know. But they seem to dislike the little children so much, I have wondered..." She shakes her head to show she's finished with the conversation and, standing from the table, she goes to Cyril's side, helps him gather blocks.

Emily and Joshua. So the nursemaid agrees with the gardener.

Feeling the side of the teapot, I can tell the tea is too tepid to drink. "I'll just go down to the kitchen and freshen the pot."

As I pass the dining room, I hear the familiar clink of a stopper being replaced in the crystal decanter. Mrs Lovejoy walks from the room, wiping her mouth with the back of her hand.

"Mrs Lovejoy," I say, remembering at the last moment to bob my head.

"Nurse..." She pauses in front of me and seems to have forgotten my name. "Nurse, tell Cyril I have to go out for most of the day, but I will visit him after supper."

I bob again and watch her broad back as she sails towards the front door. I'm surprised she's so steady on her feet, but she halts at the hallstand, rests her fingertips against it for several seconds.

"Are you in need of assistance, Mrs Lovejoy?"

She doesn't even look my way. "No, Nurse, I'm just feeling a bit tired." Her hand follows the contour of her swollen stomach, rests at its base.

I turn slowly and walk back towards the kitchen and as I reach its doorway I hear the front door close behind Mrs Lovejoy. I have to admit, I feel a little sorry for her. Despite her callous treatment of the first Mrs Lovejoy and her children, she seems to be paying a steep price now; which makes me think of those strange children again, Emily and Joshua.

"What are you pulling a face about?" asks Cook.

I laugh. "I was just thinking of the run-in I had last night with Crossley." I give an exaggerated shudder.

Cook pulls a face too, and nudges Ruth, who's back to

work in the kitchen. "Horrible beast of a man, isn't he, Ruth?"

The girl nods, her eyes widening, as she stirs batter in a large bowl.

I take a seat at the table while Cook sets the kettle on to boil for me. She points out lumps in the cake batter to Ruth, tells her to whisk harder.

"Crossley said you think he murdered the Lovejoys," I say, looking from the cook to the girl.

"Stupid creature." Cook considers for a moment. "Although he did find both bodies, and he was the one with good reason to be outside on each occasion. What do you say, Ruth?"

The girl shrugs and spoons the batter into a cake tin.

"But did he have reason to murder them?"

Cook takes a bunch of beans from a basket on the floor and slaps them down onto a board. "Master was always telling him he'd lose his job if he was caught drinking too much brandy again. Near lopped one of the master's special shrubs to the ground, he did once, when he was supposed to be pruning 'em." She smiles at the memory. "A special plant all the way from somewhere in the Orient, it was."

Her comment about the plant, of exotic places, reminds me of my friends—Pidgeon and Cosgrove and the others—and I wonder how they're getting on. I'm reminded to buy a newspaper, see if there is any news on McBride's death. I might even dash off a quick note to one of them—Cosgrove maybe—to see if their dreaded *kungsi* has contacted any of them again.

Cook refills the teapot and pours me a cup. It's very settling watching her rhythmically chop the beans, followed by five crisp carrots. No wonder Amah spends so much time in the kitchen with Agneau. Maybe I should follow suit when I return home.

Ruth swipes batter from the inside of the bowl and licks it from her finger, smiling at me. She's just pushing the bowl across the table for me to try when Nurse Marie runs into the room.

"Have you seen Cyril, Nurse Louise?" she gasps.

I stand from the table. "No. The last I saw of him he was with you in the nursery. What happened?"

"All I did was make his bed, and then when I came out again he was gone."

"And you've checked all of upstairs?"

"Yes." She hesitates. "Except for Emily and Joshua's rooms."

Ruth joins us as we weave from room to room calling Cyril's name. Nurse Marie checks behind the sofas in the drawing room while Ruth flings open cupboard doors. I make my way upstairs and glance through the nursery and bedroom. He's not there.

I meet the nursemaid and Ruth at the top of the stairs. Nurse Marie has started to breathe heavily. Each time she breathes in it sounds like a sob. Despite the looseness of my corset, my stomach constricts. She's worried something awful has happened to him, something like what happened to Margaret, to Mr Lovejoy.

I touch the kitchen maid on the arm. "Ruth, you knock on Emily's door, see if he's there. Nurse Marie, you check Joshua's room."

I turn towards Mrs Lovejoy's rooms. I know she's gone out so I open the door, stick my head in. "Cyril? Cyril?" He's not behind the sofa in her sitting room, nor is he under the table. There are no bulges behind the curtains giving a small boy away. I peer out the window down into the gardens. I can just see the roof of the outhouse, veiled in branches from the oak tree. *Please don't let us find him there.*

I walk through the connecting door into Mrs Lovejoy's bedroom and step across the thick carpet, peep under the large bed. No Cyril. I look in the wardrobe, parting the gowns to make sure he's not hiding beneath the voluminous skirts, but he's not there either. This isn't good. Where's the little brute?

My eyes take in Mrs Lovejoy's bed linen. Far too much lace and ribboning for my liking. But tucked under a mountain of pillows, so I can just see its leather corner, is a book. I lift it out. There is no title on the front and, thumbing through its pages, I see that they are covered in spiky handwriting. *June 13 1859, Erasmus says we are to…* Her diary.

Hearing footsteps approach Mrs Lovejoy's room, I make a swift decision and ram the diary into my apron pocket.

"We still haven't been able to find him, Nurse," says Ruth. Nurse Marie stands close behind her. Her face is shiny with perspiration, her hair as messy as I've ever seen it.

"Just wait a little," I say, rummaging around in my pocket. Sliding the diary in there has reminded me of the bounty I bought with Cyril the day before at the bakery. I take out a bag of hard candies and rattle them. "Cyril. Cyril," I call, standing in the doorway between Mrs Lovejoy's sitting room and the upper landing. "I have a lemon candy here for you. Be a good boy and come and collect it."

The window seat in Mrs Lovejoy's sitting room flings open from the inside. Cyril sits up, grinning. "I is here, Nursie." His fingers curl in and out like he's beckoning me. "Can I have my sweet now?"

CHAPTER 22

Peachy leaves flicker like bunting against the overcast sky. We've returned to the clearing in the park we shared with Hatch the day before, but this time I've had the forethought to bring a kerchief full of bread for Cyril to feed the ducks. I leave him by the side of the pond and take a seat on the bench.

Mrs Lovejoy said she'd be out all day, but I want to be quick, in case she returns early. I riffle through the pages, and stop at a date from almost three years ago. *It's almost unbearable to go into the kitchen with that photograph there, displayed on the wall. Me in that ghastly uniform. I begged Erasmus to insist upon it being taken down, but he thinks it's a fine joke, and I don't want to make a fuss because then those scrawny bitches will think I care.* I wonder if she means Cook and Ruth. Or is it Emily she's referring to?

I continue to leaf through the diary, my gloved fingers whisking the thick pages across. I learn that the new Mrs Lovejoy couldn't stand the housekeeper, but kept her on because Erasmus wouldn't fire her, and that she resented every cent spent on poor Joshua and Emily. She's actually kept a tally of expenses the older children incur in the top right-hand corner of certain pages and, on the 12th of June two years before, she'd listed the reasons she put forward to Erasmus for denying Joshua further schooling at the expensive college he attended.

Glancing up, I see that Cyril is almost out of bread, so I flip forward to the latest entries in the diary. I take in a sharp breath. Scrawled across the page, so deeply the pen nib has scored through the paper onto the next page, is the word *EVIL*. I turn to the page before, but it's just a recount of a meeting with Hatch, and her anxieties about being left a widow.

"Nursie, Nursie," Cyril calls, running over to me. "Nursie. No bread." He points to the pond, but the ducks are already cruising away.

"I don't have any left," I tell him. I rummage in my bag, and bring out my cache of sweets. "Why don't you sit quietly for a moment, and you can have another candy."

He puts his hand out, but I shake my head, tell him he has to sit next to me quietly. He climbs onto the bench and takes his sweet, pops it in his mouth. His cheeks and the tip of his snub nose are rosy from the cold and he beams up at me, his lips pursed shut over his treat. I really don't mind the little brat.

I go back about a quarter of the way through the diary and stop at a page crammed with Mrs Lovejoy's spidery writing. She's even written in the margins, curled her text up the sides of the page.

Today I arrived home early from the village and that vile Nurse Marie, that cursed hussy, came out from Erasmus's study again. When I stopped her last time she insisted the master was just asking after the children, but I swear, I swear on the lives of my children, that she smirked at me this time. Turned her head from me and smirked!!! I am sure of it. And when I went into his study it was so warm in there, and there was a smell, I know that smell, it reeked. I am not stupid. I am not stupid. Does he think I'm stupid? Did he not play these games with me? But he denies it, looks at me like I'm mad. That's how he used to look at the first Mrs L., the stupid cow. Am I the stupid cow now? I will kill him, I will rip apart all that he loves before I become that stupid cow! I cannot believe he would do this to me but I should have known, because isn't this how he made Mrs L mad in the end, urging me to turn the children from her and to share my bed with him while she seeped away in their bed, which is my bed now my bed my bed my bed. I feel sick. I want to fall to the floor, bring up all that I have eaten, oh Lord but isn't that how Mrs L died? Am I to be next? That TROLLOP TROLLOP TROLLOP. I wish it were her breast that I lashed right now with this pen, stealing everything from me. I won't I won't I won't I won't. They don't know what I'm capable of but they…

What madness is this? I'm torn. I sympathise with her rage, yet I'm alarmed at the tone of the passage.

I realise Cyril is tugging at my sleeve. "What is it, Cyril?" I ask, dragging my eyes from the text.

"'Nother sweet please, Nursie."

I shake out another yellow candy from the bag, hand it to him. I flick through the next few pages and find more of the same. She's unhinged. Full of fury, paranoia. By the time the boy asks for another sweet, I tell him it's time to return home. The little beast ensconces himself further into the back of the park bench and folds his arms. That stormy look descends on his face, and as much as I'd like to ignore his wails, I also want to avoid having to carry a screaming boy tucked under my arm all the way home.

"Look, Cyril, if you behave yourself, I will give you one more candy when we get home. But not before. But if you start to cry, I'm leaving you right here. The wolves can have you." He must see in my eye that I'm quite willing to leave him behind so he hops off the seat, takes my proffered hand.

We walk through the park's gates and wait by the side of the road for a carriage to pass. Once across, Cyril presses his nose against the window of the bakery, admiring the sweet buns and pastries. I wander ahead and peer into the gloom of Sullivan's rag-and-bone shop. Looks more like a pawnshop to me, the type Amah loves, where she might find a set of bone buttons or exotic coins; refuse from others' lives. I glance back at Cyril, call him to me. I won't drag him inside. It would bore him. But I do take him into the apothecary's and he waits patiently enough while I have an ointment made up. I only have to ask him four times to stop touching everything.

As we stroll along Lordship Road, Cyril lugs on my hand as he jumps over anything he deems an obstacle, be it a stick or horse manure. The journalists have moved on, and all is quiet. We're just entering through the front gate of St Chad's Lodge when I notice a person step out from behind a large elm tree. He's wearing dark clothing and a wide brimmed hat like American men sport. He looks very familiar, but out of place somehow.

"Cyril, run ahead and knock on the door," I say to the boy.

It's difficult to see from this distance, but I think the man's eyes widen in surprise when he sees that I've noticed him, and as I approach, he turns heel, runs around the nearest corner. By the time I reach the bend in the road, he's long gone, a black figure in the distance.

My cousin, Jakub. What the hell is he doing here?

I deliver Cyril to Nurse Marie who's setting out luncheon on the nursery table. Looking right and left along the corridor to make sure nobody sees me, I creep into Mrs Lovejoy's room. Standing by her bed, I bring out her diary and have one last flick through it. I pause at the word *EVIL*, shake my head. I wonder what's on the woman's mind. I'd very much like to know if she means the evil that took her husband and child, or an evil deed of her own?

I tuck the book under her pillow again, pat the bedspread across it.

"What are you doing?"

I swing around. Emily.

"You really must stop looming up on me like this." I

straighten a cushion across the bedspread. "I was just righting your mother's bedlinen. I'm afraid Cyril messed it up when he was hiding from us."

Her eyes, almost as dark as onyx, take me in. I can tell she doesn't believe me.

"Actually," I say, brushing past her, "I picked up something for you in the village."

I look back. She hasn't moved from her spot, only follows my movements with a turn of her head. "Come along," I say. Strange, strange girl.

I feel in the pockets of my coat that I've left hanging in the nursery and bring out the small jar from the apothecary's. Returning to the corridor, I find her standing by the pictures on the wall.

"Come, take a seat with me over here." I lead her to the two parlour chairs arranged neatly between her bedroom and her brother's.

She stares at me, suspicious. There's a thud in the nursery, Cyril cries out. Not until we can hear Nurse Marie murmuring endearments to the boy does Emily approach me. Even then she lowers herself slowly onto the chair, sits right at its edge.

"I bought this for you at the apothecary's." I hand her the jar. "It might help clear your complexion. The man said it was the best treatment for specks."

She takes the ointment, frowning, but says, "What business is it of yours?"

"Well, you are supposed to be in my care, after all."

She glares at me for a moment from under her thick brows, then looks down again at the jar in her hands. "What's in it?"

"I think he said it's camphor with a little lime water. Nothing harmful."

Emily thrusts the jar into my lap. "I don't want it. I don't trust it."

"What do you mean, you don't trust it? It's from the apothecary's. Of course it's fine."

She stares down at the jar, and I realise that she is actually quite eager to try it, but wary too.

"Here," I say, unscrewing the lid. "I'll put some on first." I dab a little on my finger, swirl it on my cheeks and smooth it in. "There. Now you take this jar, and when you see that my skin doesn't peel away or that I don't fall down in a swoon, you can try some too."

She takes the jar again, cradles it in her hands. Cyril squeals, and she looks up. "Aren't you supposed to be looking after Cyril?"

"Nurse Marie can manage for the moment." I twist in my chair, peep through the open door into her bedroom. I wonder if I'll ever have a chance to explore their rooms for the missing wrapper. Although if Emily or her brother did use it, no doubt they've burnt or disposed of it by now. "What do you do with yourself all day?"

The girl goes to stand up, but hesitates as she answers me. "Sometimes Josh and I play cards, but mostly I read."

"What are you reading? I love reading too."

"I like Dickens, and Braddon too."

"Oh, I adore Braddon. I just finished one of hers last week, in fact."

Her shoulders seem more relaxed now, although the expression on her face is still sour. She lowers her eyes and mumbles, "Actually, my favourite is Radcliffe."

I almost laugh aloud. Of course this poor, plain, bored girl loves Radcliffe.

"Do you get them from the library?" I know she doesn't have any funds to buy them herself.

"Yes." She nods towards Mrs Lovejoy's rooms. "She has a subscription."

"And she allows you to borrow what you like?"

Emily bows her head, like she's talking to the ointment. "If I do some chores for her, she lets me borrow one book a sennight."

"What sort of chores?" I ask, surprised.

163

"Some light mending. Embroidering the handkerchiefs and smalls. Sometimes I polish the silver, when the housekeeper is too busy. But she's gone now so I guess I'll have to do it all the time."

What an old cow that Mrs Lovejoy is, making her stepdaughter do the menial work for which she has servants. But I see an opening here. "Cannot the woman who does your laundry take care of such things?"

The girl shrugs.

"Of course, the cook did tell me of the problems you have with the laundry woman, now I think on it. It's no wonder Mrs Lovejoy doesn't trust her with the mending. Loses clothes, doesn't she? Lost the cook's wrapper, I believe."

I watch for Emily's reaction. Her eyes narrow and her head slides around to look at me, like a snake slithers in the zoo. There's something in her eyes—suspicion, anger, fright? I can't tell.

"I don't know anything about that," she says.

CHAPTER 23

I step out from the cab onto Tottenham Court Road. I've told the cook and Nurse Marie that I have an appointment with a dentist. I even try to bring attention to the chip in my front tooth, suck on it while I eat lunch like it pains me. In fact, I've received word from Hatch to meet him in town so that I can join him when he questions the servants' agency that Nurse Marie is with.

I find him outside Duke's Superior Servants' Registry. I can already see it's a cut above Bower's, the one I visited the other day, further down the street. The shop windows are elegantly curtained, the signage painted in refined, curling script.

"Thank you for meeting me, Mrs Chancey," he says. "Any news?"

"Actually, I think I have a few interesting points," I say, as two women bustle past us to enter the agency.

Hatch looks around. "It might be best if we have a cup of tea in the teashop across the way first. We can return here to ask after Nurse Marie once you've brought me up to date."

I'd much prefer to have a drink in the public house next to the teashop, but doubt Hatch will concur.

We take a seat at a window table, and Hatch orders tea. "I'm afraid you will probably only have the one more night at St Chad's Lodge."

Home. I can go back to the comforts of my home. Back to Amah. But I'm also disappointed that we haven't solved this murder yet. "That seems a pity. Is it the superintendent?"

"Yes." His voice is heavy and a little colour comes into his pale face. "If an arrest is not made by tomorrow, I am off the case." With that, he flips open his notebook, asks me to report all I have found out in the last twenty-four hours.

"You know that Cook said Mr Lovejoy had a penchant for his nursemaids?" The detective nods. "Well, I found Mrs Lovejoy's diary—the present Mrs Lovejoy. And she knew all about it. She was furious." I frown as the girl slides the tea things onto the table. I think of the disjointed sentences, the agony behind the words. "No, she was more than furious. I can't remember the exact words, but there was something about making him pay. Mr Lovejoy."

"You think it was a threat? Against him? Against their children?"

"I'm not sure. She seemed quite tormented." I pour the thin tea into his cup, then mine. "And there was another thing. She referred to the first Mrs Lovejoy's death." I screw my eyes together, try to recall what she wrote. "Something along the lines of how she died, and was she going to die the same way. It could just mean that she thought she might die from disappointment like the first Mrs Lovejoy, but I did wonder if she meant there was something more… nefarious behind her death."

He's quick to understand. "You think that they had something to do with Mrs Lovejoy's death?"

"I'm not sure." Taking a sip of my tea, I wait for Hatch to makes notes. "And I met the gardener the other night. What a dreadful creature. Are you sure he didn't do it?"

A smile hitches the corners of his lips and he nods. "Horrible man, isn't he? But yes, I've had him checked. He was at home with his unfortunate wife. Arrived at the house just after the maid found the girl and just before dawn when he found Mr Lovejoy. The nightsoil man can corroborate this."

"Was that the other person who found Mr Lovejoy?"

"Yes. On his way home, I believe."

"The nightsoil man didn't notice anything else?"

The detective shakes his head as the girl plonks a plate of soggy crumpets, already buttered, onto the table between us.

"I'll tell you what I find interesting," I say, as I stir another spoonful of sugar into my tea. "The cook, Nurse Marie and the gardener each believe that the older children are responsible. In fact, the gardener goes as far as to say he thinks that Mrs Lovejoy and Cyril are in danger of being next."

I tell him that the current Mrs Lovejoy doesn't treat Emily and Joshua well, that she's responsible for ruining their relationship with their real mother.

Hatch chews on some crumpet, wipes his fingers on his handkerchief. "And what do you think?"

I want to be fair, but I think of all the times they've crept up on me, especially Emily; his vacant stare and her sullen face covered in angry pustules. "They're quite disarming, I have to admit. Between the two of them, they could have taken Margaret, killed her and arranged her body in the outhouse. That'd be much easier than on their own. They could've overpowered their father too." Again, I imagine Joshua binding the old man's arms while Emily draws the razor across her father's throat. Unfortunately, it's an easy picture to visualise, when it involves those two.

"And Nurse Marie?" He takes another crumpet. "Maybe Mr Lovejoy didn't give her what she wanted."

"Such as?"

"Marriage? Money? Maybe she killed them in revenge?"

I fiddle with the handle of the teacup. Somehow, I don't think this is the case. A servant like her would know better than to expect so much. Money? Maybe. Marriage? No. I shake my head. "No. I don't think she would've murdered them for such a reason."

Hatch takes one last sip of tea and says, "Well, if you're finished here, we will go over and find out what we can about this Nurse Marie. See if there are any other reasons she might have resorted to murder."

We tread across the plum carpets of Duke's Registry, and wait at a desk for a number of minutes, while a clerk, her grey hair piled high on her head and the ruffles of her blouse clasped together with a cameo brooch, serves a couple who seem to be searching for work together as butler and housemaid. The clerk tells them they must be patient, that they might need to wait a while for a household in need of both at once.

Duke's Registry, just like Bower's, has posters on the wall. Inventories of available servants, but also those who are on the blacklist. I wander closer, my eyes taking in the likenesses drawn in graphite. I marvel at the pettiness of the charges against the servants, although one particular fellow, who has an almost gnomish face, is purported to have garrotted all his master's dogs before taking off. Further on, I smirk as I read of those who are "permissive" or "sinful", although my lips tighten as I gaze into the face of a pretty young girl, and wonder if her sin had been thrust upon her.

Hatch is talking with the grey-haired clerk now, but my eye is caught by a face that seems all too familiar. Yes, she's slimmer, younger, her black hair neat under a nurse's bonnet. But there's no mistaking those heavy, straight eyebrows, the handsome cast to the face. Mr Lovejoy's second wife, the present Mrs Lovejoy. My eyes skim over the words next to the likeness, and then I read it through again more slowly. *Catherine Chandler, sometimes Challenor. When not "baby farming", as it is referred to by the authorities, she finds engagements as a nursemaid. Beware.*

"Hatch." He's writing something down in his notebook. "Hatch," I say again, beckoning him.

He joins me. The woman is not far behind. "What is it?"

I point at the drawing. "Do you recognise her?"

His eyes take in the picture and the longer he gazes, the wider both his mouth and eyes become.

"Oh yes, her. Have you come across her too?" says the grey-haired woman behind us. "Had a man in a week or two ago looking for her. Mr Collins, Mr Collins," she calls out to a thin man with spectacles at the next desk to hers. "When was that deranged man in here? The one asking after this Catherine Chandler?"

The man scratches his head, takes his glasses off. "I don't seem to remember."

The woman rolls her eyes. "Well, it wasn't that long ago, Detective Inspector. He was very upset. I thought he might have apoplexy when he saw that picture. I nearly called for the doctor."

"What did this man look like?"

"A mop of white hair. Quite a bad-tempered face."

Hatch takes a page from the newspaper out of his pocket and unfolds it to reveal a picture of Mr Lovejoy. "Is that him?"

The woman's eyebrows rise in surprise. "Yes. I'm sure that is him."

Hatch and I exchange looks. "And what can you tell me of this woman, madam?"

"I heard she got six months' hard labour. For neglect, mind you, not murder. The shame of it. Women who are unable to keep their babies…" her eyes drop for a moment, "… you know the type—well, they pay respectable women to care for or adopt their little ones. But this Catherine Chandler kept the babies passed out on Godfrey's Cordial, I believe, and they died from starvation, poor mites, while she pocketed the mother's money and pawned the clothing. We heard she might have murdered—because, really it's murder, I think you'll agree—as many as eight children."

"When was this?" Hatch asks.

"Oh," her face wrinkles as she considers. "Quite a few years ago now. Maybe five, six, seven? Haven't thought of her in a long time, until that man came in asking after her."

"Where did she operate, do you know?"

"Moved about, of course. But she was picked up in Willesden, I believe. A doctor became suspicious by how many death certificates he had to fill for her. The local police there might be able to help you, if you're after more information."

"Can I take this?" Hatch asks, gesturing to the drawing.

"Yes, of course," she says, peeling it from the wall. "Know her, do you?"

"I think we just might," he says, taking it from her. "Thank you for all of your assistance."

We pause on the sidewalk in front of the registry. "Well, that was quite a find, Mrs Chancey. We are lucky you have such sharp eyes."

"What would you like me to do from here?" I wonder, on returning to the house, if I will be able to hide this new-found knowledge from Mrs Lovejoy. Just how callous do you have to be to allow a number of babies to die in your care? To murder them?

Hatch stares at me for a few moments. "You go back. Keep an eye on her. She's not likely to disappear, leaving her son behind. But who knows? If she's the monster we're looking for, she might do just that. Or worse." He guides me to a cab. "I'll report to the superintendent. In all likelihood, I'll be back with some constables this afternoon to arrest her. If you can, find that diary again, before she has time to spirit it away, and I can follow up on the Willesden deaths." I climb into the cab and he closes the door on me. "What with Mrs Lovejoy's pitiless character, her fury at her husband's affair and his uncovering the truth about her past life, it looks like we have finally found our murderer."

CHAPTER 24

I have never witnessed so much wailing and struggle as when Hatch came to interview Mrs Lovejoy last night. I have been to funerals, have visited asylums, where more decorum has been shown.

As the constables dragged her into the study, Mrs Lovejoy clung to anything within her reach. She upended a plant stand, toppled side tables, scraped chairs across the floors, all the time moaning entreaties peppered with screams of protest, despite Hatch trying to assure her that he only wanted to ask her a few questions.

I'm not sure where she'd been all day, but she stank of the tavern.

Nurse Marie had to pull a teary Cyril back into the nursery while the cook and Ruth watched from the kitchen, hands clamped across their mouths. Only Joshua and Emily seemed composed, standing at the top of the staircase; Joshua as vacant as usual, head tipped to the side as he watched the show, while I'm pretty sure a slight smirk lightened the girl's heavy features.

And now, walking to the village shops, the wind is so cold and so strong, I'm sure it'll whisk Cyril's small body away if I don't hold onto his hand firmly. Oak trees rustle menacingly above us, and we need to press against the heavy gale as we stride forward. My eardrums start to ache and Cyril's eyes are watering. It's almost unbearable, but not as awful as it would have been to stay cooped up in the house.

I've left Nurse Marie in the housekeeper's room again. She's worse than when I first met her, if that's possible. Hair flopping all over the place, staring at the wall, her fingers plucking the woollen blanket I draped over her lap. As soon as Hatch left last night, and Mrs Lovejoy took herself off to bed, Nurse Marie tried to bar me from the nursery, said she was in charge of the boy. But I could tell he was afraid of her, I could see it in his wide eyes, the tremble of his lip. When I refused to fetch his warm milk, she lost her temper, stomped down to the kitchen herself. Cyril clung to my skirts as we listened to her quarrel with Cook. By the time she returned to the nursery, her composure had left her. She began weeping again, said she needed to get away, be anywhere but here in this house, so I made her a cup of tea with a slug—a very, very generous slug—of that Woodward's Gripe Water. It didn't take her long to settle down. I guided her to the housekeeper's bed to rest.

And this morning the house was freezing because Ruth was late to lighting the fires. We were lucky to get a piece of toast out of Cook, who was too busy wringing her hands over what was to become of us all, what with the master dead and the mistress losing her mind. Only when Emily came down, mild surprise on her face, asking after breakfast, like nothing untoward had happened to disrupt the morning routine, was it that Cook finally poured boiling water over tea leaves and stoked the oven.

That girl, Emily. Heart of stone. Hasn't she wondered what's to happen to her and her brothers if they find themselves without a parent?

A cab slows down, the driver asking me if we need a ride, but I shake my head. I wonder about the Lovejoys' finances. What is to happen to the children? How has Lovejoy provided for them all? I must ask Hatch to find out about his will. If Mrs Lovejoy is committed to trial… my mind jumps ahead—what if she's hanged?… Does Joshua inherit everything? Joshua, who dotes on his sister, Emily.

What do those strange children do all day? Do they sit in their airless rooms, plotting? What's really going on behind Joshua's empty eyes? And Emily's? That knowing gleam, calculating every move. I run my gloved fingers over Cyril's cap. As certain as I am that Mrs Lovejoy is our culprit, we can't leave him with those two. I'll have to bide my time until I hear from Hatch again.

We pass a tobacco shop, and I glance into its smoky depths, yearning for a lungful. I glance down at the boy and almost draw him inside. What does it matter? It's not like I'm going to be dismissed now. They might even have a bit of sherry behind the counter. But no. I'd better not. I'll sneak a cigarette at home, maybe nick some of Mrs Lovejoy's stash of sherry. I grin at the thought.

"Come on, Cyril," I say to him. "First, I'm going to look in Sullivan's rag shop over there, see if there's anything interesting, and then we're going to that teashop across the way, where you can have as much cake as fits in your belly."

We open the door, shuffle in, shutting the door firmly against a gust of wind. The shop is blessedly warm, but the air is close; has the musty smell of cast-off clothing, the staleness of unwanted detritus. It takes me straight back to the days I had to scrounge in proper rag shops, tucked away in Liverpool back alleys, looking for a decent pair of shoes or a dress without too many patches or stains upon its skirts. I remember the slippery feel of grime these searches left upon my fingertips, the itch the dust left on my skin.

"Don't like it, Nursie," says Cyril.

"We won't be long," I say, drawing him towards a glass cabinet filled with things that sparkle in the dreary light. On closer inspection, I see that it's only fishing hooks, tools I don't even recognise, and some sort of metal knobs for who knows what. On a shelf in line with my nose is a glass bowl filled with buttons made from brass, shell, wood. Next to this is an array of fans, mostly moth-eaten and faded.

"Can I ask what Miss hopes to find?"

I turn to look at the man with the gruff voice. He's big, with a barrel chest and bristling sideburns that match his thick eyebrows.

"This your shop, is it?" I ask.

He nods. "Sullivan. My father was the rag-and-bone man around these parts. Did such good trade he set up this shop. I've extended the business, I have, to include all sorts." He stands a little taller, hooks his thumbs into his trouser pockets.

"Ah, I thought it looked a little better than a mere rag shop." I cast my eyes around the small room. "I was just looking to see if you had any nice china or lacework, really. A gift for my mother."

"Step this way, Miss," he says, ushering me to the other side of the shop where clothes hang along the length of the wall. "This piece is very handsome. Bought it from a gentleman newly arrived back from Spain. He thought it was too colourful, but I think it's a very nice garment. Be perfect for a lady." His flat fingers trace their way over the crimson ribbon embroidery of the jacket's lapel.

"Very nice," I reply. There is no way Amah would wear that. "What is that coat behind it?"

He shows me a number of fur coats, but I can't bring myself to try them on. I prefer new apparel now. Clothing that has only known my skin, my scent. And Amah wouldn't wear them anyway.

"What about porcelain?" I say to him.

He leads me to a bench cluttered with gravy boats, cups and saucers, and even more saucers. I pick up a particularly pretty bowl with a willow pattern. A slight chip mars its edge, but I love the intricate pagodas, the costumed fellows crossing the neat bridge. Maybe I'll get it for myself, for I know Amah will turn her nose up at it, say it's like no Orient she knows.

I glance into a glass-top cabinet, my eyes taking in the cheap trinkets on display. Tarnished bangles and rings with dull crystals. At the back of the cabinet, though, is an assortment of quite decent snuffboxes—one with mother-of-pearl inlay—and a prettily carved tortoiseshell comb next to a silver brush and mirror set. I look around for Sullivan, just about to ask him to show me the silver, when my eyes take in the weapons mounted on the wall before me. Between a long sword with a rusty handle and a pistol blackened with age is a *kris*. I take in the wavy blade with the dragon's curves engraved into the iron, the garnets that wink dully at me from the handle. My *kris*. It's my *kris*.

"Where did you get that?" I ask, pointing. I'm so dismayed that I squeeze Cyril's hand a little too hard so that he uses his other hand to prise my fingers away.

"That?" Sullivan stares at me, calculating, for a few seconds. "A gentleman I met at the docks brought that back all the way from China. Very valuable, it is. You can see, here, on the metal…"

I frown at him, placing my free hand onto my waist. "As a matter of fact, it's from Java and I know exactly how much it is worth because it was stolen from my home."

He looks shocked, then laughs. "No. How can you be sure?"

"Of course I'm sure."

He's looking at me suspiciously, now. "Well, how did you come to own such a piece?"

"A gift from my uncle," I say, confident. "Who brought it here from Java. It's been in my family for many years, only to be stolen from my home a week or two ago."

His ferocious brows lower into a frown too. "I hope you're not accusing me of theft?"

I roll my eyes. "No. I'm not. But if you could just tell me who you actually had it from, then I can follow up on my loss."

"The police, you mean?" His mouth clamps shut on the last word. I fear if I say yes, I might not find out who the culprit is who supplied him with my *kris*.

"The police are of no use to me," I say. "I just want to make sure it wasn't one of my friends or colleagues."

175

He scratches the back of his head as he stares at the *kris* on the wall. "I hope you don't expect me to just give it to you. I paid good money for it."

"I'll pay you for it."

He hooks his thumbs into his pockets again and considers for a moment.

"I got it from Tomkins."

"Who's Tomkins?"

"Nightsoil man. He brought it to me about four days ago. Said he found it dumped by the side of Grayling Road."

My brain is awhirl as though I've been spinning on the dance floor after too many champagnes.

My *kris* turned up four days ago. Here. Just after Mr Lovejoy had his throat cut and just like McBride before him.

I pace the plush carpet of the Lovejoys' drawing room. The *kris* lies on an oval, mahogany side table with spindle legs. I gaze down at it, take in its keen edge. I peer closer, not quite sure if the dark rim that separates the hilt from the blade is a sign of age, or worse, a residue of blood.

Who brought it here?

Who was at my soiree that night—the night McBride was murdered? My thoughts are scattered, like the windswept oak leaves strewn across the footpath outside. Cosgrove? Surely not. Hunt? No, no. Pidgeon? I shake my head, take a deep draw on my cigarette. This is ridiculous. Hopefully Hatch receives my message soon so he can relieve me of this damned *kris*, once and for all.

I lift the *kris*, and its shiny blade catches what dim light comes through the window. Smoke curls from the tip of my cigarette, hangs on the still air. Jakub. I remember how I saw Jakub yesterday. I'd forgotten to write to Amah of it. What was he doing here?

I angle the *kris* back and forth, feel its heft and the cool grip of the handle, and wonder who else has held it in the recent past. Gripping it tight, I imagine how the murderer might have grabbed a clump of hair in his left hand, bringing the blade towards his victim's throat…

The drawing room door shifts slightly. A shadow blocks the gap at the door jamb, then is gone. I go to place the *kris* back on the table, but hesitate. I don't want to carry such a deadly thing around with me, but I don't want it to go missing again either. I slip it under a cushion on the divan and then hurry into the corridor.

I'm just in time to see Emily bound up the stairs. I follow her, lugging my heavy skirts high as I take two steps at a time. I've almost reached the landing when she rushes from the nursery, Cyril tucked under her arm. By the time I reach her bedroom door, it clicks shut in my face. I knock loudly on it, shout her name. Shout for Cyril.

"What are you doing in there, Emily?" I call between bangs, pressing my ear to the timber. I can hear voices; Cyril's high-pitched questions, low murmurs.

My heart judders in my chest. Is this how it will end? I rattle the doorknob but it's locked. What will I find in there? Crimson streaks flash across my mind. Please, no. I kick the door until my toe throbs.

"What is it, Nurse?" asks Nurse Marie behind me.

"She has Cyril." Stepping back, I stare at the closed door. "I don't know why."

Nurse Marie's slightly puzzled. Her eyes look strange, glossy. The pupils are huge, cover her blue irises. She's taken something, laudanum probably. Swaying, she lowers herself into one of the chairs.

I take to knocking again. "The police will be here soon." Was that the wrong thing to say? Will it hurry the girl along in her dastardly plan?

"Emily, don't hurt him. Please, don't hurt him."

The door is wrenched open so quickly, I lurch forward, nearly crash against her.

"What do you mean?" she demands, her eyes scanning my figure. It's the most emotion I've ever seen from her.

The pimples on her face are livid, flare red from her pasty skin.

She grasps a pair of scissors in her hand.

I put my hands up between us. "I just want to know why you have Cyril." Over her shoulder, I see Joshua standing by the bed. He has his hands resting on Cyril's shoulders, keeping the little boy in place.

"I think you should return the boy to me, Emily." I'm trying to keep my voice smooth, calm, but it resonates in my ears, sounds almost childish. "He needs to go back to the nursery now."

She looks to the side, sees Nurse Marie. Her eyes harden. "I'm not leaving him with you mad bitches. He's safer here with me and Josh."

I blink. "What are you talking about?"

She brandishes the scissors between me and the nurse-maid. "At first I thought it was you," she stabs the scissors in Nurse Marie's direction, "who killed Father and my sister Margaret." She swings the scissors around towards me. "But you! Turning up out of nowhere, and all your snooping about at night."

"But, Emily…"

She interrupts me. "And I saw you just then with that knife. I saw you! You're getting ready to kill someone else, but it won't be us." Slamming the door shut, she shouts, "You said the police were on their way. Well, I hope they arrive soon."

CHAPTER 25

"I've explained to both Emily and Joshua the circumstances that brought you here," Hatch says, hitching his trousers up at the knees before taking a seat in the drawing room. Weak afternoon sunlight streams through the windows. "But I think they're still uneasy and feel it's best if their little brother stays under their care for the moment. At least until we know what's going to happen with Mrs Lovejoy."

I've been waiting, twiddling my thumbs, while he was locked away in Emily's room, interviewing them about our misunderstanding over the boy and our respective weapons. "You haven't made up your mind about her?" I ask.

He shakes his head. "It was hard going, last night. She was too far gone on sherry, I'd say. I'm going to question her right after this."

"And my *kris*? How do you account for its presence here?" I ask.

He takes to his feet again, and stands looking down upon the dagger where it lies on the side table. "Very puzzling, isn't it?" He brings out a magnifying glass from an inner pocket, studies the *kris*. "You're sure it's yours?"

"Yes. It went missing on the night McBride was murdered outside my house."

"Which was after Miss Margaret was killed in the outhouse?"

"Yes."

He stares across at me. "And the fellow in the shop said a nightsoil man found it after Lovejoy's murder?"

I nod.

He frowns down at the *kris* again. "So it may link Lovejoy's murder to McBride's. But not necessarily to Miss Margaret's."

I've had a little time to think on this, and have come to the same conclusion.

"I think it might be best if you follow up on Nurse Marie, while I contact the detective on the McBride case, see which one of us will question this..." Hatch glances down at his notes, "this Tomkins. The nightsoil man." He tears a page from his notebook. "The clerk at Duke's Registry supplied me with the directions of a special servants' home where you might find more information on Nurse Marie, although now I'm not convinced it's necessary. But I won't know for sure until I've seen Mrs Lovejoy."

The cab is buffeted by the strong wind as it pauses at a crossroads. I glance down at the slip of paper Hatch pressed into my hand as I left St Chad's Lodge. On it is written a White Lion Street address.

I decide that after my work with Hatch today, I'll return to Mayfair, finally have a full night's rest. I don't relish another evening in the nursery, and anyway, Cyril is in Emily's charge now. My eyes follow a man being driven down the street by gusts of wind, his hand clamped against his hat, and wonder what Hatterleigh is doing. Has he tried to contact me in the past few days? Has his brat been born? I turn my head, gaze out the other window. What do I care?

Finally, we pull up in front of a building made of bricks the colour of biscuit, with crisp, white window frames. According to Hatch, it belongs to an organisation that helps "fallen servants" find their way again. After paying the cabman, I rap on the brass knocker.

I smile up at the middle-aged woman who opens the door and introduce myself. "I believe Detective Inspector Hatch has written to you in regard to my visit," I say. "You had a nursemaid named Marie Brown."

"Yes, yes," she says, ushering me into the hallway. "I'm Miss Agnew. I can tell you what you need to know."

I follow her through a doorway to the right, where she asks me to take a seat. The room is cold and quite bare, furnished with hardback chairs and a table covered with skeins of wool and unfinished baby booties and bonnets. Miss Agnew's a large woman, very tall. The ringlets in her short, brown hair fall loose and her mouth purses over bucked teeth. Her eyes are bright and friendly.

"What did you want to know about dear Anne-Marie?" she asks me, folding her hands neatly in her lap.

"Anne-Marie?"

"Oh, yes. That's her full name, and how we always re-ferred to her here. Anne-Marie Bromley. Although I have heard she prefers just Marie now. I can't think why. Anne-Marie is such a pretty name, I think you'll agree."

"That is strange," I say. "We call her Nurse Marie. And I'm sure the detective said her surname was Brown."

"Yes, yes." Miss Agnew's head bobs side to side. "Often the girls like to use new names when they leave here. The stigma, you know, if they were to be connected to their pasts."

"Their pasts?" I know what she's talking about, but would like her to clarify.

She sucks her cheeks in for a moment, so that she looks like a duck. "With child, but without husband, if you know what I mean."

"That's how Nurse Marie—Anne-Marie—came to be here?"

"That's correct. She was with us nearly seven years ago."

"And you still remember her?"

She nods, vigorously. "Oh yes. I'd just started working here, you see, and then what happened to her... so awful." Miss Agnew sits forward, looks around. "I forgot to bring the tea things in. Would you like a cup of tea, Mrs Chancey?"

I do, but not as much as I want to hear the rest of her tale.

"No, thank you." I wait for her to lean back in the chair. "You were saying…?"

"Ah yes. Anne-Marie. Well, as you must surmise, she came to us heavy with child. She was a nursemaid for a well-to-do family in Somerset, and had managed to convince her mistress that her dying mother needed her home for four months."

"Her employer didn't suspect the truth? Surely she was showing by that stage?"

Miss Agnew thinks for a moment. "She was quite a large lass, Anne-Marie. I don't think she would have looked that much different attired in a wide skirt and apron."

I think of Nurse Marie, of her sinewy arms, her gaunt face. I can't be sure we are talking of the same woman until Miss Agnew says, "The last time I saw her, though, she was a mere shadow of herself. As thin as straw. She never was her jolly self again after what happened." She shakes her head sadly.

"What happened?"

"She had a lovely little boy. Matthew, she called him, after her own father. Well, he wasn't the bonniest baby you've ever seen, but very placid, like his mama, I used to say to her. She stayed on with us a matter of weeks—maybe three, four? Usually, after confinement, the girls stay for only a fortnight at the most before they return to work, but Anne-Marie was a bit sickly, so she stayed on."

"And the babies? What happens to them when the women go back to work?"

Miss Agnew sighs. "Yes, well, that's the problem, isn't it? We are able to help unfortunate mothers-to-be through confinement, but we are not set up to care for the newborns, so sometimes we send them on to church organisations we know of, or to an orphanage run by an affiliate group of ours. And, of course, sometimes, the mother is fortunate enough to find a man to marry. But that's quite rare, sadly."

"And Nurse Marie?"

"Anne-Marie was smitten with her baby. They all are, you

know. People don't realise how harrowing it is for these poor women to give up their babies. Most only see the children as the bruised fruit of sin, to be discarded, hidden. But these women really want to keep their babies, they really do." She takes a deep breath. "Nobody more than Anne-Marie."

"But she couldn't?"

"No. Not if she was to return to work at her former station. And she had to. It was the only way for her to make any sort of income to support the baby. It's a terrible bind."

"So what did she do?"

"It was my fault, really. I told her of certain women who look after babies for a fee. I knew of quite a few mothers who used this type of service so that they could still be the child's mother, visit them once in a while, despite being unwed and working full-time." Miss Agnew stared into the empty grate. It was nearly a full minute before she spoke again. "Anne-Marie found an advertisement in the newspaper for just such a service and contacted the woman. A very respectable-looking woman she was, too. I saw her myself." Again she paused, shook her head. "Broke her heart to give her little boy up. But I put my arm around her shoulder, reminded her that she could visit the boy whenever she wanted. Then Anne-Marie went back to work as a nursemaid for the lady in Somerset. It was maybe four months later I saw her again. She was in a terrible state, just terrible. Told me she couldn't find the woman or her son, and asked me if I knew anything. But, of course, I didn't. I took her straight around to the police."

"And?" I begin to see the end myself. Things I've learnt over the last couple of days are coming together in a dreadful kaleidoscope.

"And," her voice is hollow. "They'd recently arrested a woman for neglecting children in her care. They took poor Anne-Marie to somewhere north of here, had her look at the bodies of two children who'd starved to death in this woman's care. Little Matthew was one of them."

My heels click along the pavement as I strive to keep up with Hatch. His strides are long, but he doesn't seem to notice how I struggle to match his pace. His chin is tucked into his chest, his hands deep in his pockets as he walks, deep in thought. What I've told him has given him much to think about.

After my interview with Mrs Agnew earlier I had the cab drop me at Sullivan's rag shop again, where I made a special purchase. By the time I returned to St Chad's Lodge, my mind was seething with notions. Hatch was still with Mrs Lovejoy in the study, which was fine with me because it gave me time to ask Cook some things while she prepared a chicken for dinner. I then checked on Cyril, who was playing in Joshua's room with his siblings.

"Are you leaving now?" Emily asked. Her tone was nonchalant as she looked at me from behind the novel she was reading, but her dark eyes were sharp, maybe a little anxious.

"Not until everything is resolved." But would it ever be for these children? I looked at Joshua, who was writing something at his desk, and Cyril, who looked up from his picture book and said, "Milk, Nursie?"

I knew that there would definitely be more trouble ahead for them, but hopefully the loyalty the two older children had shown to Cyril earlier in the day would carry them all through.

"I'll ask Ruth to bring you some, Cyril," I said. Then to his sister, "Keep this door locked, Emily. Stay together. Until you hear otherwise from Hatch, don't talk to anyone except Cook or Ruth."

Joshua glanced over his shoulder at me and Emily frowned. They both nodded, and watched as I backed out of the room.

Trotting along now next to Hatch, I ask him how far away the nightsoil man lives.

"Not far at all. I have it from the local constable that this

Tomkins lives just down this alley," he says, turning to the left.

The low-set homes look more fitted to a stable yard than to a row of human dwellings. We pass five doors before Hatch stands back, looks a squat building up and down. "This is it, I think." He knocks, and then has to knock again before the door is answered.

"Tomkins?" he says.

The man squints, and his eyes are bleary. His brown hair is snarled close to his skull like sheep's wool, and his thin wrists poke out from his coat sleeves. "Yes. Who may you be?"

"Detective Inspector Hatch. I have some questions for you."

Tomkins's eyes widen a little, but he gestures for us to follow him inside. "We have to be quiet though. The missus is just trying to settle the children."

We find ourselves in a cramped kitchen so clotted with smoke it's like we're caught in a thick fog. The beams and chimney flue are as black as tar and the floor is unboarded. I take the one seat at the rickety table, while Hatch leans up against a bench. Tomkins stands by the closed door to the other room.

"Who's she?" Tomkins asks, looking at me.

"A witness of mine," says Hatch. "She's found some items we thought you might be able to help us with." Hatch lays a bundle of cloth on the table and unravels it until the *kris* lies sparkling in the gloom. "I believe you sold this to the rag shop in the village?"

Tomkins stares at it, and nods. "What of it?"

"We'd like to know where you acquired it in the first place, Tomkins."

"Well, it's mine, isn't it? Been in the family for years. Yes, years. And I didn't want to sell it, but things have been very slow for me lately. Usually I'm a labourer, earn a tidy living, what with that during the day and my nightsoil work at night. But I hurt my back a few months back, had to give up the labouring. And the missus just had another baby. Have to keep the bread on the table, so I sells that there knife to Mr Sullivan." He sucks his bottom lip when he finishes speaking.

A baby mewls in the other room, and the longer I sit here, the harder it is to ignore the reek of human waste.

Hatch stands to his full height, the top of his hat brushing the ceiling. "Tomkins, we know this short-sword was stolen from its rightful owner. I do not, for a moment, believe that you ever owned such a valuable item."

"But I did, I..." he protests. He looks Hatch dead in the eye and it's as though the fight leaves him immediately. "All right. All right. I'll tell you the truth. It's not a family relic. I found it, long ago. On my rounds."

"Long ago?"

Tomkins nods, vigorously.

"Where?"

Tomkins screws up his face. "I think it were down on the riverbank, I found it."

"And yet Sullivan says you found it within the last week in Grayling Road." Hatch's pale skin almost glows in the dark kitchen and the nightsoil man looks up at him, fearful. "I have to warn you, Tomkins, you keep this up and I'll be forced to arrest you for theft. Now, unless I hear some truth come out of your mouth, you won't be around much longer to support your missus and children."

I'm surprised at the detective's intimidating manner, but it seems to work. Tomkins wilts, runs his hand over his face.

"I found it on the roadside. Last week."

"When, exactly?" I ask.

"Several mornings ago. Yes, Monday, it were, because I don't usually work of a Sunday night, but Driscoll couldn't work on account of being sick."

"And where did you find it?" Hatch asks.

Tomkins gulps, as though he's swallowing a lump of bread. "Lordship Road."

"Speak up. Did you say Lordship Road?"

The nightsoil man nods.

"Whereabouts on the street did you find it?"

"Well to be precise, it were at the corner, where the road crosses the next street."

"Just on the ground?"

"Lying in the grass, for anyone to see."

"Was this after or before you found Mr Lovejoy's body?"

Tomkins runs his hand down his face again. "Before, it were. The sun weren't quite up."

"But why, Tomkins, didn't you report it straight away to the police when they were called?"

"Well, it were difficult, weren't it," he says, his tone lifting. "On our rounds we often find things we can pawn or sell to the ragman. People usually give us a bottle of gin for our troubles, but that Mr Lovejoy had a tight purse. So when I saw that knife, I could tell straight away that it would fetch a pretty penny, so I swiped it, hid it in my bag, I did, so's the others wouldn't want a share."

"And later? After you found Lovejoy?"

"Do you know how horrible that was to find a dead man, his head near sliced from his shoulders? What with that and running for the police constable, the knife went clean out of my head, it did."

"And when you remembered it? It didn't occur to you that it might have something to do with the man's death? That you should hand it in?"

Tomkins sags against the closed door. Something bumps in the next room, one of the children squeaks. The planes of his gaunt, starved face catch the shadows. "I didn't think it would do any harm, me keeping it. The whole village knows it's one of them crazy Lovejoy children who've murdered the child Margaret and their father."

Hatch presses his lips together as he regards the other man. He shakes his head and says, "This won't do. It won't do at all. You might be in for some serious trouble for withholding this evidence, Tomkins."

The nightsoil man bows his head, clutches his forehead in his hand. I wonder if he's crying, and I feel a small stitch of sympathy.

"I'll tell you what, Tomkins," says Hatch. "I have one more thing to ask you about. If you tell me the truth—no prevaricating, mind you—I will see what I can do so that the authorities are lenient. How does that deal sound?"

Tomkins stares at him. "What do you want to know?"

Hatch nods to me. "I want you to tell us about this."

I reach into my bag and bring out an item wrapped in a handkerchief. As I place it on the kitchen table, Tomkins gasps.

CHAPTER 26

It's late by the time we return to St Chad's Lodge. The household's already eaten supper and Mrs Lovejoy has passed out in an armchair by the fire in the sitting room, the whisky decanter nestled in her lap.

All is quiet upstairs, and as we walk down the hallway, Ruth peeps around the corner of the kitchen door at me, only to be pulled back by Cook. I knock on the housekeeper's door.

"Nurse Marie?" I call lightly. I turn the knob, let myself into the room.

She's seated in that chair again, staring out the window into the darkness. As I draw nearer, I realise all she can really see cast against the glass by the candlelight, is her own reflection.

"Nurse Marie," I say. "I wanted to discuss something with you."

She doesn't say anything, doesn't move.

I place the tortoiseshell comb on the little table by her chair. "Do you recognise this, Nurse Marie?"

Her eyes swivel down, fix on the comb.

Something clangs in the kitchen, the back door claps shut. I can smell remnants of their roast chicken dinner and I feel queasy, for the task ahead of me is exhilarating, yet daunting. "Do you recognise it?"

Her head swings slowly side to side.

"No?" I say.

She continues to shake her head. Her lips are so chapped, I can see the keen fissures sliced into the skin.

"Cook says it's yours. She recognised it straight away," I tell her, picking the comb up again. Its teeth are spindly, more rounded than usual. Carved into the tortoiseshell is an intricate pattern of flowers and leaves, while at its centre, wings spread, is a swooping swallow. "Cook said your uncle brought it back for you from his travels and that it was your most cherished belonging. She also said she hasn't seen you wear it since… Well, for quite a while."

I've left Hatch standing on the other side of the door, which is ajar. I told him that I thought she was more likely to speak to me if I appeared to be by myself.

"That's not mine," she finally manages. She keeps her gaze on the comb in my hand.

"Do you want to know where it was found?"

Her eyes find mine and I think there's a flash of entreaty there and, in light of this, I almost hesitate, think of calling Hatch in to finish for me. But I pull another chair forward, across the timber floor, until I'm sitting opposite Nurse Marie.

"We—the Detective Inspector and I—went to visit a man named Tomkins."

"But why? What do you have to do with the police?" she asks.

"I was placed here to keep an eye on the household, Nurse Marie. By the police."

She's slumps back into her chair, and seems to shrink the more I speak.

"When we visited this Tomkins—he's one of the nightsoil men around here, you know, and he explained to us that he's the holeman, the one who has the delightful job of being lowered into the pit," I say. "Well, according to him, he came across this comb—your comb—in the muck of the outhouse directly after the morning Miss Margaret was found, dead. He's a very poor man, you know, open to temptation, so he wiped the blood and the mud from it and sold it to Sullivan."

190

Her hollow eyes stare out at me. I'm becoming frustrated by her lack of reaction. "He says he knows it wasn't there the morning before because he was on duty that day too. And, of course, the outhouse wasn't used for a day or two after Margaret's little body was found."

"I lost it the day before." Her voice sounds strangled. "It must've dropped in when I was helping Miss Margaret use the lavatory."

I consider for a moment. "No. I don't think so. Cook and Ruth are quite certain it's only since Margaret's death they haven't seen your hair tucked in with that comb. They thought you'd just put it aside in your grief." I smooth my thumb across the grooves of the comb. "This is quite compelling evidence, you must see, that you took the life of little Margaret."

"Ridiculous." The nurse draws herself up for a moment, squirms her shoulders against the back of the chair. A ghastly smile trembles on her lips, and heat flushes her face. "Why would I do that?"

"We know about Mrs Lovejoy, Nurse Marie." I think of the home for fallen servants. "We know about Mrs Lovejoy's days as Mrs Chandler, about the children she took into her care."

The nurse's head rears a little and she sneers. "Care!"

I want to place my hand on her knee in sympathy, but stop myself. "We know about Matthew, Nurse Marie."

She stares into the black glass of the window, her bottom lip twitching. Finally, she says, "So you know what that woman did to my son?"

I nod. "We do. And we're very sorry for your loss, as was Mrs Agnew. But tell me, how did you find Mrs Lovejoy again? How did you come to be here too?"

"I saw her, walking along the path in the village, with the children and a nanny." She squeezes her eyes together, as though she's trying to see that day again. "I'd recently taken a post with a family in Dalston, and my mistress had asked me to come into Stoke Newington to fetch some linen she was in need of." Her eyes open. "I was horrified when I saw her— *her*, Mrs Lovejoy—strolling with the children. I thought she was up to her old tricks again. I thought she was going to harm those small innocents. But when I pointed her out to the draper, she told me that she was the very respectable Mrs Lovejoy, living in the grand house on Lordship Road." She runs her fingers through her greasy hair, clutches at the strands, before relaxing her hands again. She shakes her head in disbelief. "She told me that those healthy, beautiful children were her own."

"What did you do?"

"Left my household in Dalston and watched the Lovejoy family. The nursemaid took the children for a stroll every morning after breakfast and it only took me a matter of days and all of my savings to convince her to leave. She recommended me for the position."

I suppress the urge to look around at Hatch, but I can sense him scribbling down this information. No doubt he'll want to track down the former nanny.

"And then?'

"Then..." She shrugs.

"How long before you and Mr Lovejoy...?" Her eyes find mine. "The other servants have told me that you and Mr Lovejoy were in an intimate relationship."

She lifts her hand to shield her eyes, but not before I see a look of distaste sweep her face. "I don't want to talk about that."

"But that was your first revenge, yes?" I push. "To catch the eye of her husband?"

Her hand flaps.

It occurs to me that she might have been planning more. "Anne-Marie, were you hoping to become pregnant to him? Was this to be your revenge?"

"I can't talk about it. I won't," she whispers.

"Ah." The awful truth of her position finally dawns on

me. "But you didn't become pregnant, did you? Mrs Lovejoy did. She was going to have another bonny baby, and you were still without."

Her hand falls at the same time as a tear tumbles down her cheek. "She didn't deserve another child. She didn't deserve another baby to hold and love and..." She holds her hands out, rigid, emphatically, entreating me to understand. "She'd murdered all those babies. She'd murdered my Matthew. How could God reward her with so many beautiful children? How? And leave me with nothing?"

I take a deep breath, let it out again. She's right. Life has been terribly cruel and unfair to her. "Did you leave a note for Mr Lovejoy? On the terrace?" I'm thinking of the time Mr Lovejoy sat in my drawing room; of how he told Cosgrove and Pidgeon of the threatening letter he'd received.

She looks puzzled.

"A warning of some sort?" I prompt. Signed with a figure that looked a lot like an "A", the sign of Pidgeon's evil *kungsi*, but also the initial of Nurse Marie's real name—Anne-Marie.

"Is that where it went?" Her eyes fix onto a spot on the floor. "I wanted to caution *her*," she won't use Mrs Lovejoy's name. "I wanted her to feel that trickle of dread, the constant worry of the unknown. But the letter must've fallen from my pocket. I did better than that in the end, anyway."

My heart rate picks up pace. "What?"

"I told Mr Lovejoy of her previous life. Her former profession." Her voice rings with malice, her eyes hard. "He didn't believe it at first. But I pointed the way for him."

"To the servants' registry?"

She nods.

"What happened?"

"Nothing. I think they quarrelled about it—I heard raised voices from her sitting room, thumping on the floor. But that was it. He didn't leave her. She wasn't thrown out."

Her lips tremble again and she clamps her lips together between her teeth.

"What did you do then?"

She shakes her head.

"It must have been so difficult for you. Seeing that woman with her children. Having to follow her orders, after what she'd done to you."

"I couldn't sleep." Her voice is barely a whisper. "I couldn't sleep. Her words, her deeds, the injustice of it all. I felt I was going mad." With the flat of her hand, she taps the side of her head. "The constant thoughts throbbing in my mind." She grabs onto her hair again, close to her scalp, tugs. "She only got five months of jail time for the babies' deaths. Did you know that? Only five months! They called it neglect, but it was murder. It was murder."

"So what did you do, Anne-Marie?"

Her hands fall. Straggly strands of hair entwine her fingers. She doesn't answer me.

I wait. The clock on the mantelpiece ticks the seconds away, and I hear the slightest rustle from the doorway, maybe Hatch turning a page in his notebook. I wait half a minute, but she still doesn't speak.

"I wonder if I can guess what happened?" She doesn't answer, doesn't even look my way. "I think that you realised there was only one way you could really hurt Mrs Lovejoy. One way she would truly understand the grief she has put you through."

Nurse Marie raises her eyes to the ceiling.

"Maybe you chose the girl because you couldn't bring yourself to hurt the boy—a boy like your own Matthew who was taken from you."

"No."

"You waited until the deadest part of the night, maybe around four in the morning, and you lifted that little girl from her bed and carried her down to the lower floor." Her gaze is still on the ceiling, but tears now brim her eyes. "Maybe she woke, and you assured her you were taking her to the lavatory. That she needed to relieve herself. But going through the house you had the forethought to put on Cook's wrapper." I'm not sure if this was before or after she'd fetched the girl, but it shows a degree of planning. This was no spur-of-the-moment crime.

Still, she says nothing.

I continue. "The fire is almost always alight in the nursery, isn't it? To stay nice and warm for the children. How easy to throw the wrapper amongst the flames, destroy the evidence."

She blinks, forcing the tears to fall.

"And the drawing room doors. Jimmied on the inside and out. I think you found yourself locked into the house. Only the housekeeper and Mr Lovejoy had the keys, so you had to break your way out. And then you scraped the panelling on the outside too, to confuse the police, make it appear like an intruder forced his way in."

Nurse Marie swings her head back and forth, slowly, like a muzzled beast trying to break free. "No," she moans. "It didn't happen."

"But it did, Nurse Marie. You carried poor Margaret to the outhouse and you murdered her. You wanted her mother to know the terrible anguish she'd put you through. What did you use, Nurse Marie? When you cut her little throat? Was it Mr Lovejoy's razor? That would serve him right, wouldn't it, Nurse Marie? Wouldn't it?"

Nurse Marie clamps her hand to her face, squishing her nose and cheeks, and lets out a groan. The door creaks, and I see Hatch hovering. I shake my head at him, turn back to the nursemaid.

"Is that how it happened, Nurse Marie?" I ask her again, but she doesn't answer.

"And Mr Lovejoy? Why'd you take his life?" I'm quite sure she didn't, but I have to be certain.

The woman lifts her haggard face to me. Her mouth opens and closes, trying to force words out. She lets out a pitiful "No."

"You didn't murder him?"

She sinks her face back into her hands, still shaking her head from side to side. The sobs shudder in and out of her skinny frame, and it takes a good five minutes before she is almost calm again.

"I think you'll have to go with the police now, Nurse Marie," I say to her. "Are you prepared?"

"I need a drink." Her voice is hoarse as she pours water from a small jug into the drinking glass beside her on the side table. Her hand is shaking so hard, the china rattles against the glass.

"I will fetch the Detective Inspector," I say, standing.

Out of the corner of my eye, I see her lift a small brown bottle. "Just to calm my nerves." Instead of a drop or two, she splashes the rest of the bottle into the water.

I only have a moment or two to react. I know the contents of that bottle must be her stash of laudanum and she's tipped a dangerous amount into her drink. A deadly amount. Part of me sees the sense in what she is doing. Not only that, I feel bad for the sorry creature, and I understand it might be the most humane way to see this through. But what of young Margaret, robbed of life because of her mother's sins? Surely she deserves some sort of justice?

I step forward, slide my hand in between the glass and her mouth just in time. She tries to resist, but her strength is feeble, and as I wrench the drink from her hands, laudanum and water dash across my skirts.

Hatch arrives by my side. He draws the nursemaid to her feet, and leads her away by the upper arm. She's not crying anymore.

CHAPTER 27

It's quite late by the time Taff picks me up from St Chad's Lodge. I feel flat, a little sad, as the coach rumbles home. I left Hatch to deal with the nursemaid and, as he handed me into my carriage, he congratulated me on finding the comb. Said I made a fine detective.

Usually, after such a satisfactory ending to a case, I'm jubilant, ready to toast with a glass or two of champagne, but not tonight. As I sway against the side of the carriage, I think of how ghastly young Margaret's last moments must've been, of how her life was sacrificed because of the activities of her mother. And what of Nurse Marie? Doesn't she deserve my sympathy too? I wonder if the anguish she now lives with, having murdered such an innocent, will ever be worth avenging the death of her own baby. Remembering her trembling fingers, the lips stretched awry as she tried to speak, I think maybe not. It might've been better for her own soul if she'd just taken Mrs Lovejoy's life and been done with it.

Which reminds me of Mr Lovejoy. What with solving Margaret's murder and finding the *kris* so close at hand, his slaying continues to be a mystery. As Taff helps me climb down onto the path in front of my home, I think again of how this has not been a case of three interconnected murders, after all. Lovejoy and McBride. McBride and Lovejoy, linked by the *kris*: my *kris*.

"Good evening, Bundle," I say, as he opens the door, the hallway cheerfully lit behind him. "Home at last."

"Mrs Chancey," he replies, taking my luggage from the coachman. "We did not expect you home tonight. You'll find the drawing room sadly chilly, but there's a nice little fire lit in the parlour."

"Is Amah in?" I ask, as I strip my gloves off.

"I believe she retired a couple of hours ago, Mrs Chancey."

I nod and make my way to the parlour. As I pass the display cabinet, I glance in to where the *kris* used to be, but Bundle or Abigail have rearranged the ornaments to cover the gap.

Taking a seat on the divan by the fire, I lean back into the cushions, watch the black tips of the flames lick the air. I run my fingertip over the velvet upholstery, back and forth, its soft, layered texture comforting somehow. Fatigue presses against the back of my eyes, but thoughts continue to tick away in my brain.

"A light supper for you, madam," Bundle says from behind, as he places a tray on the table. "And I'll just leave all your post here for you to read at your leisure."

I look around at him and smile. "Thank you, Bundle. Why don't you take yourself off to bed now? It's late. I won't be far behind."

He gives a slight bow and walks from the room.

The clock chimes ten o'clock before I manage to haul myself up from the divan. I inspect the soup—chicken and vegetable, cooling now—and, ignoring the tea tray, I move to the side table, half fill a tumbler with scotch. Sipping it, I sort through the post Bundle has left me. First, I pick up a package and, peeling away its wrapping, reveal a small, flat box. Lifting the lid, I discover powdery squares of my favourite sweet—Turkish delight. I dab my finger against the chalky sugar, touch it to my bottom lip where my tongue seeks it out. With it is a note. *Dearest love, I hope this small treat finds you well, Hatterleigh*. Hatterleigh.

I'm so tired, I almost can't be bothered being annoyed with him anymore.

I then open three invitations to card evenings, one to a fancy-dress ball and four to fancy suppers. Maybe that's what I need to take my mind off these things: convivial evenings with women of my own sort, and the admiring men who surround us. As I drop Queenie Martel's missive onto the table, bidding me to attend her next euchre night, I notice a letter with familiar, bold, loopy handwriting. Sir Thomas. I tear it open and my eyes skim over the contents. It's dated a week earlier.

My dear Mrs Chancey,

I hope I find you well. Detective Inspector Hatch informed me that you took up the nursemaid position in the Lovejoy household after all. I won't interrupt your commission for Hatch, but thought I'd send this letter to you in the hope you read it when you do eventually find yourself home.

A little while ago you recommended my services to a certain Sir Henry Pidgeon. He has since apprised me of the truly horrifying events surrounding McBride's death and the involvement of a group of dastardly Chinese fellows who seem set upon a path of revenge. Unfortunately, I will be leaving for Scotland in the morning with two of my employees. We are to keep an eye on a certain doctor, suspected of murdering his wife and servant. As you know, normally I do not undertake the groundwork myself, but I find this contract to be an excellent opportunity to spend some time with my daughter's family in Glasgow. Therefore, I was unable to help Pidgeon besides providing him with Bob Beveridge—you might remember Mr Beveridge? You worked with him on the Knightsbridge case. Bob will keep an eye on Pidgeon's home, and guard his daughter. My request of you, provided you arrive home in South Street before I return, is to contact Pidgeon, perhaps check up on him and his daughter? I feel it might be best if Mr Beveridge joins us in Glasgow as soon as possible to assist in this murder case. Of course, you will be reimbursed at your usual rates.

I will call upon you as soon as I am returned.
Yours Sincerely,
T. A.

Poor Pidgeon. I run my tongue across the chip in my tooth as I think of his distress. That Beveridge creature won't be much help to him, from what I remember of the man. Most of the time he was "corned", as Taff likes to refer to it, lurching from the job at hand to the nearest tavern, and back again. I really should've mentioned it to Sir Thomas, but one day Beveridge's wife turned up, a little one clutching her skirts, asking after him. I didn't have the heart to jeopardise their income.

I'm just picking up the next letter in the pile when I hear a soft rap against the front door. I frown, wonder if I could've heard correctly, but then, the sound is repeated.

Recalling that I've sent Bundle to bed, I step out into the hallway. As I approach the front of the house, a shadow falls across the glass of the sidelight. I shade the glass with my hand, peer outside. My heart lifts, races a little, when I recognise the familiar shape of square shoulders, the smooth jawline and temple beneath the top hat.

Swinging open the door, I say, "Cosgrove." I smile up at him. "A little late for a visit, isn't it?"

I move back to allow him to step into the hallway.

"Didn't your butler tell you I have come by several times over the last few days? Pidgeon let slip you were helping the police on the Lovejoy case, which made me very curious for news."

He stands rather close to me. I'm aware of his scent, how tall he is, his eyes on me. Turning away, I close the door.

"I was just on my way to Motts, actually. Wondered if you'd like to join our party again. I'm to meet the others there. You can fill us in on the gossip." His smile is as relaxed as ever, reaching his blue eyes.

I glance down at my dress. I haven't changed since my long day with Hatch, and I'm weary. Well, I *was* feeling weary, until Cosgrove's presence cracked through me like a sapling spark in a bonfire.

"You do look a little fatigued, however," he says. "I will leave you alone and visit again tomorrow. Maybe you can share a little of your news then." He makes for the door, places his hand on the brass handle. "It's just that I've become a bit worried about Pidgeon. I'd like to discuss it with you also, sometime soon. I fear for poor Isobel."

"Well, in that case, don't feel you need to leave immediately." It's not just an excuse to make him stay. I am interested in Pidgeon's predicament. I am. "Have one drink before you go to Motts."

He takes me in for a moment, then shrugs off his overcoat. I hang it up for him, and he places his gloves and hat on the hall table. I lead the way to the parlour.

"We can sit at the table or by the fireplace. Your choice," I say, lifting the decanter. "Whisky?"

"Yes, thank you." He takes a seat at the foot of the divan, leaving the side with the recline for me.

I sit next to him, my wide skirts encroaching upon his thigh. I try to move back, but I am quite ensconced against the side of the divan as it is. I place the box of Turkish delight on a lacquer side table. "Tell me about Pidgeon."

"Ah, yes." He sits forward, elbows on knees and gazes into his glass. "The morning after we met here in your drawing room, he received a threatening letter that was almost identical to the one I received. The poor fellow has become quite unhinged by the matter. You haven't heard from him?"

I shake my head. "No. I have only returned home this evening. I must go around first thing tomorrow morning," I say, recalling Sir Thomas's request of me. "Is Isobel not one of your party tonight?"

"No, Pidgeon has become increasingly paranoid. Won't

allow her to leave the house. Has some drunk guarding the front door."

"I know. I've just read a note from Sir Thomas. I'm acquainted with the man he's put with Pidgeon. A lush buffoon." I shake my head and take a sip of my whisky.

Cosgrove turns his head to look at me. His fine lips curl into a smile, and I have an urge to run my fingertips across the texture of his face, the evening bristle.

"Tell me about your time at the Lovejoy residence," he says.

I sigh, raising my eyes to the ceiling, conscious of his gaze resting on my profile. "It was quite exhausting really." I tell him of Cyril and the drinking habits of Mrs Lovejoy. I make an amusing tale of the gardener startling me that night and befriending the vicious hound. I finish with an account of visiting the servants' registry and the information we gleaned that helped to unravel the mystery of Nurse Marie.

"But why did she murder Lovejoy? Why not just kill Mrs Lovejoy and be done with it?" he asks, putting his empty glass down on the side table.

"But that's the problem. We don't think she did, after all. I'm quite sure she murdered the little girl, but we can't hold her responsible for Mr Lovejoy too." I place my hand on his arm, draw it away quickly. "Remember that *kris*? My *kris*, from the cabinet in the hallway?" He nods, frowning. "It was found at the scene of Lovejoy's death. His murder must've been committed by whoever killed McBride, not by the nursemaid."

Cosgrove looks bewildered, draws back. "But I haven't seen any word of this, that the *kris* was found. In fact, the police were quite sure the Lovejoys' deaths were connected."

"Yes, but the nightsoil man found it that morning near the body, although he pawned it almost immediately. Sold it to the local ragman, without reporting it to the police."

"Outrageous. Didn't the blasted ragman make the connection between the knife and Lovejoy's murder?"

"I think he did, but he wanted the sale."

Cosgrove folds his arms, stares into the fireplace, and is

silent for half a minute. "Are you quite sure, Heloise, that the *kris* went missing the night of your soiree? I'm just asking because it really does appear to be that we're dealing with that *kungsi* Chinaman who's trying to finish us off, one by one. There's no chance he could have sneaked in here that night? Nobody who works here who might've smuggled it out to him?"

I give a sharp shake of my head, a little offended. "Of course not." Surely not. Bundle's very efficient at keeping the house safe from intruders. And the staff? Why would they bother? I must remind myself, though, to question the butler regarding any tradesmen or labourers that might have had opportunity to nick it at the time.

Cosgrove brings out his pocket watch and glances at the time. "The others will be at Motts by now. I really should go."

"Of course." I feel a little disappointed at his leaving, and wonder if I should quickly change into a more festive gown, but I'd only hold him up unnecessarily. "Please, before you leave, have a slice of Turkish delight." I reach across him, and pick up the box.

As his teeth sink into the pink square, the gold pin with the blue stone that holds his tie in place twinkles in the gaslight. Feeling bold, I lean towards him, and touch the stone.

Looking up at him, I ask, "What sort of gem is this, Maurice? I've never seen such a thing."

I go to withdraw my hand, but he catches it in his. "It's called lapis lazuli. I brought it back from my time in Mandalay."

I'm so close to him I can smell his cologne, and something beneath that, something male, earthy.

"It's lovely. I must find myself a piece of this lapis lazuli," I say. A dab of powder dusts his lips. "But you must go, sir, mustn't you? Your guests wait."

He smiles. "Yes, you're right. I'm very late." Yet he doesn't make a move. Instead, he stares at me with those blue eyes of his, and then cups the side of my face in his hand, his thumb softly sweeping the skin below my eye. I turn my head, kiss the base of his thumb, tracing the flesh with the tip of my tongue. With a soft choking sound, he pulls me to him, and presses his lips to mine. I taste the rose water, and feel the prickle of his stubble against my mouth.

I grin as I gaze into the mirror of my dressing table. All around my mouth, and a little bit on my chin, I have a rash from the hour or so my lips were crushed against Cosgrove's. Heat rises up through my chest and into my face as I think of his hardness pushed against me, of his lips brushing the flesh of my breasts. But I didn't take him to bed. Not yet. I have to be sure of him first.

"Yes?" I call, when I hear a light scratching at my door.

The door opens a few inches and Amah peeps in. "You are alone?"

"Amah, yes. I am. What are you doing up so late?" She does not look well. Her skin is pallid and she's taken off weight in the short period I've been away. "But what is the matter? Have you been ill?"

She stares at me for a few seconds, her mouth ajar like she might say something, but she just shakes her head. "No. I am fine. It's just this horrible cold weather. Who can rest with its nipping?" She rubs her hands together so they make the sound of rustling paper.

"Well, at least take a seat and I can tell you all that has happened while I was away." I pull an armchair close to the fireplace for her, which she ignores.

"Tell me of your case," she says, as she takes up my brush.

Taking a seat again, I close my eyes. How nice it feels, how comforting, to have her sweep my hair back from my face. Every few moments I feel her cold fingers skim my scalp, and I can smell her fragrance, something of teak tea chests and jasmine. It's not often she brushes my hair so gently, with such reverie.

"Tell me," she repeats.

"It was the nursemaid."

A sharp intake of breath. Her eyes meet mine in the mirror.

"What wickedness," she says.

I watch as she places the brush back onto the dressing table, and I see how dry and chapped her fingers are. Urging her to take a seat on the armchair, I kneel down and try to apply my special ointment to her skin. She waves me away, taking the jar, and rubs and rubs the substance into her hands as I tell her of what happened at St Chad's Lodge. The whole time I speak, she continues to massage the ointment in, as if she's polishing the silver, only pausing once, when I mention the *kris*.

"The *kris*?" Her voice is hoarse.

"Yes, awful, isn't it? So, of course now it seems obvious that whoever killed McBride also killed Lovejoy." I turn back to the mirror. "And the strangest thing, Amah, I'm sure I saw Jakub in Stoke Newington. But then I realised it was impossible." I swathe cold crème across my forehead, swirl it into my cheeks. It's made of opium and lemon water and something else that smells so sharp the rose perfume can't hide it, but I've been assured it will keep my skin pale and blemish-free. "Jakub's still abroad, isn't...?" But the bedroom door clicks shut. Amah's gone.

For days Amah has hunted for that boy. She's searched the West India Docks and the shops of Limehouse. She smelt cargoes of spice, the greasy fumes that billowed from the ships, the body odour of the sailors, but all she's managed to collect are memories of a past she's striven to forget.

Towards the end of that long voyage on the *Dukano*, when they made their way across the ocean to this place, Mrs Preston was very sickly. Most of the white people had terrible dysentery—the stench, as the servant boys ran past with overflowing buckets, that mixed with the sweetness of the *nilam* oil the white men used to keep the bugs from their bedding—even now Amah's stomach recoils. She'd never seen anything worse.

Day after day, Mrs Preston lay in her bed, panting, only half in this world. Amah had to gather up all their linen, Mrs Preston's leather shoes, books, spare candles and tuck them into the bedding with her mistress, under a shroud of netting so the rats wouldn't chew on all of their things or maybe even Mrs Preston's flesh. Every afternoon, Amah lifted her mistress into a chair and turned her mattress, lined it with fresh sheets, so that when she lay down again she had some relief from the heat. While the sun was high in the sky, Amah fanned Mrs Preston's face. She watched as the woman mumbled in her sleep, her cheeks flushed. She only really found peace late at night, when the sea breeze whispered through the open doorway. It was on one such night, when the lanterns had been extinguished and the men were bedded down in the saloon, that he found Amah there.

The waves lapped the side of the boat, the timber floors and beams creaked. But still, she heard his soft tread find his way across the cabin. The dark was so complete, Amah had to blink a few times to make sure her eyes were open.

She was not sure if his plan was to attack Mrs Preston or her, but he stumbled, cursed in his white tongue, and landed atop Amah. Her breath came out in a loud huff, and she doubled over, trying to clasp her stomach. He grabbed her arm and held her pinned with one hand, while his other covered her mouth. She struggled against him. She strained to reach the knife that lay close by where she'd been slicing pineapple for Mrs Preston earlier in the day.

Amah doesn't know how long this went on for—a minute, ten?—it was like the darkness allowed no certainty, no record. But the smell of him, the feel of his flesh. She made sure that she would know this man again.

CHAPTER 28

Over breakfast, I open the rest of my post. Second from the bottom is a letter from Pidgeon. His handwriting is not much better than a scrawl. He writes of the threatening message he'd received, the same one that Cosgrove told me about the evening before. He complains of Bob Beveridge and how unhelpful the police have proven to be. The letter is closed with the words, *Heloise, do you trust this Sir Thomas implicitly? Something troubles me greatly, and I need to share it with someone. I think I might know why McBride had to die—indeed, why we are all marked to die. Maybe when you return, you can visit me, tell me of this Detective Inspector you have been working with.*

How very odd. I smear Gentleman's Relish across my buttered toast. But very interesting too. I need to find out what is haunting Pidgeon. I'm sure I'll be able to draw it from him.

The morning sky is so clear I decide to walk to Pidgeon's house on Derby Street. Under my cloak I'm wearing a new walking dress. The full skirt, spruce green, has a handsome Swiss waist. The white bodice is neatly trimmed with embroidered seams and has pretty, billowing sleeves. Besides my small bag, I clasp a lace handkerchief, chiefly because it matches my bodice, but also to hold to my nose if the air becomes too foul.

I pass a small bakery and it reminds me of Cyril. I smile and wonder how the little brat is doing. Pausing, I look through the bakery's window, but they only carry bread and some plain pastries, no sweets, none of the hard candy the boy enjoyed so much. My silhouette makes a smart reflection in the glass, but maybe, just maybe, it's missing his small figure by its side. My fingers curl, as I remember the boy's small hand tucked in mine. Pliable, trusting, insistent. Sticky.

Curzon Street is filled with the sounds of coachmen, carmen, and, in the distance, I can see three ladies leaving the chapel. A butcher's boy makes his way to a large house on the corner, a dog trotting along behind.

I stop short at Derby Street. The narrow road is blocked by a number of carriages and a uniformed policeman argues with a fishmonger trying to gain access.

"Sir, I won't repeat myself again," the constable says. "You cannot pass through this street until the Inspector says you can."

The fishmonger, red in the face, turns back, rolls his eyes at me. "Somebody dies, and the world has to shut down."

I glance over his shoulder to the row of houses. Anxiety taps its claw against my ribcage. "Who died?"

"They found some chap dead in his coach. Alls I wants is to deliver this fish to Mrs Poole at number 19, but I just can't get through. Tried the other side too, I did. This fish won't stay fresh all day, you know. And Mrs Poole is very particular."

The fish's grey carcase lies limp in his basket, its middle partially covered with a red and white checked kerchief. A globule of blood seeps from its gills and its mouth gapes. A whiff of its damp, raw odour reaches my nostrils and my stomach turns.

Thankfully, the fishmonger walks on, leaving me staring into Derby Street, trying to discern which coach might hold the corpse. I can see the top of the white portico that fronts Pidgeon's home, which seems to sit at the centre of the tumult. The claw of anxiety tightens its grip on my chest.

"Mrs Chancey," a familiar voice hails me from behind. I

turn, and look up into Detective Inspector Hatch's pale face. "What are you doing here?" he asks.

"Inspector, who has died?" I hold tightly onto my purse and handkerchief to stop myself from grasping his sleeve. "I have friends—the Pidgeons—who live in that house, there. Please tell me it's not one of them."

Hatch's thin face seems to lengthen as he watches me.

Two gentlemen stroll close by, crane to see into the road. A cab slows down for the driver and passengers to stare out at the commotion.

Hatch steers me by the constables guarding the road, gestures for me to hop up into the police buggy. "Please sit, Mrs Chancey. I'm afraid I have some bad news for you."

I'm glad of the seat because my knees feel weak. I hadn't really noticed how cold the morning was before, but now I feel as if my limbs are made of ice, that my lips are frozen.

Hatch's words are hushed and swift. "I'm afraid your friend, Sir Henry Pidgeon, has been found dead in his carriage."

My mind is awhirl, as though a flurry of snowflakes fills my head. "But how?" I manage to ask. *Please let it be an apoplexy or a lung fever. Not…*

The Detective Inspector leans forward and briefly grips three gloved fingers of my left hand. "You must be strong, Mrs Chancey. What I have to tell you is not for the faint-hearted, but I believe I can use your services again. And I know Pidgeon was a good friend of yours."

I'm conscious of how dry my lips are, but can't summon the will to lick them. I just stare at Hatch and nod.

"It appears Pidgeon has been murdered by the fiend who killed both McBride and Lovejoy."

I let out a long breath. I breathe out for so long, my corsets conflate with my stomach. My breath in is too short, and the next, and the next.

"Was he…?"

Hatch nods. "He was murdered in the same manner as the other two men."

Pidgeon. With his mournful, hound-like face. Doting father, loyal friend. The terror he must've felt.

"Mrs Chancey, are you all right?"

I nod. Closing my eyes, I try desperately to think of something pleasant, something reassuring that will help me right my breathing. I try to imagine I'm by a bright fire, that I'm safe, home in Mayfair. I imagine there are strong arms wrapped around my shoulder. I think they might be Hatterleigh's, but no. Cosgrove's? I frown. No. And then I realise they're Amah's.

I open my eyes. "I apologise. This has been quite a shock. For that poor man to die in such a terrible manner." I shake my head. "I can't fathom it." I glance over at the carriage. Three men have unharnessed the horses and lead them away. Two constables guard the carriage doors, and Pidgeon's driver stands close by, staring into the gutter, puffing on his short pipe. "What is it you needed of me?" I dab my lips with my handkerchief and my hands quiver only a little.

"Please come inside and sit with Miss Pidgeon. You will only need to stay with her until her aunt arrives from Croydon. Obviously, she is in quite a bit of shock." He climbs down from the buggy and takes my hand as I take the two steps down onto the road again. "Maybe you can find out if she knows something that can shed light on this affair."

He steers me in a wide semicircle around the carriage so there is no chance I might accidentally see inside, but just as we reach the bottom of the Pidgeons' front steps, his driver greets another man on the pavement, and I hear him say, his voice low yet urgent, "His head had fallen fair in his lap, Roddy. In his lap! I'm not lying to you." The driver lifts his pipe to his lips with shaking fingers.

I almost glance back at the carriage, but Hatch takes my arm, says, "No, Mrs Chancey. You don't want to look."

I look up at him. "Is it true?"

He nods, as he leads the way into the house. "I'm afraid so. One of the more vicious crime scenes I've ever seen."

Isobel appears at the top of the stairs on the first landing. "Heloise. Heloise," she moans. I hurry up the stairs to her.

I wipe Isobel's hair back from her forehead. It's damp with perspiration and tears. She lies along the sofa, and her head rests in my lap. Besides stroking her hair, I don't know what to say to her as her tears seep into my skirts.

Anger builds inside me the longer I sit here. I don't know much about McBride and Lovejoy, but who would want to kill Pidgeon, who was such a harmless, well-loved man? Fury billows up from my stomach through to my chest. Isobel's sobs stoke the rage, until I feel the pressure of it in my head, in my fingertips and my jaw aches. I want to burst out onto the street and scream, "Who did this?" Closing my eyes, I imagine forming a fist and smashing it into the murderer's face. But the picture shifts—the cheekbone, the chin, the eyes—for I don't know yet who is the culprit. Is it really a Chinese person, as Cosgrove and the others suspect, or is it someone else?

I glance back down at Isobel. I won't trouble her with these questions. Her father is dead, and that's all that matters to her, not the how and who.

Picking up her left hand, I gently squeeze her fingers. "Why are your fingertips so orange, Isobel?" She still has an apron over her skirt, and she smells distinctly of something like mutton stew and onion.

She sniffs, wipes under her nose. "I was teaching Cook a recipe for a curry I learnt while we lived in Burma." Rubbing her fingertips together, she says, "It's from the paprika. They don't make curry quite like that at the Oriental Club, and as it was Father's favourite, I..." She presses her hands to her face and sobs quietly. I rub her shoulder, helpless.

Isobel's aunt arrives about an hour later, and I leave the two women to weep together on the sofa. The carriage has been cleared away, along with poor Pidgeon's body, and only one policeman remains, stationed on the bottom step leading onto the pavement.

"Where is everyone, Constable?" I ask him.

"The Detective Inspector has returned to the station, madam," he says. He's rugged up in his heavy uniform overcoat, but his cheeks and nose are pink from the cold. "Down on Vine Street."

I thank the man and walk home as swiftly as I can. My eyes tear up against the rising wind, but also from my sorrow for Pidgeon and his daughter. I bow my head as I make my way, wishing my hat had a veil attached that I could pull down over my face.

Flinging open my front door, I call for Bundle. "Can you let Taff know I need the carriage as soon as possible?"

I run up the stairs to my dressing room and sweep through my drawers until I find a short length of Chantilly lace, black with a pattern of roses, that I can swathe over my hat. I then return to the hallway and pace the floors, waiting for Taff.

When I hear my carriage pull up at the door, I hurry out, call up to Taff, who's seated on the driver's box, "Don't bother getting down, Taff. I'll be fine. Take me to the police station in Vine Street, please." A young couple passes by my house at that moment, and the man looks as though he might offer me his hand, but I manage to haul myself and my skirts into the carriage.

I look out the window as we make our way, but I don't really see anything. I'm anxious that Hatch might have left the station before I make it there. I want to know more of what happened and if they've managed to find any clues as to who has done this horrible thing. I feel if I don't keep moving, keep busy, there will be nothing left for me to do except allow the tightness in my chest to dissolve so that I'm capable of nothing but blubbering on my bed.

The police station is hidden behind a forbidding brown façade. The strident windows are covered with black metal bars and a large lantern perches over the entrance. A constable leads me down a dingy corridor and leaves me in a poky room, windowless, and only furnished with a table and four sturdy chairs. I'm reading the names nicked into the table-top when Hatch enters the room.

"Mrs Chancey." His expression is slightly surprised, but without reproof. "How can I be of assistance? I only have a moment, I'm afraid. How is Miss Pidgeon?"

"Not well. But that is to be expected. I left her with her aunt." I watch as he takes a seat opposite me. "Have you any clue yet to who may have done this?"

He takes in a big breath and lets it out noisily. "We are back at the beginning, I'm afraid."

"What do you mean?"

"Well, I first questioned Pidgeon's butler, and it seems Pidgeon received a message earlier in the morning that caused him to finish his breakfast abruptly and call for his coach."

"Did you see this message?"

Hatch nods. "We found it in Pidgeon's pocket."

"And...?"

"What can you tell me of Jedediah Hunt?"

Hunt. I think of the last time I saw the older man—his whiskery face, his loud, querulous voice—in my drawing room the night McBride was murdered on my doorstep. "Not a lot." I tell Hatch that he's just one of the group of explorers who frequent my soirees. "I think there was talk of a time when they were all stationed together in... was it Mandalay or Sarawak?" I try to think back to the night at my place, but what with the amount of champagne I'd had and McBride's death, the evening is a bit of a blur. "Why do you ask? Was the note from him?"

Hatch doesn't answer, he just frowns down at the table, traces his finger across the word "hell" that's been etched into the timber.

"And the *kris*," he finally says. "You are sure the *kris* we found is the one from your display cabinet?"

I nod. "Quite sure. But, if you want to confirm that, you are welcome to show it to Bundle, my butler. He will know."

"Yes. I was going to question your servants today, in any case."

"Were you? About the *kris*?" I stiffen a little, wondering how poor Bundle and Agneau will take to being interviewed.

"Yes. See if they saw anyone suspicious around the time of McBride's death." He shifts in his chair. "The thing is, if the *kris* was from your home, then the culprit had access to it. I'm afraid I'll have to question both your servants and your guests."

I swallow. "What of the coachman? Did not he see who murdered Pidgeon?"

Hatch blinks twice as he stares at me. He seems to be weighing up how much to tell me. "He says he was sitting on his box, thought he felt a bit of a commotion below in the coach but put it down to Pidgeon just trying to make himself comfortable. He didn't know anything was amiss until he was pulling out from the kerbside and a man jumped from the carriage and ducked around the corner."

"Could he describe him?"

"Said he looked Asiatic."

I take a sharp breath in. "The Chinaman."

Hatch shakes his head. "I'm not so sure, although I'm no expert on the subject." He's frowning again. "When I asked him to elucidate, he said the fellow was dark and tall, and had a long red cloth of some kind swathed around his head."

I try to picture what he's described.

"Fortunately, at that precise moment, a midwife was leaving a house further down the road and told the constable on duty that she also saw the man lurch from Pidgeon's carriage. Her description was similar. Tall, dark man. Long loose clothing. Foreign. But she called his head covering a turban. Said she'd worked in a household once who employed Indian servants. She was sure the fleeing man was of Indian blood."

I sit back in my chair, flummoxed. "Well, that's a strange twist."

Hatch's frown takes on an irritated cast. "Yes. Just what I was thinking."

CHAPTER 29

As Bundle lets me in through the front door, I feel faint, jittery, and I realise it's late afternoon and I've not drunk or eaten since a cup of tea and toast at my dressing table this morning. My face feels flushed, but at the same time as if all my blood is dropping to my feet. As I peel off my gloves, I see that my hands tremble.

"Bundle, Detective Inspector Hatch will be here sometime to talk to you and the staff. Please let Agneau and Taff know. It's about the *kris* that went missing."

"And Abigail, Mrs Chancey?"

I'd forgotten Abigail. "Yes, her too. Although, Bundle, I'm not sure he'll need to talk with Amah."

Bundle just bows and returns to the back of the house. How thankful I am for the man. He always understands me.

Amah appears at the top of the stairs. "What is it, Heloise?"

I beckon for her to follow me into the drawing room, where I sink onto the sofa, and say, "Pidgeon is dead. Murdered."

Amah pauses by the card table.

"Did you hear me?" I say, exasperated. "I said Pidgeon was murdered this morning. Just like McBride and Lovejoy."

She shakes her head slowly. "Terrible. Do they know who did it?"

I shrug. "The coachman and another witness claim it was someone of Asiatic appearance." Asiatic. The general term for a brown foreigner. Lucky the midwife knew a thing or two. Or did she? Really, she might have been as mistaken as anyone.

I stare down at my bag, at the embroidered leaves that match the colour of my skirt. I remember that Amah never liked the Pidgeons. She probably doesn't care. But when I glance back up, her face is as pale as rice pudding, and a small frown flickers between her brows.

I sit forward. "Take a seat, Mama. You don't look well at all. What is the matter?"

"Nothing, it is nothing, Jia Li," she says.

Abigail treads past the open doorway with a heavy pail that swings against her knees. She opens the front door, closes it behind her and we can hear the brush's bristles scrub across the tiles of the front steps. A bit late in the day for that, I would've thought.

"I need to go out, Heloise," says Amah, as she walks from the drawing room. "I might be late home."

"But where...?" She's already trotting up the stairs and out of earshot. I roll my eyes. What bee does she have in her bonnet this time? I pull the box of Turkish delight onto my lap.

Bundle places a cup of tea on the side table, already sugared, and I smile my thanks to him.

"Maybe you would like an early supper, Mrs Chancey?"

My stomach rumbles at the thought, despite my low spirits. "Yes, please, Bundle."

After a few sips of the sweet brew, I can feel my heartbeat settle, my fingers steady. Placing the cup back in the saucer, I pick up a square of Turkish delight and take a bite. Licking the powder from my lips, I am transported back to the night before with Cosgrove.

Cosgrove. I wonder if he's heard from Hatch. If he's heard the terrible news.

I take to my feet, almost upsetting the box of sweets. I quickly sip more of my tea and then pop the rest of the Turkish delight into my mouth as I hurry into the hallway.

"Bundle, Bundle," I call, walking towards the back of the house. "I won't need my supper just yet, thank you. Can you tell Taff I am very sorry, but can he take me out again?"

Bundle appears in the kitchen doorway. "I'm afraid Amah just left with him, Mrs Chancey. I assumed you knew."

I'm nonplussed. Amah must be very flustered indeed to take the coach without letting me know. "Not to worry, Bundle. Can you please fetch me a cab, then?"

The cab passes along a line of identical Georgian terraces in Holborn. Luckily, I know Cosgrove's directions from the frequent times I have needed to address invitations to him, and the driver leaves me outside a house with a door painted the shade of a glossy horseshoe. I rap on the knocker, glancing left and right. The sun has set, and I wonder if Cosgrove would be embarrassed if his neighbours were to see him receiving a solitary, female visitor.

A middle-aged man with short, dark hair oiled flat to his head answers the door, but almost immediately Cosgrove is at his elbow, saying, "Heloise, Mrs Chancey, this is a surprise. Meadowes, there's a good man, fetch us some tea, would you?" He ushers me past his man into a room to the left.

I find myself in a small sitting room that also functions as a study. A desk, piled with books and loose sheets of paper falling to the floor, sits under the front window, next to an overcrowded bookcase, its glass doors ajar. In a semicircle before the fireplace is a setting of two lounge chairs the colour of oxblood, which are divided by a low-set marquetry table. A fine Turkish rug covers the floor. The room smells of smoke, books and leather.

Cosgrove pulls the curtains together across the window to the street. "Take a seat, Heloise." He lowers himself onto the lounge chair opposite to mine. "To what do I owe the pleasure of your company?"

His words are polite, yet the gleam in his eye is cheeky, gives a hint of other pleasures. My chest feels heavy. He mustn't know about Pidgeon.

I reach out, place my hand on his knee. "Maurice, have you not heard from the police?"

A slight frown. "No. Why? What has happened?"

At that moment, Meadowes enters the room, bearing a tray of tea things. I draw back into my chair, wait for Cosgrove's man to lay out the cups and teapot, the plate of bread and butter.

When Meadowes finally leaves, closing the door behind him, Cosgrove repeats, "What's happened?"

"Pidgeon is dead." I can't think of any other way to say it. I can't see him appreciating me trying to soften the blow. "He was found this morning."

"But how?"

"The same as McBride." I don't want to describe the ghastly details, give word to how my good friend—our great friend—was murdered. As I watch Cosgrove's head sink, as he covers his face with his hands and groans, "No", I again feel anger rise in me. Who is the bastard who killed poor Pidgeon?

I stare down at the carpet. The white fringe has grubby ends, and in the port-coloured weave there is a patch worn thin from silverfish.

Cosgrove's face is red when he lifts his head again. "What of Isobel?"

"She is fine. She's still at their home but will travel to her aunt's house tomorrow."

Cosgrove's face is haggard as he stares at me. "Where was he when it happened?" he asks, through clenched teeth.

"Outside his home, in his carriage. He seemed to be in a hurry to meet someone."

"Whom?"

"I think it might have been Hunt, but the Detective Inspector wouldn't elaborate."

"Hunt? Do you know where they were to meet?"

"No." I shake my head. "And like I said, I cannot be sure it was him he was called on to meet."

"Surely someone saw the culprit this time? It was morning, you said."

I nod. "They did. Said he looked to be from the East." He

opens his mouth to say something, but I cut him off. "No, not the Chinaman, apparently. Someone from India maybe, foreign clothing, a turban on his head."

He stares at me. "What new devilment is this?"

I just shake my head.

"And Isobel? How is she?"

"Not good." I lift the teacup to my lips and am mortified when my fingers tremble so that some tea sloshes into the saucer.

Cosgrove takes the cup from my hand, clasping my fingers. "This must have really distressed you, of course." He draws me to him.

I'm happy to be ensconced in his lap but loath to have him believe I am too weak to cope with this situation. "No," I say, laughing a little. "No, it's just that I haven't eaten today. I'm feeling faint from lack of food." I lean over and take a slice of bread. "I will be right after I eat this, I'm sure. Then we can plan how we are to go about finding Pidgeon's murderer."

I'm torn—I know it's almost indelicate to eat at such a time, but I'm really hungry.

He squeezes me tight, burying his face against my throat. His body is rigid with grief and fury, his eyes are pressed shut. I'm sure he must be thinking of his friend. Like a prickle in my brain, it occurs to me for the first time that he might also be worried for his own safety.

Dropping the bread back onto the plate, I nuzzle into the hollow of his neck, breathe in his scent. His lips find mine and for a few minutes we sink into each other, our unspent rage finding passage in desire. His hands snake up my thighs and I yank his collar apart so his blue lapel pin hangs loose. I kiss his smooth chest, his muscles quivering as I slide my hand across his warm flesh. He lifts me from the chair, lays me down onto the carpet, and we fuck until we're spent and panting amongst the silks of my skirts and petticoats.

He rolls onto the floor beside me and we lie like that, the warm fire crackling next to us. I'm just thinking of retrieving that slice of bread and butter when Cosgrove's head lifts. "Did you hear that? Someone at the door?"

"No, I didn't hear anything," I say, alarmed. I sit up, straightening my stockings and pulling my skirts down. I back up to the armchair and heave myself into it.

"I'm sure I heard something." Cosgrove gets to his feet and walks to the door, buttoning his trousers and readjusting his collar.

I try to neaten my hair, while taking bites of bread. I hope it's not Hatch. Surely, though, Cosgrove wouldn't expose me to another man's censure.

I'm putting an extra teaspoon of sugar into my tea when Cosgrove returns. My hand pauses, the teaspoon mid-stir, when I see his face. "What is it?"

"Meadowes found this slipped through the mail slot. A message from Hunt," he says, showing me the slip of paper. "He wants to meet me."

"When?" I ask, glancing down at the note. *As soon as possible*, is written in neat copperplate. And, sure enough, it's signed, *J.D. Hunt*.

I look up at Cosgrove. "But you mustn't go. It might be another trap."

He frowns down at the note. "By Hunt? I've known him many years now, and I cannot believe he's responsible for these deaths. I cannot. He might be in danger himself."

"But it could be from someone else," I say, following him into the hallway. "It might be the same person who murdered Pidgeon, tricking you into meeting him, by posing as Hunt. At least show it to Hatch first. Let him accompany you."

Cosgrove casts around for his hat, which he finds on a small escritoire. He shrugs into an overcoat. "It says to come now. I must go. You can wait here for me, if you like, or fetch your Hatch and tell him what is going on."

I hurry back into the sitting room and jam my bonnet onto my head. Taking up my coat, which lies on the floor where it was discarded, I pull it on. "I'm coming with you.

221

But first, do you have a firearm we can bring? I've left mine at home, unfortunately."

It takes the cab driver nearly an hour to find the meeting place in the East End. Cosgrove curses, wonders why Hunt or "whoever the damned scoundrel is" who wrote the message chose such an out-of-the-way location to meet.

"It must be a trap," I repeat.

But as we draw nearer to our destination, Cosgrove wrenches the cab window open, peers out at the dreary street. "My God," he says. "I remember this place."

"What is it?" I ask.

"It's where we found a group of those *kungsi* rascals living. Years ago. Tried to bribe Pidgeon, they did. Hunt too."

"The Chinese from Sarawak? Why would they try to bribe Pidgeon and Hunt?"

He's silent for a few moments. We bump against each other as the cab trundles across cobblestones. "I was never quite sure, Heloise. All I know is we rooted them out." By the light of the street lamps outside, I watch his hands clench. "Hunt must've found something."

The cab halts at the corner of a narrow alley. "Far as I can go, sir," calls the driver.

Hopping down into the road after Cosgrove, I repeat my question. "But what on earth did they have on the likes of Pidgeon?"

"I was never quite sure, Heloise," he says again. "Pidgeon, Lovejoy and Hunt—and that fellow McBride—were very quiet about something to do with that riot in Sarawak. I've never been sure of what it was. I was newly arrived in Kuching, and although we have been great friends since..." he pauses. He's probably thinking of how those friendships are in the past, now that the others have been murdered, "I was much younger than they, new to their expeditions. I have heard them talk about the wonders of antimony, though, which is mined in Sarawak. They had a good laugh about it, but didn't explain the joke to me. Lately, since these murders, I've begun to wonder if they were hiding something."

"Like what?"

He shakes his head, and lifts his hat to push his hair back from his forehead. "Maybe they knew the Chinese were going to attack. In fact, maybe it was arranged so. With Crookshank and Wilkins out of the way, a negotiator with good business acumen could arrange a tidy deal with the local *kungsi* for the antimony mines. Yes, but maybe the Chinese were double-crossed. Antimony has only increased in value, tenfold probably, in that time. I wouldn't be surprised if that is why the *kungsi* keep sending men in to finish off those that tricked them. Maybe they hope to recover the mines."

"You can't mean Pidgeon was a part of this? He would never!" I say. But then I remember that twice he's tried to tell me of something that was troubling him. If not involved himself, he might have had information against the other men.

We stare down the murky alleyway we must enter. There's a strong whiff of ordure and river rot, and damp stains the walls of the hovels that line the road.

"Damn. I should've brought a lantern," Cosgrove says, glancing up at the sky. The night is cloudy, dimming the moon's glow. "You should have stayed behind, Heloise." His voice is rough and, for the first time, I think that maybe I should have.

"Do we go down here?" I ask, taking the first step into the alley.

"Yes."

I step over a pile of turnip ends and mouldy cabbage and God alone knows what else. I whip the lace from my hat and clamp it lightly against my nose with freezing fingers. Cosgrove grunts and curses as he steps in what I think is human shit and, by the slit of moonlight that finds its way past the ramshackle buildings, I momentarily mistake a de-composing cat for a discarded fur tippet.

The further we walk, the more I can smell something gas-like.

"What a peculiar place to have a pond," I say, walking towards the body of water that marks the end of the alley. By the light of a single lantern hanging from the balcony of a shack on the corner, the water seems to be the shade and consistency of tea. Two rows of houses back onto the pond, while the alleyway snakes off to the right and left, forming the shape of a T. A very low archway leads the way into the lane to the left, its interior swamped in darkness. The lane to the right is a little wider, uncovered, with a long row of terraced shanties on each side of the dirt path.

"He said to wait here."

I wander closer to the pond. It isn't surrounded by any greenery—no grass, no shrubberies—and its banks have been trodden into mud that spreads its sludge onto the path's flagstones. The reek of gas becomes overbearing and I realise what I'm looking at.

"It's some sort of cesspool," Cosgrove says behind me.

A faint light glows from one of the houses that backs onto the pool as a woman opens her back door and throws the contents of a bucket into the water. The slopping sound, the fresh, foul stench, leave no doubt as to the contents of the bucket. At the same time, a little girl, maybe seven or eight years old, sidles up to the edge of the pool. Keeping a wary eye on us, she bobs down and dips a tin cup into the water and then quickly turns about, returns to a house several doors down. I gag so strongly that tears form in my eyes.

"Where is Hunt, blast him?" says Cosgrove, taking his pistol from his pocket. "Heloise, it's best if you wait over there." He points to the archway leading to the left. "Hide yourself. If anything is to happen to me, find your way out, alert Hatch."

I know from his voice that there will be no negotiation on this, so I take my place in the dark folds of the tunnel as quickly as I can. As I press myself and my wide skirts against the damp wall, I can just make out two figures walking towards us down the opposite lane. Each of them carries something over his shoulder—shovels, maybe, or rakes? They pause by a doorway, knock, and that's when I see another shadow, taller, solitary, moving up the lane behind them. Cosgrove steps back, by the side of the pool, so that he's out of sight.

The lazy clip-clop of a horse's hoofs draw near. I think the sound is coming from the alleyway we followed from the main thoroughfare. In the distance, a coster, selling some sort of fare, clangs metal together while calling out something indiscernible. The shadowy man in the opposite lane pauses for a moment. A crunching noise behind me. I swing around as a creature scuttles from sight; but not before I see the sheen of its bulbous eye. A rat. Fleeing from a carcase, pink and unrecognisable, that lies not two feet from me, left to desiccate in the open air. Even as I watch, though, two more rats creep close, inspect the mound. A hacking cough echoes down the tunnel, hacking and hacking as the person tries to expel the poison from within, catch their breath. I'm just turning away, pulling my veil across my mouth and nose, when something even darker than the gloom cuts through the air, knocks me into oblivion.

CHAPTER 30

The first thing I notice when I open my eyes is the smoke billowing around my face. Someone puffing on a cigarette nearby. I turn my head, the uneven cobblestones bumping against my skull. I pull myself up onto my elbows. Not smoking, just my warm breath suffusing the chill air.

The pong of filth and excrement rises around me and I remember where I am. The lane beside the cesspool. Sitting up, my fingers find the ache at the back of my head, carefully prod the swelling that's as big as an egg.

I want to stand, but for almost a minute all I can manage is resting forward on all fours. Trying to ignore the sludge that films my hands and gown, I have to squint against the terrible pain that slices through the right side of my head. I sway like that until I hear a voice cry out. Looking up, I can see that someone is crouched low near the cesspool. I struggle to my feet and lurch towards him, but stop short, my mind whirling, when I see by the feeble light thrown by his lantern that it's not Cosgrove. He's a young man, with beefy shoulders and a flat face and, as I stare at him, a boy steps out from behind him.

The man puts his hands out. "Miss, you shouldn't come any nearer."

"What do you mean?" I manage to croak, stumbling forward until I can see outstretched legs and well-shod feet in the shadows between him and the pond.

"Miss, you really don't want to see this," the man repeats,

but as I come closer he steps out of my way rather than touch me.

I look down upon his body. Cosgrove's body. I know it's him, despite the dreadful absence of his head.

"Where's his...?" I whisper.

"It rolled into the pond when we checked on him. Shook him, we did. Thought he was just passed out or something."

The banging in my head becomes unbearable and I fall forward onto my knees again and hack up onto the road, heaving until a line of spittle dangles to the mud. My finger-nails scrape the dirt. I wipe my mouth down the side of my sleeve.

The man tries to pull Cosgrove's body away from the edge of the pond. I reach my hand over.

"No, no. Don't touch him," I say. My nose is running and my eyes water from the cold and sorrow. "Fetch the police. Tell them to find Detective Hatch. Vine Street Station."

The man sends the boy, who scampers away down the main alleyway, unperturbed by the dark.

"Did you see who did this?" I ask the man.

He just shakes his head. "By the time me and Jimmy came out, the murdering bastard—excuse my language, Miss—was running down the lane."

"You didn't see what he looked like?"

"No..." The man lifts his cap for a moment, scratches his head. "It was like his head was big, you know? Like too large for his shoulders, if you know what I mean."

As though he had a turban on.

A family of five come out from a nearby house and two men peer from a doorway before approaching. The man holds them all at bay. I hear him murmur the words "murder" and "fell in the pond". A stout woman lets out a short squeal, cups her hands over her mouth, shrinks back into the arms of another woman.

I stay huddled near Cosgrove's body, but I can't look again, not further than the bottom of his right shoe, which I can see out of the corner of my eye. A thin man limps by, lantern swinging, and, by its light, I see a piece of paper screwed up on the ground. I lean forward, pick it up. It's the note from Hunt, but I can barely read it, I'm shivering so hard.

"Here, Miss, take my coat." The young man holds it towards me.

"No, no, I couldn't," I say, my teeth chattering so violently I think I might bite my tongue.

He shoves it towards me again. "Here, take it. Just until the police come."

Relenting, I pull the coat over my shoulders. Drawing it close, I bury my nose into the rough tweed and find comfort in its odour of sweat, ale and tobacco.

By the time the first constable arrives on foot, a small crowd has formed. But by the time Hatch arrives, the lanes are quite clogged with onlookers. Four policemen hold them at bay, push them back from the vicinity of the body.

Hatch draws me to my feet, leads me towards the alley.

"Mrs Chancey, what happened here?"

I open my hand, reveal the crumpled note.

Hatch takes in a sharp breath as he reads. "From Hunt again."

"Yes, but I don't think it could really be from him. I think this whole thing was trickery." I look around for the young man, whose coat I have wrapped around me. "That man over there, the one in the grey shirt, he described the killer to me. Sounds like the man in the turban."

Hatch catches hold of a constable, tells him to escort the witness to the station.

Turning back to me, he asks, "And why are you here, Mrs Chancey?"

I peer hard at him to see if suspicion lights his eyes, but it's too dark, and my eyes are dry and cold, making my vision hazy. I blink, trying to cast my mind back to earlier in the evening. Cosgrove's port-coloured carpet, frayed at the edges. Bread and butter. His heavy body pressed against mine in front of the warm fireplace. "I think…" Pidgeon's death. Head toppled off in his carriage. "I visited him to see if he'd heard about Pidgeon. And while I was there, he received that message."

The three detectives who arrived with Hatch gather by the side of the cesspool. They're accompanied by an old man who holds a long rake of some kind.

"Well, you're right about the note not being from Hunt," says Hatch, shoving it into his side pocket. "We've since found out that Hunt is safely away in Bernissart, Belgium. It looks like we are back to an Asiatic culprit. Chinaman or Indian, I still can't place."

A cry of triumph by the side of the pond is accompanied by a hush from the others. The old man lays his pole down, next to a dark, muddy lump. I turn away, gripping my waist, dry retch against the side of a brick dwelling.

Hatch's hand falls onto my shoulder. It's reassuring, but has weight too. "I think you'd better go home, Mrs Chancey. But I will need you to come in for an interview tomorrow. Is that all right?"

I nod. As he escorts me to the main road, we pass Cosgrove's body again. Circles of light from lanterns held high by the police and the many onlookers bob amongst the shadows. As the detectives roll Cosgrove's body onto a stretcher, his gun clatters to the cobblestones from his lifeless hand. By the lanterns' glow, his blue pin glints against the dark, dark stain that has leached into his collar.

CHAPTER 31

Taff reins the horses into the kerbside along East India Docks Road. Amah hops down from the carriage, ignoring his loud entreaties to just wait one moment, darn it, and he'll escort her. She turns into the same street she has haunted over the last few days. Despite the late hour, quite a few people stroll up and down the road outside Kung's shop. A group of sailors make their way in the direction of the docks, while a vendor offers sweet buns to others who pass by. A young couple—him Chinese, her white—are seated on the front steps of their home, dandling a thickly swaddled toddler between them.

Amah's heart lifts when she sees the shutters are finally up at Kung's shop. She pushes the door open into a shallow front room. The walls and floors are bare of decoration and the only furnishing is a timber bench that once housed some sort of produce from far away. A bright, lacquered altar sits on the floor to the left. Smoke rises in a wisp from the joss sticks planted in sand next to a sad-looking orange, dimpled and shrunken.

A door opens and a Chinese man steps through. He stares at Amah out of his one good eye; the other is swollen shut, and there's a nasty graze above his brow, which she assumes is a result from his altercation with Sin Hok.

He says something, but she can't understand him. She shakes her head, says, "English?"

"I say Ayah Hostel in Jewry Street. Men only here."

Amah tries to look over his shoulder. "I am looking for Jakub Chee."

He grunts and turns back through the doorway. She peers past him, into the half-darkness beyond. Divans and beds are crammed up against each other, arranged like a maze, with only just enough space to inch around. The man calls out something unintelligible, then, "Chee". Several heads lift, crane around to see Amah, but only one figure, in the furthest corner, rises and makes his way to them. Jakub.

She'd forgotten how tall he is, how fine. His shoulders are slender but strong, his waist trim. She always calls him a boy, thinks of him as a boy, but really he's a man. A young man who doesn't look as pleased to see her as she is to see him.

Taking a seat on the bench, she indicates for him to sit next to her. Jakub hesitates, until he sees her lifted brow. She doesn't like the petulant lift to his mouth, the frown in his eyes, but he must know that she can do testy far better than anyone.

"Why have you been leading me on this merry dance, Jakub?" she says. "We've all been worried about you. Me, your mother, your father."

"Ha," is all he says, staring across at the altar.

"Why do you say this?"

He just shakes his head.

"And what do you have to do with this man, Sin Hok? I was told he's a very bad man. A criminal, in fact. Just look what he did here." With her chin, Amah indicates into the other room to where Kung is playing mah-jong with three other men.

"Who'd you hear that from?"

"A man at the Strangers' Home told me. Cardigan, his name was."

"Cadogan. That weasel." Jakub folds his arms. "He's cross because Sin Hok won't be converted. Sin Hok's just a trader. He's like Kung, in there, or…"

"Or who?"

"I was going to say Papa, but I mean Chee. Your uncle."

"But he is your papa. You must call him that. Disrespectful not to."

"Is he? I don't know who anyone is anymore." He clenches his teeth together so she can see the bulge of his jawline.

"Of course he is. Why do you say these things?"

"I know that Miriam is not my mother."

Amah nods slowly. "Uncle Chee said you thought this. Why, Jakub, why do you think this?"

Jakub's dark eyes study the older woman for a moment. He takes a notecase from his coat pocket, flips it open. "Do you remember this?"

He places a photograph onto her lap. The print isn't clear. It's as if the posing couple stands amid a light fog. Amah squints. It takes her a moment to work out who the strangers are in the picture, but then she recognises the tattered pheasant feather poking up from the woman's bonnet, the bonnet that was so cherished because it had once belonged to Mrs Preston. Li Leen. It was a photograph of herself, many years beforehand. Standing next to her, a very young Chee. No gut yet, smooth skin like Jakub's. His hair braided into a long queue, which hangs over his shoulder, snakes down his front, reaching just above his hip.

Amidst the wonder, Amah feels a dip of sadness to see her young face. Oval, like her mother's. "I can't remember ever seeing this." She smiles, thinking of the day Chee corralled her into the stall at the fair, how she'd grumbled that the devil would take their souls. Oh, that day, it was so cold. Much colder than today. Down by the docks in Liverpool it was always icy, even when the sun peeped out and the locals shed their coats and rolled their sleeves up. She can almost feel a shiver tickle up her spine as she thinks of it.

Then her eyes catch what she's holding, bundled in her arms. A baby. Its dark eyes gazing into the camera.

"That's me, isn't it?" he asks, pointing at the child.

There's no use denying it. Even in such an old, faded

photo, it's clear that the angles of the skull, the ears as neat as a shell, are Jakub's. "Where did you find this?" she asks.

"In the pocket of an overcoat Papa gave to me to take on my travels. He said the coat served him well when he was on the seas, himself. I suppose he'd forgotten the photograph was in there."

Amah thinks quickly. "Yes, he visited me with you. In Liverpool. To give your poor mother a rest."

Jakub shakes his head slowly. "No, Auntie Leen. Papa didn't even know Mother then."

Amah frowns. "But of course he did."

Again, Jakub shakes his head. He points once more at the photo, this time at Chee. "I've heard Mother say many times that she never knew Papa with his long plait. That he had already chopped it off by the time they met here, in Limehouse."

Amah leans back against the wall. She stares down at the photograph and lets out a long breath. Miriam, and her constant chatter.

Her eyes find Jakub's. "So what do you think this means?"

"I think..." His eyes fall from hers. "I think you're my mother."

His mother? Amah? Out of all the scenarios she'd mulled over and over again, she never thought the silly boy would come to that conclusion. "What?" A smile creeps to her face, but she can't help herself, it's so ridiculous.

Uncertainty puckers his brow. "You're my mother."

Taking his hand in hers, she rubs his skin. "No, no, Jakub. I am not your mother." She wants to say she has always loved him as a mother would, that one of the saddest days of her life was when she was parted from him, but the words stick in her throat. Tenderness has never come easily to her; she prefers to use words that bite, that are as sour as a green nectarine. Words that guard her innermost feelings.

The door creaks a little as a gust of wind whistles through, and the men in the next room start up a new game of mah-jong, stirring the hard tiles around on the tabletop.

Jakub withdraws his hand from hers and crosses his arms, tucking his fingers into his underarms. "I know the truth, Auntie Leen. Papa told me of the ship you came in. I've been to Liverpool and seen the passenger list."

"But why? What does that prove?"

"I needed to find out who my father was. Even if he is a blackguard."

Amah shakes her head, frowning. She doesn't understand him.

His eyes search hers for a moment, then flick away again. He mumbles something that she doesn't quite catch.

"What?"

"I said, Papa told me of how on that voyage one of the English gentlemen attacked you. Of how you didn't say anything because what notice would they take of two Chinese servants?"

Amah recalls that black night. The sharp stench of smoke-stack fug, the dusty floor, the brandy on his breath as he slobbered against her neck.

"No, no." She goes to grasp Jakub's hand again, but they're still shoved into his underarms, away from contact. "You have it all wrong, Jakub. And in any case, even I am not certain who it was that came to our cabin that night."

"But it must have been one of them," says Jakub. His eyes are red, entreating. "Lovejoy, McBride, Hunt…"

Amah covers her mouth with her fingers. Her eyes are wide as she watches him. She thinks again of how he's no longer her boy, her sweet boy, but a man, and what is a man not capable of? "What have you done, Jakub?"

His head hangs low so that his dark hair flops onto his forehead.

The mah-jong players stand from their table, chat to a group of men seated against the wall. They pull coats on and form a straggly procession to the door. Kung is the first through, says something to Chee, mimes the eating of soup.

Chee waves his hands, no, and the men go on their way. As they trudge through the front door, cold air blasts through the gap. Amah watches the closed door for half a minute before turning back to Jakub.

"What did you do, Jakub, when you found out about these men?"

"The first one I tracked was McBride. He was still in Liverpool. I hadn't been watching him for half a day before he rushed off and caught the stagecoach to London. I caught it too, and I tried the whole time to build up the courage to speak to him, to ask him of that time, but I couldn't." He stares between his knees at the floor. "He booked into an inn in Soho, but I lost him when he ran for an omnibus. That's when I went in search of Pidgeon. His whereabouts weren't too difficult to discover. I thought I might find something at his house that linked him to that voyage—to you—but just as I was jimmying his window open he arrived home. Scared the life out of me." A ghost of a smile plays at the corner of his mouth. "So I returned to Soho, waited for McBride to come back. The next thing I knew, I was watching him enter Heloise's house." His eyes swivel around to Amah. "And I thought that confirmed it." He holds his hands to his temples. "Why else would he be at Heloise's home, if not to visit you?"

Amah shuts her eyes. "I always knew Heloise befriending those men would lead to trouble." She opens her eyes again, letting out a loud sigh. "She met that Pidgeon first. I don't know where. At one of those ridiculous scientific lectures she sometimes attends. I think she liked that he had visited our part of the world—the East Indies. She's never ventured there, herself, but she's always been fascinated by it. Always pestering me for stories." Amah thinks of the first time she glanced through the peacock's tail into Heloise's drawing room and recognised Pidgeon's long face and Hunt's wiry figure, although his cleft chin was obscured by the grey whiskers he now sported. The shock had shuddered through

235

her body, ringing in her chest, her fingertips, her ears. Later, she'd berated Heloise for inviting them, but that girl always did whatever she wanted. And Amah couldn't bring herself to explain why the men had stirred such terrible memories.

Her mind returns to the evening when McBride visited Heloise's. "I saw you that night, standing on the corner," she says to Jakub. "I thought I was mistaken, and when I saw McBride... What did you do then, Jakub?" Her heartbeat quickens. She wills him to get to the point, tell her what he did. But she wants him to not tell her too.

"I waited. When McBride left, he was escorted to the door by another man. I heard him mention the name Lovejoy several times. Another name from that passenger list."

"And then?"

"I followed him back to the main road. He stopped in a coffee house for nearly an hour, writing something, and then returned to South Street—your house—but this time he just stood out the front by a street lamp."

"What was he doing?"

"Waiting for something."

"And you?"

"It was awkward. He was watching the house, I was watching him. And it was bloody freezing. So I loped off home. Spent the night in Limehouse."

She searches his face for signs of a lie. His face is relaxed though.

"And Lovejoy?" That little girl, cut throat. Lovejoy, the blood spilled on the ground. Sliced almost to the bone. The *kris*. Did he steal into Heloise's house and take the *kris*?

He shrugs. "Took me a few days to find out where they lived. I didn't realise that he and his daughter had been murdered." His hands drop to his lap, where they lie open.

"You saw Heloise?"

He looks up at her, surprised. "Yes. I did. That was a shock." His eyes search hers for a moment before dropping to his hands again. "That's when I really thought I was on the right track. That you two were still in touch with these men for some reason." His voice has become tight, his brow creased, he looks sad. "But what I really couldn't understand—can't understand—is why you got rid of me? Why didn't you keep me, like you kept Heloise? Now that I know Papa—Chee—isn't really my father, it makes so much sense. Why he always disapproves of everything I do, that I say, that I think, even. Why didn't you keep me in Liverpool with you? Why did you send me away with him? Is it because you couldn't stand to be reminded…"

"No, Jakub, no." This time Amah catches his left hand, presses it in hers. "No. You have it all wrong."

Her eyes follow the fine hair on the back of his hand, the calluses on his fingers. His nails are chewed to the quick, so that the flesh swells bulbous at the tips, and folded into the creases of his skin are fine lines of dirt. At any other time she would flick his ear, ask him if he was a monkey or some other animal and tell him to wash.

She clasps his hand once more, then takes her hand back, and laces her fingers together in her lap. Turning slightly away from him, she stares at the lit joss sticks, at their glowing, red tips.

She'll have to start at the beginning. She'll have to revisit that time on the *Dukano*. She tells him of Chee fetching her from her stepfather's house, of how she became Mrs Preston's maid on the boat. Of the English words Mrs Preston taught her, of the pretty finch she kept in a cage. Her voice falters over the riot in Sarawak, and she doesn't mention the night she was attacked at all. She pauses for a moment as two men return to the hostel, walk through to the back room, closing the door behind them.

"I was a stupid girl, Jakub. Just a stupid, young girl." Amah's voice is hushed. "I didn't recognise what was happening right in front of me. I didn't realise…"

"What?"

Amah thinks back to the damp sheets, Mrs Preston

writing in them, tearing the bedding from the mattress. "She was so sickly. So ill, for so long." The stench that came off her skin. Sweet, but not a pleasant sweet. More feral, like the smell of rotting fruit.

"What was she sick with?"

"They were all sick. Dysentery." Shit and vomit everywhere. In the corridors, soaked into the carpets, splattered on the porthole windows from men leaning over the side of the boat.

Everyone's guts bloated with their illness, ready to burst. And Mrs Preston, her small stomach bulging, even though she hadn't eaten or had anything to drink for days. A puzzlement to young Li Leen. "I was so stupid. I knew nothing."

"Nothing of what?"

Of the dark whelp that slipped from Mrs Preston's lower body, wet and shining and mewling.

"She was pregnant. My poor Mrs Preston was with child and I didn't know it."

They're both silent. Someone moves furniture across the wooden floors in the next room, voices are raised on the street.

"You're saying...?"

"I'm saying," Amah's voice is heavy, "I'm saying Mrs Preston was your mother."

"But..." Jakub lifts his hand, turns it over, gazes at his olive skin that is far darker than Heloise's. Heloise, with her twilight eyes, her golden skin. She'd always taken after her father.

"Chee is your father." She thinks of that morning when her Uncle Chee came into the cabin with a bucket, how he dropped it so water sloshed across the floor, his wide eyes when he spied the wriggling creature in Amah's arms.

Jakub's mouth remains open as he gapes at her. "Papa?" And then, "Mrs Preston?"

Amah nods. "Jane. She was a very special lady. I loved her very much."

"What happened? Where is she now?"

Amah's chest constricts. Mrs Preston's fingers were so cold, so weak, when she took hold of Amah's wrist and whispered in her ear. *Li Leen, my dear friend, you must keep him. Make sure he is safe. My family would never understand our love.* Her hot breath smelt of decay, weeping sores spotted the corners of her mouth. It was the only time Amah had ever seen her Uncle Chee weep, knelt by the bed, his head next to Mrs Preston's on the pillow.

Mrs Preston knew she was dying. Who could survive such a loss of blood, such a high fever?

"She only lived for one more day, Jakub. Luckily we were not far off Liverpool then. I pretended you were mine. Nobody really cared." Except for Luba, the head cook and barber from Africa, who kept them supplied with what little fresh water he had, some flour, a little treacle for the baby. "So, it was not me who deserted you, Jakub, it was your father who wanted you back. As soon as he was married to Miriam, and knew he could look after you, he came and took you from my care." Amah remembers the day, a bright day, the sky almost white it was so blinding. She knows it was just one occasion of many that helped form the fibrous scar tissue over her heart.

She stares down at the photograph again, at the baby's little coffee-bean eyes that are so like his father's. Has he never noticed this?

"Come back to your papa's house, Jakub, and we will tell you all. They have been missing you." She touches his wrist. "We can eat some of your mother's dumplings."

CHAPTER 32

The rest of that evening is very bleak indeed. Having returned the kind young man's overcoat with Hatch, I shiver
the whole way home in a cab. When I arrive, only one lamp's
alight in the front hallway. Before taking himself off to bed,
Bundle must have assumed I'd be away all night. It's an
occurrence that happens often enough, after all.

I stare up the stairs for a good minute before I can drag
myself to my bedroom. Everything feels cold: my feet, the
silk of my dress, the banister as my fingers brush its surface.
I hold my palm to the tip of my nose. Icy. Pausing halfway
up the staircase, my eyes take in the rosy carpet, but really, I
see the claret stain again, smeared across the throat I had run
my tongue along not five hours ago.

Luckily, when I reach my room, embers still glimmer
in the grate, so I throw more wood on top, stoke the
fire. Looking down, I can now see clearly the patches of
mud—and worse—caked into the skirts of my gown, and a
crimson blotch lines the rim of my hem. I tug at the buttons,
loosen the stays, until the gown falls to the floor, closely
followed by my petticoats and undergarments. Shrugging
on my dressing gown, I stare into the flames and think of
Cosgrove's hand, drooped over the side of the stretcher,
pale, bare…

"Heloise, you are home late." Amah stands in the doorway.
She has a woollen shawl thrown about her shoulders and her
hair is tied in a plait. In one hand she holds an ivory bonnet,

and in the other, the silk thread and needle with which she is embroidering it.

I nod, plonking myself down into the armchair. "Why are you still awake?"

Amah walks into my room. "I got home late. I visited Uncle Chee's. Jakub was there."

"He's back? So maybe that was him I saw the other day." My brain is so muddled with weariness, shock, grief, it takes me a moment to realise the meaning of this. "But why would he be in Stoke Newington? Near the Lovejoys'?"

Amah stares down at me for a few moments, then pulls the dressing table chair close by me. She settles into it, her back straight. "It was him. I was very afraid," she says, "very afraid he was involved in your business, but I have found out what was going on. He was only…" she thinks for a moment, "sulking. We have talked now."

"Tell me, Mama." My head feels so heavy I rest it against the armchair, the pressure of it reminding me of the bruise at the back of my head. Shifting my head so it's in a more comfortable position, I peer at Amah through half-closed eyes.

She doesn't speak straight away. She rubs her face with the flats of her hands, up and down. "I'm so tired." Picking up the embroidery again from her lap, she pulls the thread taut, ready to sew. "That boy. He's been avoiding me. Us. I thought—I really dreaded—that he was behind the violence against those men."

"Who? You don't mean McBride? Pidgeon?"

Amah nods, then shakes her head. "All that talk of a Chinese man wanting revenge, threatening them all."

"But why would Jakub care about these men?" How silly of her to jump to that conclusion. There are plenty of other Chinese men who could be responsible. "And in any case, if you were with Jakub this evening," I glance at the gilt clock on the mantelpiece. It's almost 1.25 a.m., "it could not have been him."

"Why do you say this?"

"Because Cosgrove was murdered tonight. The same as the others." My hand reaches for my throat and my stomach clenches tight. I will miss him. I will miss the excitement that trembled in my belly whenever I encountered him, thought of him. Such a beautiful man. Wasted. But I can't let my feelings overcome me in front of Amah. She wouldn't understand. Worse, she'll think I'm being ridiculous.

I swallow, glance at Amah. "And we now think that the culprit might be an Indian fellow. Someone who wears a turban. You know these Londoners, they think all us brown foreigners are much the same." My eyes are dry and scratchy, and sadness scorches my chest. I know it's Cosgrove's death that upsets me, but I take my shortened temper out on Amah. "You didn't answer me. What interest does Jakub have in these men anyway?"

Amah adds a few stitches, then rests the bonnet back into her lap. "You know I told you once that I thought I recognised that man Pidgeon?"

"Mmm. From your voyage here? But that was years ago."

"That's correct. Well that Lovejoy, and McBride too, were on the ship."

"No!"

"Yes, they joined us in Sarawak. A whole party of Englishmen set sail with us, fleeing Kuching."

My eyes widen and I sit up again. "I heard them talking of some riot. Was it after that?"

"Yes." Amah's eyes fall to her embroidery.

"What about Cosgrove? Hunt? Were they there too?"

An irritated frown creases her forehead. "I don't know, Heloise. I was very young then. Hadn't seen many white men. They all looked the same to me. Tall, the colour of a knob of garlic, hairy faces." She runs her thumb across the silk thread that forms the petal of a chrysanthemum. "But I know many of them died in Kuching. I saw it with my own eyes. The local overseer, his wife, some miners, the doctor.

242

Mr Preston. Mrs Preston told me it was caused by the local *kungsi* fighting the Englishmen over an antimony mine, but Uncle Chee always said it was over a woman."

"Why is Jakub interested in that time?"

Amah's shoulders lift a little, tense. "You might as well know. You will hear it from your Aunt Miriam soon enough. That woman, she's worse than the local newspaper. Limehouse Bugle I used to call her."

"I remember," I say, my voice dry. I've never understood her dislike for Aunt Miriam but, pressed upon it, she always denies it. "What is it she might tell?"

My mother has never spoken much of her journey here, except to say that she was a maid to a British woman, Mrs Preston. She now tells me that Jakub suspected Uncle Chee wasn't his father, that one of these British men were.

"Who did he think was his mother then?" I ask.

Her lip lifts as she meets my eye. "Me."

"But why on earth would he think that?"

A log dislodges in the fireplace, falls to the side with a crack. She hands me her embroidery and then lifts out the poker and prods the log back into place. Settling into her seat again, she says, slowly, "He knew that something terrible happened on that voyage. Uncle Chee had told him—I think to stress to the boy that there might not always be justice at hand for people like us on these long passages."

I can see she's not telling me something. She's choosing her words too carefully. "What happened?"

Her mouth twists to the side as she contemplates me. "A man tried to violate me. One night in our cabin."

I put my hand over my mouth. "Oh no." Oh God, and I remember that night long ago. That carriage. Not my mother too? "But he didn't..."

"No." She shakes her head. I think I see a flash of something—fright? apprehension?—in her face. "He attacked me in Mrs Preston's cabin. She was too far gone with fever to hear."

"But you managed to get away?"

And then there's that familiar look in her eye — the unblinking disdain of a black cat, a warning twitch of its tail. She nods.

"Who was he? You must've found out who he was?"

She shakes her head. "No, it was too dark to see beyond a shadow. And we had much more important things on our mind after that. The next morning is when poor Mrs Preston had her baby. When our Jakub first entered this world."

Amah is sure it won't be too difficult to find sleep tonight. She's found Jakub. They have sorted out their misunderstandings. Foolish boy.

Even the reminder of that evening on the *Dukano*, when that scoundrel tried to take what wasn't his to steal, doesn't speed her heart, can't force her heavy eyelids open.

In fact, her lips lift in a smile when she thinks of how that meeting came to an end. Of how her reaching fingers found the handle of her paring knife, how it made a clinking sound against the china plate as she drew it forward. One of his hands held Amah down, pressed against her throat, but his other hand was what…? Untying his cravat? Raised to strike her? All Amah knows is it was at that moment she managed to stab him. She meant to thrust the blade into his chest, but it went straight through the palm of his hand. He reared back, bellowing like a slaughtered ox. Devil. She's never been troubled by the likes of him again.

Amah hears a slight bump below, in Heloise's rooms, and realises that her daughter is still awake, pondering the death of those men. Heloise has never learnt to walk away, to not involve herself. Always has to be part of an adventure. Isn't that how she first came to work in the alley, setting up skittles at only ten years old; how she was tricked away from Amah by that cherry-lipped vixen from the tavern?

When Amah thinks of Heloise, it feels like a snake awakens in her chest, uncoils itself, raises its coffin-shaped head. There are months, years even, of her daughter's life that Amah knows nothing of. Even if Heloise has learnt to protect herself, Amah's afraid that fate's greedy fingers still seek her out, will catch her one day.

CHAPTER 33

"Amah," I say, pushing open her bedroom door.

The room is quite dark, apart from a gentle glow from the grate. I pull the curtains apart. It's so overcast, it's almost as if the sun hasn't yet risen, despite it being past the hour Amah usually wakes. It's a very rare occurrence, indeed, that I am up before her.

She lies on her side, nestled into her bedcovers, the blanket pulled up over her ear so that only a narrow strip of her face is apparent. One dark eye blinks at me, and she yanks the covers over her nose. She mumbles something I don't catch, as I light the lamp next to her bed.

"What did you say?"

She flings her arm out and rolls onto her back. "Why are you up so early?" she says. Her eyes scan my gown. "Why are you dressed already?"

"It doesn't matter. I have things to do." I've already had two cups of coffee, but I know it's not just the brew that's left me feeling skittish. In the dead hours before dawn, a jumble of nightmares and tangled images seem to have fermented my blood, so that I can feel it rushing in my fingertips, sparking in my mind. "But first, I can't find my damned atlas. Tell me, do you know where Mandalay is?"

Amah rises onto her elbow, frowns up at me. "Burma. But why…"

"Just as I thought. Thank you, Amah," I say, as I leave her room.

At the bottom of the stairs, Bundle helps me into my overcoat.

As I tuck a hat made of sable with silk sashes onto my head, Bundle says, "Taff has the carriage ready outside, Mrs Chancey, waiting your convenience."

I gaze into the mirror of the hallstand. The soft fur tickles the tips of my ears, and although the bonnet frames my face nicely, I can see the bruising under my eyes from lack of sleep. I don't look my best. How could I? Snatching up the matching sable muff, I hurry outside.

First, Taff waits for only a matter of minutes in Holborn as I have a word with Cosgrove's man, Meadowes. Then we make our way to Vine Street. I tell Taff I might be some time, so he jumps down from his box to lead the horses up the road.

A constable leaves me in the same small room from the last time I sought out the Detective Inspector, but it's not long before Hatch joins me.

"Mrs Chancey?"

I stand so fast the chair teeters behind me. "Detective Inspector, do you think I might look at Cosgrove's body?"

Hatch's sandy eyelashes positively flutter with surprise. "You want to see his body?"

I nod. "I think there might be a clue to the killer."

He stares at me. Maybe he's shocked at how unladylike I am, or worried I might faint. He might be offended that I think I can be of assistance. A uniformed policeman passes the open doorway, and one door, then another, slams shut down the corridor. Finally, he blinks, says, "Right you are. Follow me."

I am close on his heels as he makes his way out through the front door and turns to his left. Three doors down, he crosses the road, his arms out to bar oncoming traffic so that I can pass with him, until we reach a low-set building.

"In here, please," he says, bowing me in before him. "You might need your handkerchief to mask the smell."

As soon as the words leave his mouth, a bloody awful odour slams my nostrils. I bury my nose into my muff.

My eyes water, the stench so sharp, so thick, I'm surprised the air before me is clear, not a soupy miasma of filth and poison.

"What is this place?" I ask, wisps of fur catching in my mouth.

"The closest thing we have to a morgue. Be thankful it's winter."

He leads me down a short hallway. We pass three doors, and I can't be sure if I'm just imagining that the closed doors bulge slightly against the weight of gaseous pressure from within. I choke against the fur of my muff.

In the end room, a body is laid out upon a bench, a white shroud across its length. On a table close by, ensconced in liquid like a pickled cucumber, is his head, his longish, dark hair floating like seaweed. I grimace, but I don't back out. Either the sickening smell has faded in this room, or I have become somewhat accustomed, although an underlying scent of raw meat makes my stomach heave. I lower my muff.

Gazing down at the shroud, I ask Hatch to remove it.

Below the jagged flesh at his throat-line, which I take pains to not stare at, the corpse is still attired in shirt and trousers. The lapis lazuli pin is fastened to the filthy collar.

My hand hovers over it as I look up at Hatch. "May I?"

His eyes are bulging, but he nods.

I draw out the pin, slowly, and attach it to my bodice. Then I part the top of his shirt. The flesh of his chest, marble-white, is covered in a robust mat of brown hair. So it's true. I am right.

My eyes find his lifeless fingers. I inspect the neat blue fingertips, stiff now, and note the unblemished skin on the back of his hand. Taking in his other hand, I see that it's much the same, apart from a torn fingernail. I step back from the table. Each time my suspicions are confirmed, it's like a heavy stone is wedged into the pit of my stomach.

I glance up at the head in the jar. Its face is turned away from me, but I've seen enough.

"This isn't Cosgrove."

CHAPTER 34

I expect Hatch to exclaim, to baulk in surprise, but he just nods slowly, frowning. "How do you know?"

I gesture towards the corpse's hands. "Cosgrove has scars on his left wrist, and a knife wound," I point at the unblemished right hand, use my fingernail to indicate where a slice an inch long should be, "on the inside of his palm, and the outside, from the time a pirate drove his knife through." I don't feel the need to mention the smooth, almost hairless skin of Cosgrove's chest. My fingertips find the pin, now attached to my bodice. "This stone, it confused me for a little while. That, and the shock. But eventually last night I remembered his hand," I nodded towards the body, "when it dropped from the side of the stretcher. It was pale and unblemished." Looking up at Hatch, I ask, frowning, "But you are not surprised? You knew it wasn't Cosgrove?"

Hatch ushers me from the room, doesn't speak until we've escaped the stink of the corridor and are standing back out on the side of the road. Taff is still walking the horses, turning them at the next junction.

"I did wonder," he says. "Amongst Pidgeon's papers we found an interesting letter from McBride. Written the night that he died."

"What did it say?"

"That he knew who the rascal was who set up the riot in Sarawak."

"Who? Not Cosgrove?" With each revelation, the heavy

sensation of stones in my gut stretches, gathers weight. How had I been so hoodwinked by this man?

Hatch nods. "In his letter to Pidgeon, McBride wrote that he was related to a couple called the Crookshanks, who were stationed out there. They both died in that riot. When McBride returned five years later, he found their diaries, had a word with the servant who was with them at the time. According to the servant, the whole thing was set up to look like a riot over a mine of some sort, but really, a young man—who he said was named Morris," Hatch spells the name for me, "organised it to cover up his affair with Mrs Crookshank, and the murder of Mr Crookshank. McBride wrote that at the time he'd completely forgotten about Cosgrove—his presence in Kuching, and how he joined them at the last moment on the ship to travel home—until he saw him at your soiree. Apparently, Cosgrove, *Maurice* Cosgrove, was very young then, not really a part of their group."

The leaves of a young ash tree rustle above us and two sparrows hop across its branches. I take a deep breath in, wonder at how blank my mind feels.

"Why pretend to be dead? Why murder..." I wave my hand in the direction of the makeshift morgue.

"Perhaps he knew it was only a matter of time before we caught up with him. He shut McBride up on impulse with the *kris* from your house and then had to continue with this revengeful Chinese gang subterfuge. And Pidgeon was troubled, obviously, maybe confused as to whether a Chinese man was the culprit or if it could really be his friend Cosgrove. Although he was hesitant to come to us, he did reach out to you and Sir Thomas. Unfortunately, Cosgrove must've clocked his suspicions. And who knows? McBride might have written to Hunt too, but the post missed him before he went to Belgium. In fact, I sent a constable around this morning to check all Hunt's mail."

"This morning I spoke with Cosgrove's servant," I say. "He knew nothing about the note Cosgrove received last night. I think Cosgrove must've written it himself, to lure me to his special denouement. He wanted a witness who would swear the body in the cesspool was his. All Meadowes—Cosgrove's man—knew, was that Cosgrove sent him out with a message for someone else. A man named Thatcher. Cosgrove instructed him to hand it to him personally." I look behind me at the morgue. I think of Thatcher—Cosgrove, Webb and Milly's "friend"—who always leered at me with his wet lips. He was a gross creature, but damn, he didn't deserve to be lying in that pestilent hell. I shudder, clench my fingers together deep in my muff. "The message must have lured Thatcher to the East End."

Hatch turns on his heel and moves back towards the police station. We leap over a pile of horse manure to gain the road, and he says, "Cosgrove must've known it'd only be a matter of time before that man's head would be found and cleaned, identified by someone. So what's he up to?"

That's exactly what Cosgrove needed, I realise. Time. Just enough to make his next move.

"I think I might know."

The police buggy pulls into the kerb of Derby Street before us. As I hop from my carriage, Hatch steps from the buggy. In front of Pidgeon's house is a large travelling coach, and Isobel stands on her front step, directing the driver where to deposit two hatboxes.

"Where are you going, Isobel?" I ask, striding towards her.

Two footmen, wearing bottle-green aprons and long cuff shields over their sleeves, struggle down the steps under the weight of a large trunk.

Fright widens her pretty eyes. "I'm going away. The stress…"

Hatch steps close, sends several constables into the house.

"But what are you doing?" Isobel asks, her gaze following the policemen.

"We have reason to believe that a certain Maurice Cosgrove

252

might be upon the premises," says Hatch, his voice heavy. He starts up the front steps to follow his men.

Isobel's eyes fly to her coach. I look too, just in time to see one of the footmen climb into it, leaving his partner to heave the trunk alone. Picking up my skirts, I run to the coach and, just as I reach it, the valet leans out the coach's doorway, shouts up to the driver, "Leave now, Sharpe! There's an extra twenty guineas in it for you!"

Cosgrove. He's in servant's dress and his hair has been darkened to the colour of boot polish, but I can see it's him. How could I not recognise those blue eyes?

I grab onto the door handle and holler for Hatch, but before I can think, Cosgrove swings out, hauls me into the coach just as it careers out from the side of the road. I push and kick at him, but only manage to get tangled in my damned petticoats as the coach lurches at top speed down the street. Finally, he pushes me into the seat next to him.

"What are you doing here, Heloise?"

"We know everything, Cosgrove."

He rests back in the seat next to me, his body swaying as the coach's wheels grind over uneven ground. "Ah. You think I murdered him? You have it all wrong. I fear for my life. That murdering Chinaman has me in his sights for his next kill. I'm trying to escape, incognito." His handsome face softens. "It was a terrible thing that he mistook that poor man for me. As soon as I knew it was a trap, I fled." He smiles, rueful. "I called for you, but when I received no answer, I figured you'd run off too."

"You're taking Isobel?"

"Well, it's become impossible to retrieve what funds I have, and she has just inherited a tidy sum, after all. She's always had a soft spot for me. Knew her in Mandalay, many years ago, you know. Young thing she was then."

For a moment, I wonder if I should go along with his story, pretend I believe it. Maybe a part of me wants to believe it? But no. I can already feel scorn harden my face. He sees it too, and as he makes a move for me, I hold myself steady against the seat and rake my fingernails down his cheek. He slaps my hand away and lifts a dagger between us.

My eyes are trained on the knife's edge as he pulls me against his chest so that I face away from him. The coach heaves to a stop. I feel the dagger's cold blade against my cheek. By the time the coach pitches forward again, one of Cosgrove's arms holds mine pinned to my sides, the other holding the dagger close to my neck.

"It's a pity you saw through my latest disguise," he says, the tip of his dagger digging into my high collar so that I can feel the prickle of the collar's lace against my skin. "Made a change from being the Indian suspect. Nothing easier than donning a turban, like I did last night. Just wind a scarf around the head and it's done." The coach hurtles left around a corner and the weight of his body slams me against the side of the carriage.

My voice is constricted as I say, "We know about Sarawak, about McBride and the Crookshanks. But why kill Lovejoy? And poor Pidgeon?" I struggle to twist towards him, so he can see the anger in my eyes. I can smell him—his familiar scent, of forest and something musky, and a momentary pinch of regret squeezes my heart.

His grip on my arms tightens. "Had to keep the pattern going, didn't I? The vengeful letters, the *kungsi* murders. I left your *kris* behind when I murdered Lovejoy in the hope the murders would be linked to their ridiculously sinister Chinaman, but I couldn't account for the nightsoil man filching it."

Shouts are heard over the loud rumbling of the coach. Slowly, the coach eases to a stop and, out my window, I can see Hatch's buggy pull in a few metres away.

"Maurice, you have nowhere to go," I say through clenched teeth, straining away from the blade.

"You blasted woman," he breathes, hot against my ear. "Why couldn't you just let things be?"

Hatch runs towards the coach but sees me through the window, sees the blade held to my throat. He halts, flings his arms out, blocking the other policeman from approaching.

"How'd you find out so quickly it wasn't me on the slab?" Cosgrove asks. He taps the glass of the window with the pointed end of the dagger, to ward off Hatch and his men, then returns it quickly to my neck. "I thought the blue pin would trick you. I knew you wouldn't study the severed head. I had the idea that night at the theatre, when you said everyone would recognise you once you donned the red riding cloak. I made sure you knew me from that damned blue pin."

The pin with the lapis lazuli stone. Attached to my bodice. I wriggle against him. His left hand has the dagger firmly pressed to my throat, but his other hand only manages to clasp my right arm tight, leaving my left arm loose. I'm able to bend my left arm at the elbow, slide the pin out from my bodice and hold it firmly between my finger and thumb. I think of jabbing it into his arm but that might not be enough to stop him from sinking the blade into me, so I swing the pin upwards, stab towards his face, feel the sharp end break skin, and then the long, thin shaft slide right through to the hilt.

Cosgrove's scream is high-pitched, sickening, as the dagger clatters to the floor. I wrench open the coach door and, looking over my shoulder, I see Cosgrove clutching his hands over his left eye, as a thin trickle of blood slips down the side of his cheek like a tear.

CHAPTER 35

By the light of an oil lamp, I peer into the mirror, my fingers picking at the lace of my collar where there is a rent in the fabric. Stroking the unscathed skin of my neck beneath it, I think of how much tougher the cotton lace is compared to my smooth flesh; of how lucky I am that the dagger hadn't pressed any closer.

Cosgrove must've become very well-practised at be-heading, after taking so many lives. I imagine his left hand creeping up the back of my neck, his strong fingers running through my hair—for a moment my mind grapples with the pleasures this once evoked—he would've grabbed hold of a large clump of my hair in order to steady my head, as his other hand swept the knife's edge across the front of my throat.

No. No. He would've had to unhand me first to do that. Surely in those precious seconds I would've managed to pull away, defend myself? I close my eyes, concentrate on the blank canvas, blood-red, of my closed eyelids, until the gruesome pictures subside.

"Heloise, what are you doing?"

Amah stands behind me in my drawing room, holding a tray of tea things. As her eyes travel across my face, I feel weary, I feel what she can see.

"You need to eat and drink something," she says, placing the tray on the table. She crosses the room to close the curtains against the darkening sky. "And I don't mean whisky."

I glance down at the crystal tumbler in my hand. I'd

poured it for myself as soon as I entered the room, but, in truth, I don't have the stomach for it. I place it on the shelf of the china cabinet and pick up the pile of post awaiting me.

"Sit, sit," she urges, taking a seat herself on one of the armchairs. Leaning forward to pour tea, she asks, "You don't have guests tonight?"

Dismay fills my chest. "But what day is it?"

"Wednesday."

I stare down into the teacup she passes me, watching the lazy swirl from where she's stirred honey into the milky tea. "I don't think so. I remember there's a masked ball on Thursday, but…"

"What about Hatterleigh?"

I lean back into the sofa, resting the teacup and saucer in my lap. Hatterleigh. I'm not even sure if he's back in town or not. There might be a missive amongst the post before me on the table, but I haven't had the time or desire to check. He'll want to know all the news, about Pidgeon, and Cosgrove. Usually, I take glee in relating my adventures to him, but in this instance, I won't. How do I account for Cosgrove with a straight face? Do I act shocked? Like I'm telling him nothing worse than a ghoulish tale? Or no, maybe better to act like I always knew Cosgrove was up to no good. *Surely you noticed how reserved I was around the man, Hatterleigh?*

"Heloise, what is it? Where were you all day?"

"Hatch and I found out who has been murdering all these men."

"The Indian?"

A scornful "Ha" escapes my lips. "No. And not a China-man either. It was none other than Cosgrove, one of the gentlemen of their own set." I tell her of how Hatch had tracked down the incriminating letters from McBride and that latest body wasn't Cosgrove, as we were meant to believe.

She doesn't ask me how I know this, only blinks slowly. "Why was he at Isobel's? I always told you that girl couldn't be trusted."

"Oh, Mama," I say, taking a sip of my tea. "The poor creature had no idea what he'd been up to. That's why I am so late today. I had to accompany her to the police station while she was questioned by Hatch. She thought she was helping Cosgrove escape from the monster. She didn't realise he was the monster; hadn't yet heard he was meant to have been the latest victim. They knew each other in Mandalay when she was young. She had tender feelings for him, I'm afraid." Poor Isobel. Feverish circles on her pale cheeks, nose and eyes almost raw with weeping. She's lost two men she loved in a matter of days.

"Is that why you asked me about Mandalay? And Burma?" Amah asks.

I nod. "I'd heard Cosgrove talk of Burma, and the last time I saw Isobel she mentioned a curry she learnt to make in Mandalay. Cosgrove was great friends with the Pidgeons," my lips compress into a bitter line for a second, "so I thought that maybe they spent time together there. I wondered if he might find shelter with her."

"What did the letter say, that Hatch found?"

"That Cosgrove had arranged the riot to cover up his affair with a married woman, or to finish off her husband."

Amah nods. "So, Uncle Chee was correct. It was all over a woman."

Cosgrove and women. I feel like I should've known. But, of course, I did have an inkling all along; I just chose to ignore it. Didn't I wonder if Milly was his lover? Didn't I fall for him myself? And I consider myself very well-seasoned in such things.

A veritable Casanova, Cosgrove. But ruthless. The dead wife in Sarawak. Prepared to take advantage of sweet Isobel. And that crack he gave me over the head in the alleyway, near the cesspool. Looking back, he must've used his gun to knock me out. My stomach sinks. Fortunate he needed a witness, that he didn't press it to my temple, then and there, finish me off.

Looking up, I find Amah staring at me. "You are troubled?" she says.

I shake my head, more to dispel my horrid thoughts than anything. Amah pours herself some more tea, black, with a squeeze of lemon in it. My tongue puckers at the thought.

"And you, Amah?" I say, reaching for a piece of Madeira cake. "What have you been up to lately, in and out at all hours, I hear." It's only now that I recall her story of Jakub being Mrs Preston's son. Like him, I'd always thought dear Aunt Miriam was his mother. "Chasing after Jakub, I think you said. I cannot believe the cheek of Uncle Chee." I grin, licking powdered sugar from my bottom lip. "Dossing down with the boss's wife."

Amah's lip twists, reprovingly. "He loved her very much, Heloise. We both did."

I pull a face. "Still rather brave, if you ask me." Resting my head back, I close my eyes. "I think we should take some time away, Amah." I open one eye, peep at her. "Maybe Venice? I've noticed the picture book you borrowed from the library." With portraits of canals, grand churches, decaying courtyards. "By the time we are organised, the weather might be more clement there, too, for you. Thaw your bones," I grin. "You can get your sea legs back again on the steamship over."

Her cacao-bean eyes gleam back at me. She doesn't say anything, but I know she's pleased, by her short nod.

I will have a glass of something, after all. Not the whisky; something sweeter. I pour myself a generous portion of sherry, which I sip as I tear open the first letter on the pile.

Hatterleigh.

Dearest Heloise,
I will be back in London by the 3rd. I'm having a devilish time getting away from my estate. Work work work. Kennard, my foreman you know, will not let me alone. If it's not roofs that need thatching, it's harvests that need collecting. He

seems to think he needs my nay or say in everything he does, despite my assurances to him that he is much better suited to making those decisions than I am. I know I must be thankful, though, that he's not a thieving rascal.

It's so horribly cold at the moment, I really think you and I should escape to France for a few weeks when I return. The champagne we can sip! The love we can make! The gougère to grease our lips! I have heard of a wonderful chateau we can stay at in the Loire Valley. And, of course, I know you love the theatre life in Paris. Remember those girls, you minx, in Haymarket, flashing their fannies? Maybe you could learn some of their ways? I am laughing here, my dear. You are far more alluring than they, even covered in yards of silk. What do you say? I say yes! Cherie, mon amour, mon coeur, please say yes too.

Yours

Hatterleigh.

I fold his letter into two, then over again. I glance at Amah, who has thrown my shawl across her knees and calmly embroiders a bird of paradise with yellow silk. Folding the letter once more, my mind races. Paris with Hatterleigh, or Venice with my mother? The tug of loyalty, of obligation, between these two people spirals through my mind. Picture galleries with Amah. Paris nightlife with Hatterleigh. Love, or riches? Contentment, or pleasure?

Or both?

Surely I can manage both. A merry foray into Paris on our way to restful Venice.

Smiling, I toss the letter into the fire.

ACKNOWLEDGEMENTS

Thank you, again, to Legend Press and Pantera Press, for your continued faith in my Heloise novels. Special thanks to Lauren Parsons, for her careful, thoughtful editing of my work. Works by Lee Jackson, Liza Picard and numerous others are integral to the research that goes into my Heloise novels, and some might recognise references to George R. Sims' *Living London* (1900).

I would like to thank the Queensland Writers Centre, Sisters in Crime (Aus) and Byron Writers Festival for their ongoing support. Thank you to all those who have helped me shape this book, especially Emma Doolan, Laura Elvery, Kathy George, Vivienne Muller, Fiona Kearney and Andrea Baldwin. Thank you to both Emma and my mum, Margaret Boland, for being the usual suspects (guinea pigs) to read my first drafts. Finally, I am forever grateful for all those who love and encourage me in all my endeavours, especially Jim Riwoe, Mum, Elis, Tina, Liam, Amy, Damien, Dave, Bianca, Jett and Mae.

We hope you enjoyed *A Necessary Murder* as much as we did here at Legend Press. If you want to read more about Heloise Chancey, here's an excerpt from the first novel in the series, *She Be Damned*.

I'm surprised to find two men in my drawing room. Sir Thomas Avery I know well. He is a man of maybe forty-five years, a little shorter than me, with thick, frizzled mutton chop sideburns. He steps forward and takes my hand in greeting. He then introduces the stranger standing by one of the windows which overlooks the street below.

"This is Mr Priestly," he says.

The other man doesn't approach me but bows his head. "Pleased to meet you, Mrs Chancey," he says.

His lips widen a little, but he makes no real effort to smile. A thin frame and large ears preclude Mr Priestly from being a handsome man, but he is well, if soberly, dressed and gentlemanly. His eyes flick over my figure and then, with more leisure, he looks around my drawing room.

His gaze follows the pattern of the Oriental rug, the scrollwork on the mahogany side board and the richly damasked sofas with intricately worked legs. He takes in the assortment of Chinese blue and white vases in the dark cabinets and the jade figurines on the mantelpiece. Finally his gaze rests on the large mural that adorns the furthest wall. A painting of a peacock, sat on a sparse tree branch, fills the space. The peacock, a fusion of azure, green and gold leaf with a regal crown of feathers, displays its resplendent train so that the golden eyes of its plumage can be admired. It might be a trick of the light and artistry, but the peacock's tail feathers seem to quiver.

"How very... exotic," he says.

He moves towards the fireplace and studies the painting in

the gilded frame above it. The portrait is of a young woman dressed in Javanese costume. Her hair is pulled into a low bun, silver earrings decorate her lobes, and she holds a white flower behind her back. Richly decorated batik is wrapped around her breasts, and a tight sarong swathes her lower body.

"Is that you?" he asks me, surprise in his voice.

"Yes." I stand by him and look up at the portrait. "My friend Charles Cunningham lent me the fabric for the sitting. His father brought the lengths of silk and batik back from Java, after one of his assignments with Raffles. Such beautiful, earthy colours, aren't they?"

Mr Priestly steps a few feet away from me. "I'm afraid I don't follow this fashion for aping savages."

I feel a prick of resentment at the insult to my drawing room and portrait – the insult to me. But I learnt long ago to hold my temper in check, I have learnt to behave with decorum, for I no longer work in a Liverpool back-alley. Smiling sweetly as I lower myself and my wide skirts carefully onto the sofa, I say, "Oh, don't feel bad. Not everyone can be *a la mode*, can they?"

Sir Thomas clears his throat loudly. "Maybe we should discuss the purpose of our visit, Mrs Chancey."

"Yes, let's," I answer, patting the sofa cushion next to mine. "Please have a seat."

Sir Thomas sits down and looks at Mr Priestly expectantly. However, rather than speak himself, Mr Priestly gestures for Sir Thomas to proceed.

"Well, Mrs Chancey," says Sir Thomas. "I have come to ask you to do a spot of work for us again."

"Wonderful. Who will I need to be this time?"

Sir Thomas smiles. "Certainly your prior experience as a stage actress has benefitted us, Mrs Chancey. And it is true. We do need you to do some covert investigating for us."

One of Sir Thomas' many businesses includes a private detective agency. Although he has a surfeit of male detectives, he has found it very difficult to find females willing or able to sleuth. Having both the willingness and ability, I've worked on and off for Sir Thomas over the last eighteen months. I've posed as a sewing woman to gain access to a noble house, I've rouged and revealed myself as a street prostitute in order to spy on a group of young men and I have even performed as a harem dancer in order to reconnoitre at a foreign embassy.

Sir Thomas clears his throat again. "Yes. Well, maybe the task we ask of you this time will not be so enjoyable, I'm afraid."

He glances at Mr Priestly, who nods him on.

"As you know, we are investigating the deaths of several women in the Waterloo area."

"How did they die?" I ask.

Sir Thomas waves his hand. He won't go on.

Mr Priestly stares hard at me for a few moments. "Sir Thomas assures me I can broach any subject with you, Mrs Chancey."

"Of course," I smile. He means because I'm a whore, of course, but I won't let him think his sting has broken skin.

He turns and gazes out the window as he speaks. "It seems that each of these women – well, really, they were prostitutes – had terminated a pregnancy and died soon after from blood loss and infection."

"Well, unfortunately that happens far too frequently."

"That is so, but luckily the body of the last prostitute who died in this manner was taken to the hospital to be used as a specimen, and they found that…" He glances over at me, his eyes appraising.

"What?" I ask.

"They found parts of her body missing."

"What parts?"

"Her uterus was gone, but so were her other… feminine parts."

Revulsion curls through my body and I feel the pulse of an old wound between my legs. I glance at Sir Thomas whose eyes fall away from mine.

"What makes you think her death is connected to the other deaths in Waterloo?"

"It was the fourth body they had received in this condition in the last seven weeks."

"What? And was it not reported to the police?" My voice rises in disbelief.

Mr Priestly shrugs. "Well, they were only prostitutes, after all. At first the hospital staff thought they were the victims of amateur hysterectomies, but when they found that each of the women was also missing…"

"Missing…?" I shake my head a little, hoping I'm not about to hear what I think is coming, although a part of me, tucked away beneath the horror, wonders how he'll describe it.

Mr Priestly straightens his collar. "Apparently all their sexual organs were missing. Inside and out. I am positive you know to what I am referring, Mrs Chancey."

I can't help but press my knees together. I nod.

"Accordingly, it became apparent that there was a pattern to these deaths," he continues.

"And what do the police think now?"

"Obviously someone in the area is butchering these unfortunate women, whether accidentally or in spite is uncertain. However – and it's not surprising – the police don't want to waste too much time investigating the deaths of prostitutes when the rights of decent, law-abiding Londoners need to be protected."

Indignation sharpens my thoughts, but I command my body to relax. After all, what else is to be expected? If I'm to mix in polite society I need to mimic their ways. I force a languid smile to my face, eyes narrowed, as I watch Mr Priestly. "So, what on earth do you want to look into these deaths for? If the police are not interested, why should we be?"

"A friend of mine heard of these cases and has become immensely interested. It is on behalf of my friend that I have engaged Sir Thomas' services."

"And why has your friend become so interested?"

Mr Priestly takes his time seating himself in an armchair,

crossing one leg over the other. He scrutinises my face for a few moments before answering. "My friend has a special concern. It is for this reason we ask for your assistance."

"What is this special concern?"

"My friend is a respectable gentleman, well known to his peers. A short time ago he found out that his daughter was in an unhappy condition. She is not married." Mr Priestly pauses to let the awful truth of his statement sink in.

"Ah, I see. And what did he do?" I ask.

Mr Priestly frowns. "Naturally he disowned her. He allowed her to pack some of her belongings and had her taken to a convent near Shropshire."

"Naturally," I repeat, my voice dry.

"Yes, but she did not make it to Shropshire. She bribed the coachman to take her to a hotel in Charing Cross, and from there she has disappeared."

"Do you know why she wanted to be left at that hotel?"

"Apparently her... the other party... was staying there. He is a Frenchman." He nods, as if this fact alone throws light on the cause of her predicament.

"But nobody knows where she is now?"

Sir Thomas takes up the thread of the story. "At first Mr Priestly required my men to look into her activities at the hotel, but upon questioning Monsieur Baudin, we learnt she had left his care most swiftly."

"I suppose he did not want her now she was in trouble?"

"Something like that, it would seem. Since then he seems to have flown the coop," says Sir Thomas. "My detectives have since found out that the young lady took a cab to Waterloo where she spent a little over three weeks in a boarding house before moving into another well-known establishment nearby."

"What establishment?"

Mr Priestly purses his lips for a moment. "A house of ill-repute, it would seem. She moved to an abode owned by one Madame Silvestre."

"Ah yes, I'm aware of her services," I reply, thinking of how it's been many years since I have had the pleasure of the old cat's acquaintance. "Do you need me to fetch her?"

"If only it were that easy. It seems she has since disappeared. Nobody knows where she has gone."

The sudden realisation dawns on me. "Are you concerned that she too has been mutilated?"

"We are not sure what has become of her," says Sir Thomas. "Madame Silvestre might just be hiding her, or maybe the young lady has moved on to another place."

"Or maybe she is one of the butcher's victims," says Mr Priestly. He withdraws a card case from his pocket and carefully takes out a small photograph. He hands this to me. "Eleanor Carter."

The likeness is of a very fair, young woman. Her face is small and serious and the bodice of her gown is buttoned tightly to the base of her throat.

"How old is she?" I ask.

"She is only seventeen. She is quite small and pretty – this photograph does not do her justice," says Mr Priestly. "My friend is worried for her safety."

"He might have thought of that before he threw her out onto the street," I say, before I can help myself.

Mr Priestly's brow lifts as he looks across at me coldly. "Although it is out of the question for her to return to her familial home, naturally my friend is troubled. He would like to see her ensconced safely at the nunnery."

I glance from Sir Thomas to Mr Priestly. "You want me to find her?"

Sir Thomas sits back into the sofa and extends his legs out before himself. He studies his shoes as he says, "Well, as you now know, I have already had my detectives scouting for information on Miss Carter, but they have failed to find her."

"And you think my womanly touch might avail?" I ask, amused.

Sir Thomas resettles himself again. "As simple questioning

has not sufficed, we wondered if you could possibly discover Miss Carter's movements with more covert methods."

"Such as…?"

Mr Priestly makes an impatient motion with his hand. "You seemed interested in picking up the mantle of another character again, Mrs Chancey, and that is what we are asking of you. I believe it won't be too much of a stretch for you, for we would like you to pose as a…" he glances at Sir Thomas, "a 'gay girl', I think they're called."

I stop breathing for a moment as annoyance flushes through my body. It's true that I posed as a street prostitute for Sir Thomas, but that was just a lark, and it's also true that in the dim past I'd worked in many places, both good and bad, but I choose not to think of that now. So, for this absolute pig of a man to refer to me as a mere gay girl makes me angry. I'm no longer a lowly *grisette*, willing to flatter or implore my way to a few more pennies or ribbons while I try to hide my desperation.

I lift my chin. "You want me to pose as a prostitute?"

"Precisely."

"At Madame Silvestre's?"

"If they would have you, certainly," says Mr Priestly, his voice even. "What better place for you to be situated in order to find out where Miss Carter is?"

I heave myself up from the sofa and stride to the bay window. My skirt bumps a side-table causing a figurine of a Chinese goddess to totter. Go back to work in a brothel, for the sake of a little detection? I'm not so sure.

Sir Thomas puts his hands out entreatingly. "Mrs Chancey, not only can you investigate the disappearance of Miss Carter, you can also look into the other deaths. You can try to find more information about the monster who is harming these women."

"Who knows?" interrupts Mr Priestly. "You could even pretend to be pregnant and see where that takes you."

"Be your bait, you mean?" I ask, my voice flippant.

"Whatever it takes, Mrs Chancey, whatever it takes."

COME VISIT US AT
WWW.LEGENDPRESS.CO.UK

FOLLOW US
@LEGEND_PRESS